A Higher Justice

The Trials of Kit Shannon
Book 5

James Scott Bell

Compendium Press

Originally published by Bethany House Publishers

Scriptures taken from the Holy Bible, King James Version. Public domain.

ISBN 10: 0-910355-21-5
ISBN 13: 978-0-910355-21-6

Human beings do not ever make laws;
it is the accidents and catastrophes of all kinds
happening in every conceivable way
that make laws for us.
—Plato

Part One

Chapter One

The morning that was to shatter Winnie Franklin's life forever began as one of the happiest she'd had in months.

Since her husband's untimely death a year ago, which had left her a widow at age twenty-six, Winnie's life had been a series of blows. Thank the good Lord her sister and brother-in-law also lived in Los Angeles and took her and Sammy in without a qualm. It couldn't have been easy to allow a widow and her four-year-old child into their modest home on Fullerton Avenue. Not when they had four children of their own.

But just yesterday Winnie had gotten word from the Broadway Department Store that her application for employment had been accepted. She would begin work next week in the fabric department. At long last she'd found work and could help with the expenses.

So, in celebration, she gathered up the money she'd been saving in the tin sewing box—money to buy Sammy a new set of clothes—and headed out with him for the two-mile walk downtown.

Sammy held his mother's hand and chatted with an

excitement he could barely contain. "Will I get a suit, Mummy?"

"Yes, sweet. A suit."

"Just like Daddy?"

Holding back a tear, Winnie nodded. Sammy loved to look at the photographs of the father he hardly remembered. He told his mother he wanted to look just like him when he grew up. And a new suit would certainly make him look like a man, wouldn't it?

The Broadway had a special going on. *Brand-New Suits for the Little Fellow,* the advertisement in the *Examiner* said. *The latest fashions for 1906! From $2.95!*

Winnie had seen the perfect suit in the ad. A brown-and-gray wool one, with plaits and slash pockets on the coat, and knickerbocker pants with a hip pocket and buckle at the knee. With the addition of a silk tie, Sammy would look like a miniature of Nevin.

Her husband, God rest his soul, would have been so proud. Nevin Franklin was a real man's man, not well educated yet always trying to better his lot. He read books and worked hard. He was a highly regarded cooper, able to repair almost anything made of wood. He hoped, through industry and enthusiasm, he could start his own company someday. "Something to pass along to Sammy," he had liked to say.

Turning at last onto Broadway, Winnie saw that it was another busy Saturday in Los Angeles. Fine ladies with their parasols were out for strolls and shopping. Men in suits, wearing derby hats or straw skimmers, talked together on street corners, some of them disappearing into barrooms and pool halls.

The street teemed with horse-drawn carriages and a few gasoline-powered autos, as pedestrians crisscrossed the streets like so many ducks waddling to various ponds. The loud clang of a bell told everyone in the street to watch out for the electric trolley rushing through.

Sammy looked at it all, his eyes wide with fascination.

Winnie was content to take her time on this trip. She and Sammy would spend the day together. She would spoil him rotten and have fun doing it. In fact, it was only an hour until lunchtime when Winnie stopped at the corner of Broadway and Fifth and bought Sammy the latest fad treat—a scoop of ice cream in a waffle *cone*. The St. Louis World's Fair had first introduced the novelty, though it was Los Angeles, with its arid temperatures and dry desert winds, that had adopted the cool delight as its own.

As Sammy happily licked the strawberry ice cream, Winnie realized she was, for the first time since her husband's death, happy. Perhaps there would be a promising future ahead for her after all. Maybe a widow with a son could forge a good life in the America of Roosevelt, one of progress, of increasing opportunity for women.

Perhaps Sammy would, after all, have a chance at a successful life.

At the same time Winnie and Sammy walked up Broadway, Kit Shannon, a Los Angeles attorney, was getting pinned.

"This will be the most beautiful wedding dress of the season," Mrs. Norris said, admiring her work so far. Her dress shop on Hill Street was the most popular in Los Angeles.

Corazón Chavez, Kit's able assistant in everything from the running of her law office to investigations, agreed. "You are the most beautiful lawyer in the city!"

Kit laughed. "That is not saying much, is it?"

"Be still," Mrs. Norris commanded. She was an energetic, gray-haired mistress of the needle. And she had outdone herself this time.

The bridal gown was made of peau de crepe, trimmed with silver cross-stitching. The skirt was gauged in sections, trimmed with three deep tucks; the waist tapered down into a belt of liberty satin, and the bishop sleeves were delicately puffed. Kit was more than pleased. She was ecstatic, for she wanted nothing else than to be a vision for Ted Fox. He deserved no less.

"Your dear aunt would have been proud," Mrs. Norris said. Indeed, Kit's great-aunt, Freddy, had immediately commissioned the dressmaker when Kit first arrived in the City of Angels three years before. Kit's meager wardrobe had been "a scandal," not proper for a young lady of high society. That Kit had resisted Freddy's attempts to "womanize" her was not forgotten. At last Kit was going to be married. Freddy, looking down from heaven, must have been pleased.

"She always wanted me to have a big church wedding," Kit said.

"There!" Mrs. Norris stepped back. "Perfect. You are a picture of loveliness!"

"And feeling like a pincushion." Kit smiled at the dressmaker. "Are we finished for the day?"

"You are free to go," Mrs. Norris said. "Don't muss it!"

Outside, comfortable again in her walking suit and shoes, Kit said, "Shall we lunch at Mrs. Olson's?"

"*Sí,*" Corazón replied.

"Do you want to drive?"

"Oh no!" Corazón shook her head. "Not yet."

Kit tied the copious sash of her hat under her chin and climbed into the new Model F Ford automobile parked outside Mrs. Norris's dress shop. Kit, with Ted's prodding, had decided that it was time to step up to the age of the auto. Even though a few loud voices held that the horse would never be truly replaced, Kit sensed the inevitable. Besides, it was the most efficient way to see clients and get around town.

Shopping for the auto had been something of an experience. Gus Willingham, Ted's friend and chief mechanic on the aeroplane project, extolled the virtues of the Peerless. While it cost $3900, it was the car with the most luxury. Certainly finer than the Winton Model K, at $2650, or the Buick Runabout for $1150.

Kit was not looking for ostentation, however. She had her sights set on a Rio Light Touring Car for $1350—that is, until a Ford ad in the *Times* caught her eye.

Economical, reliable, and speedy. The Model F, only $600!

This was the one Kit had picked. "At this price," Kit

remarked to the garage owner, "everyone in Los Angeles may soon own one."

"I hope you are right," the owner said. "The more autos the better, if you ask me."

Maybe not, Kit thought as she drove with Corazón toward Broadway. Too many autos might cause chaos. It was hard enough these days getting a horse to stay calm on the city streets, what with all the people and trolleys.

As if to prove the point, Kit had to pull the hand brake hard to keep from being slammed by a trolley as it clanged madly down the middle of Broadway. She glared at the motorman, who was oblivious to her presence. He was talking loudly with some of the men on the trolley and laughing it up.

"Everybody is in a hurry," Corazón said.

These days, Kit said to herself, that was exactly true. America was on the move, and Los Angeles seemed determined, in its own fashion, to lead the way.

Winnie Franklin held Sammy's hand—sticky from the ice cream—and crossed Sixth Street. A small crowd had gathered on the other corner. An organ grinder and a monkey! Winnie hadn't seen one in years. Sammy's face lit up.

"You may give the monkey a penny," Winnie told him, handing the boy a coin. The monkey, seeing what its master had trained it to see, brought its tin cup over with a chattering insistence and held it up to Sammy. The boy dropped the coin in with a *chink,* and the monkey doffed its cap.

"How big he's growing!" a voice said.

Winnie turned and saw a familiar face, Beatrice Beatty. She was a neighbor of Winnie's in-laws, a friendly, matronly woman who had taken an early interest in Sammy's well-being.

"How nice to see you," Winnie said. "I'm taking Sammy in to get fitted for his first suit today."

Sammy was still fixated on the monkey. A merry tune issued from the hand organ.

"Quite the little man," Mrs. Beatty said. She was dressed in a heavy wool ensemble and appeared to have corseted herself quite enthusiastically. Her face looked flushed as tiny pinpoints of perspiration glistened under her eyes. "My, it's hot today," Mrs. Beatty added.

"Indeed," Winnie agreed. "May I recommend a serving of ice cream?"

Beatrice Beatty laughed and then patted her stomach with a gloved hand. "I'm trying to keep my figure for Mr. Beatty," she whispered. "He prefers the slender type. He'd have me be a Gibson girl! Pshaw!"

Winnie smiled. Out of the corner of her eye, she saw a boy of ten or so throw something into the street. A coin?

"We must have tea soon, eh?" Mrs. Beatty said. She looked at the sky. "So hot."

"Yes, it is." *Why doesn't Mrs. Beatty have a parasol?* Winnie wondered.

"I must ..."

Suddenly Mrs. Beatty began to swoon. Winnie clutched at the woman's arms. Mrs. Beatty fell forward, heavily.

Winnie went down, her ample neighbor on top of her. She then felt a forest of legs and arms closing around, trying to help. Voices shouted. Someone called for a doctor.

Stunned, Winnie lost her breath for a moment. She watched as two men struggled to get Beatrice Beatty off of her. Finally relief came as Winnie herself was lifted to her feet again.

"Are you all right, miss?" A gentleman with a gray mustache doffed his derby.

"Yes, thank you." She looked down at Beatrice Beatty, now in a sitting position. A woman knelt and waved her fan in front of Beatrice's face. Her eyes slowly blinked. It appeared she would be fine.

"Sammy?" Winnie spun around to the spot where Sammy had been standing.

He wasn't there.

A fluttery disquiet hit her as she looked frantically for her boy among the crowd.

"Sammy?"

No answer. No sign.

A bell clanged. A trolley. It jarred Winnie. It sounded like a death knell.

A woman screamed and shouted, "Look out!"

Winnie froze, her body shaking, because she knew—just somehow knew—it was Sammy. She charged toward the street, knocking aside a man in the way.

She saw Sammy, then, standing in the middle of the tracks, looking at something in his hands.

The trolley was not going to stop.

"Sammy!"

"What is this crowd?" Corazón asked.

Kit looked up ahead and saw the throng gathered in the center of Broadway. "Who knows? Maybe a horse kicked someone."

Kit chugged along behind an ice wagon pulled by a slow nag. The character of the crowd ahead, however, was not good. Men were gesticulating wildly. Kit could see a woman with her hands pressed over her mouth.

And the Broadway trolley. It was on the other side of the crowd, not moving.

That's when she knew it was another trolley accident. They happened with too great a frequency. Kit prayed that it was not fatal.

She parked the car on the east side of Broadway for there were, at the moment, too many people to get by. She heard loud cries from the middle of the knot of people.

Leaping out, Kit tapped a tall, angular gentleman on the shoulder. "Can you tell me what has happened here?"

The man's thin face was downcast. "A little boy," he said. "A poor little boy."

Chapter Two

The woman screamed.

Kit saw her, on her knees, holding the boy's head. She rocked back and forth, crying, inconsolable. There was blood on the ground, the boy, and the woman's dress.

A cop, his billy club in his hand, was trying to get the people standing around the woman to back up. Kit knew the policeman, as she did many on the force. His name was Jimmy Leeds.

Kit assessed the situation. The trolley was stopped a little bit ahead, with the position of the boy's body dreadfully consistent with a trolley accident.

The same trolley she'd seen speeding down Broadway earlier.

Suddenly the motorman appeared in the crowd, horror-stricken at the sight.

"He ran out in front of me," Kit heard the motorman say. "I couldn't stop in time!"

"He was going too fast," a woman muttered close to Kit.

Since 1903, when she came west after completing a women's law program in New York, Kit had observed human behavior closely—in court and out. Her mentor, the famous attorney Earl Rogers, had taught her the key to getting at the truth was in one's gaining insight regarding human nature, what he called the Rule of Human Probability. A subset of that rule, which Kit had learned through experience, was that human witnesses often proved to be frail. Two people could see the same action yet have completely different recollections of it.

When self-interest became part of the equation—as would be the case with the motorman—there was another variable to consider.

All of this rushed through Kit's mind as she watched and listened. But most of all she wanted to help the woman who cradled her dead son. She wanted to give comfort and protection.

"The poor mother," Corazón said.

"Wait here," Kit said. Wading through the crowd, she reached Officer Leeds. "Jimmy, can I help?"

"Miss Shannon!" he said, sounding relieved. "Can you stay with this woman, keep her from getting hurt? I got me hands full."

"Did you call for a doctor?"

"Somebody went to fetch one."

Kit knelt by the mother and put her arm around her. She jerked at Kit's touch.

"Breathe deeply," Kit said quietly.

The woman looked at her with raw, red eyes. "My son ..."

"Yes," Kit said, stroking the woman's back. She said nothing more but just stayed with the woman, whose body would not stop shaking.

"The future of this country is written in the rails," Stanton Eames said. He made a waving motion, leaving a trail of cigar smoke across his large body. At sixty he was a man who liked to eat as much of the finest food as his intestinal system could absorb. What was the point of having millions in the bank if one did not indulge, he believed.

Three other men, also puffing Cuban cigars, sat in plush leather chairs in the library of the Eames mansion that sat atop Crescent Heights. Eames looked into the eyes of each of them, lingering longest on Mayor Wilfred Tillinghast, looking for signs of dissent. He saw none.

"That includes municipal transport," Eames added. "Now is the time to do something about the atrocity of the automobile."

"You don't have to fear the gas buggies," Melvin Oliver said. He was the representative of Western Railroad in Southern California. "They are a gimmick, is all."

"You underestimate the American spirit," said Eames. "We are a race of individualists. There is nothing as individual as a conveyance under a man's own control." He turned to Mayor Tillinghast. "In any event, I don't want to see our city streets cluttered with autos."

The mayor, a smallish man with the spectacles of an accountant and the eyes of an opportunist, said, "No one wants to see our fair city under a cloud of exhaust fumes. But there is money being made by these auto manufacturers, you know, and—"

"Oh, hang it all, Willie," Eames interrupted. "You'll get your cut from us. So you can stop pretending to care about fumes."

The other men laughed again. Tillinghast scowled.

Julius Rhetta, the banker who was current president of the chamber of commerce, observed, "Gentlemen, we are one big happy family here. All we want is what's best for the city. Rail and water are the keys to our future."

"Finally," Eames said, "a man who knows what he's talking about. Now, what exactly can we do to—?"

He stopped speaking when his private telephone rang. The other men watched as Eames picked up the set and barked into the mouthpiece.

And as his face began to flush. The big man listened intently, his white eyebrows narrowing downward.

"Yes," Eames said firmly. "Keep me informed."

He slammed the telephone down on the table.

"We have a slight problem," Eames announced. "Julius, who's your man at the *Times*?"

"Tom Phelps," Julius Rhetta said.

"Get him."

Chapter Three

In the tombs of the county jail, one could find the occasional rat. But a mouse?

"That's what he calls himself," Smiley said to Kit. Smiley was the chief jailer, known for his toothy grin, and he always treated Kit with fairness.

In fact, he had been the one to direct the message that a man named Mousy Malloy was asking to see her.

It was Tuesday, the day after the trolley accident that killed the small boy. This was on Kit's mind as she followed Smiley—a concern for the poor woman who lost her son. The thought then occurred to her that every man locked up in here was some mother's lost son.

"But watch him," Smiley said as he pointed to a middle cell. "He's a little daffy."

Kit walked down the dank corridor filled with the unpleasant smells that went along with the caging of drunks and dirty criminals. She had gotten familiar with the odors in the past three years, though never would she be able to ignore them. Regardless, it was here that she saw the majority of her clients for the first time.

The man in the cell was as thin as a barber pole. His tufts of hair stuck out in crazy shafts like the sagebrush along the beaches of Santa Monica. His eyes were heavy-lidded, although they widened as soon as he saw Kit standing facing his cell.

"Miss Shannon?"

His breath, even from the distance of five feet or so, smelled foul and was tainted with whiskey.

"You asked to see me?"

"God bless you for coming."

The name of God coming from such chapped, puffy lips was strange. But Kit told herself to suspend judgment. How did she know what his story was?

"My name's Mousy Malloy. You heard of me?"

"Only this morning when the jailer called. I don't mean to offend, but Mousy is not your real name, is it?"

The prisoner grinned, revealing brown teeth at odd angles. "Real name's Abner. I like Mousy better. Mousies can move fast and know how to hide. Anyway, I was a fast runner when I was a young'un."

"Then Mousy it is. Why don't you start by telling me why you are here?"

"I been in and out of jail lately. Can't seem to stay out, if you know what I mean."

She did. Some men hit bottom and never got out again. "How did you happen to send for me?"

"I know your name. I heard about you." His head twitched then; he seemed in the grip of an electric shock. His whole body vibrated a moment. "Heard you is a good lawyer."

"I try to be."

"And a good woman of God."

"How can I help you, Mousy?"

"I need God's help, I do, not just a lawyer's." His eyes became watery. "My mother, sainted she was, always told me to turn to the good Lord. I don't know where else I can go now."

He ran a dirty arm under his nose.

"What is it you have been accused of?"

"They say it's attempted murder."

Kit slid a jail stool up to the cell bars. "Tell me what happened."

"That's just it, Miss Shannon. I don't know."

"You don't know?"

Malloy shook his head. "I was in a bar. I got hooched up. This and that happened; next thing I know I wake up in here."

"It's the *this and that* I want you to talk about. First, who told you it was for attempted murder?"

"A cop. I think his name's McGinty."

That would be Mike McGinty, chief detective on the force. Kit could talk to him. They had tangled before and gained a mutual respect.

"What did McGinty say?"

"He wanted me to make a statement saying I tried to kill Ellis Dyke."

"Dyke? The name is familiar."

"He's from the railroad family."

"Ah. San Francisco, isn't it?"

"Yeah, and Ellis ain't shy about it. He's a loudmouth." Mousy Malloy twitched again, still in the grip of some inner tremor. He rubbed his face hard with his hand.

"His being a loudmouth from a railroad family is not a justification for murder," Kit said. "What else happened?"

"I don't know! But I can't remember shooting at him!"

"Suppose you tell me what you do remember."

Mousy leaned forward on the edge of his cot and took a deep breath, which seemed to calm him a bit.

"I remember going to Doogan's Saloon around nine-thirty. I have my breakfast there. Usually an egg sandwich with a beer. I don't start my heavy drinkin' till later."

"What is your work?"

"I do jobs for the rail lines. Steel fixing, splitting ties, things like that. Sometimes for the Santa Fe line, sometimes for Western Rail. It's off-and-on work. I also do some fix-it work for the hotels around town."

"Go on with your story. When exactly did this take place?"

"Yesterday. Like I said, I was minding my own business when Ellis Dyke come in with a bunch of his no-good friends."

"Then you were familiar with Ellis Dyke before this?"

Mousy Malloy practically spat. "He's a spoiled-rotten rich boy. Thinks that gives him the right to push people around."

"Has he pushed you around?"

"Well, it's like this. His old man, up in Frisco, thought it'd be good for Ellis to work a little with his hands before going full into the business. Make a man of him or something. So Ellis and me ended up on the same crew about a year ago. And we got into it."

"A fight?"

"I clobbered him good." A sly smile came to Mousy's lips.

"What came of that?"

"Nothin'. Ellis was too ashamed to make a big deal out of it. But we've circled like city cats after that. Like he was waitin' for a good time to do me dirty."

"How many people knew about this fight with Mr. Dyke?"

Mousy shrugged. "I guess word got around some."

"Tell me what happened yesterday morning after Ellis Dyke and his friends came in."

"They all sidled up to the bar. I was at a table in the back, but they saw me. Ellis give me the evil eye. I give it right back to him. Then they started laughin' and jokin'. About me."

"How did you gather that?"

"The way they looked at me when they laughed. I tried not to let it bother me none, only I sure couldn't eat my breakfast in peace."

"Go on."

"Next thing I know Bill Doogan come over to my table with another beer and says it's on the house. I look over and see Ellis with his glass raised, like he's tryin' to make up. So I salute him and drink. Ellis then says to the whole place, `Mousy's a good man. But can he drink like one?'"

"How many people were there?"

Mousy scratched his head. "I dunno. A few."

"Can you remember how many?"

"I don't know. I thought a cop may have stuck his nose in."

"What?"

"A man in a uniform, at least. Maybe I was just seeing things."

"Was everyone in the place watching you?"

"I think so," said Mousy. "Anyway, Ellis orders me another drink, and Bill Doogan sets it down in front of me. Then he draws another for Ellis. Ellis looks at me and downs his beer. So I drink mine. By this time everybody is cheering."

"Let me guess—the two of you had a contest over who could drink the most beer."

Mousy nodded. "I know it was a fool thing so early in the day, but I saw Ellis making this personal and I sure wasn't gonna back down. Everything gets kind of fuzzy after that."

"I should imagine. Did you have a gun with you?"

"No, ma'am. No gun. That's what I can't figure out."

"Did Detective McGinty tell you that you actually fired a gun at Ellis Dyke?"

Mousy thought a moment. "I don't rightly remember that, either."

"I'll talk to him," Kit said.

Mousy's eyes filled with something like hope but then just as quickly saddened. "Uh, Miss Shannon, I can't pay you anything right now."

"Let's not worry about that yet. I'm only going to find out what the police have on you. I will let you know after that if I'm going to represent you or not. Fair enough?"

Chapter Four

"Well, if it isn't Miss Kit Shannon, dragon slayer."

John Davenport, the county district attorney, stuck his thumbs in his vest pockets. He looked at Kit with the disdain she had come to expect from him. It was no secret around town that Davenport loathed Earl Rogers, mostly because of Davenport's never having won a case against him. Now that animus had passed to Kit, who had yet to lose a case to the D.A. It was whispered, in fact, that the wrinkles in Davenport's face, along with his permanent frown, were caused more by the Rogers-Shannon duo than advancing age. Davenport was sixty-four and had been a lawyer for forty years.

"Good morning, Mr. Davenport," Kit said, feeling his dislike but treating him with respect all the same. It was only proper to do so, and perhaps the Golden Rule would one day have an effect on the D.A.

"Please have a seat," Davenport said, obviously behaving overly polite. "Do you mind if Mrs. Price sits in on this meeting?"

Clara Dalton Price was the lawyer Davenport had hired to try the Truman Harcourt murder case. His reasoning at the time—which had been hinted at in the *Examiner*—was that to defeat Kit Shannon, the D.A.'s office would be best served by hiring its own woman lawyer. It hadn't worked. Kit established Truman's innocence, even though Clara Dalton Price had proved a strong opponent.

"Not at all," replied Kit.

"Thank you." Davenport bowed and stepped out of the office. Kit glanced at the neat rows of law books on the shelves. California was beginning to build quite a library of official reports. The state was growing rapidly. Los Angeles itself now boasted a population of over two hundred thousand. With such growth came the inevitable increase in crimes and lawsuits and the expansion of case law.

Kit also noticed the gold-plated nail scissors sitting on Davenport's desk. The D.A. was something of a dandy in the way he dressed—always three-piece dark brown suits with dangling watch fob and the occasional walking stick—and in his immaculate grooming. But the scissors were a bit too precious for a man who fancied himself a courtroom warrior.

Looming from its perch on the wall hung a photograph of Theodore Roosevelt, president of the United States, in one of his more serene poses. He appeared dignified, with no teeth showing. The look seemed to be a stretch for him. When Kit had met him during his memorable Fourth of July visit to Los Angeles, all she could see were those teeth—grandiose, oyster white, magnificent. The papers were fond of drawing his likeness as a uniformed Rough Rider, an image "Rough and Ready Teddy" would, apparently, never shake.

Presently, Clara Price swept into Davenport's office, followed by the D.A. As usual, Price wore a hat—a small-brimmed, blue-silk affair with a bow—a pressed woolen skirt, and a shirtwaist under a coat. It was the suit of a new breed of professional women, as sparse as those ranks were. Price nodded formally at Kit, then sat in a chair by the window, looking serious and ready to take in everything that was to be said.

"Now," Davenport said as he took his own chair, which squeaked as he leaned back in it, "to what do we owe the pleasure?"

"It concerns the Malloy matter," said Kit.

Davenport shot a surprised glance at Clara Dalton Price. To Kit he said, "You're not representing him, are you?"

"I may."

"Miss Shannon, you never cease to amaze me." Davenport shook his head and slid a thin cigar from the pocket of his starched shirt. "Malloy is not one of your stray cats. He is not some poor unfortunate who has fallen on hard times. Mousy Malloy has a record of trouble and a motive for murder. Frankly, Miss Shannon, I'm surprised at you."

"Why should it trouble you, Mr. Davenport? Any accused is considered innocent until proven guilty beyond a reasonable doubt. Mr. Malloy's background does not change that."

"But it certainly gives us a basis for the charge of attempted murder," Clara Dalton Price added. She was an intense woman who had been nicknamed "The Iron Lady" early in her career. She did not like to lose, as she had made very clear to Kit when they first tangled. Kit had the feeling she was just itching to have another chance at trying and convicting one of her clients.

"Evidence of previous bad acts is not admissible," Kit said.

"Unless it relates to motive, opportunity, or intent," Price countered.

Davenport smiled at his deputy's quick answer. He lit his cigar as the two lawyers debated.

"The crime of attempted murder requires *mens rea,*" Kit said. "A guilty mind, the mental element of a crime. Can you prove that?"

"The intent to commit the act," Price responded, "is implicit in the act itself. The proper question is whether you have any proof that would defeat such a presumption."

"I have not yet begun to gather evidence," Kit said, beginning to feel a twinge of competitive heat. It was almost as if they were already arguing in front of a judge. "My purpose is to determine whether your evidence is strong enough to file the case. If it is not, perhaps another disposition regarding Mr. Malloy would be in order."

Davenport waved away a puff of cigar smoke. "You want to beat us even before the case is filed?"

"No, Mr. Davenport. I am not interested in beating anyone." That remark drew a skeptical glance from Clara Dalton Price. Kit ignored it. "Before you file an information, I am requesting that you take more time to find out what happened."

"We don't need more time." Davenport then looked at Price, who nodded in agreement.

Kit shook her head slowly. "This is not the case of the century here. Why such an interest in a transient worker named Mousy Malloy?"

Davenport's cheeks twitched. "I do not make it a habit to explain the policies of this office to defense lawyers. That would be like the chicken telling the weasel where the eggs are hidden, would it not?"

"I take it, then," said Kit, "that we shall be meeting in court quite soon?"

"That appears to be my lot in life," Davenport said.

"I also presume Mrs. Price will be handling the case?"

Clara Dalton Price nodded. "I let you get the better of me last time. This time I will not underestimate you."

Should she even take Mousy Malloy's case? Kit wondered about it even as she guided her Ford through the streets of Los Angeles toward Fullerton Avenue. The grinding engine spooked a horse pulling an Owl cab, and the driver, his whip in hand, yelled a curse at her.

Kit waved good-naturedly. *Can't blame him a bit,* she thought. *Life is changing drastically around here.*

Was she changing, too? She had made a vow to represent only those who she was convinced were innocent. Mousy Malloy had requested she come to see him, and she always answered such requests. But it certainly looked as though

Mousy was a guilty man. In a drunken state he had somehow secured a gun—he may have been holding back the whole truth from Kit on that point—and tried to shoot an enemy.

Clara Dalton Price was right in that Malloy's own conduct could be enough proof for a jury to find him guilty. And then there was the reference Davenport had made to Malloy's troubled past. Kit never held that against a client. She believed anyone could change if they turned their lives over to the care of the Master. That was always her prayer for her clients.

Still, on the issue of guilt or innocence, things did not look good for Mousy Malloy.

Kit turned down Fullerton and found the wood-frame house numbered 120. The morning *Times* had run a brief story on the accident that killed the little boy. Winnie Franklin's address was supplied.

A tall, roughly hewn man answered Kit's knock. He had large hands and leathery skin, a manner of man used to working outside. His eyebrows were dark and bushy and his eyes held no mirth.

"Good day, sir. My name is Kathleen Shannon. I have come to inquire about Winnie."

"You know Winnie?"

"I was with her yesterday."

"At the accident?"

"Yes. I sat with her for a bit until a doctor came. I just wanted to know how she is getting along today."

The big man's eyes filled with bitter sadness. "You want the truth or some stiff-upper-lip story?"

"The truth."

"Then I'll tell you. We've had to watch her all night to keep her from harming herself."

"I'm so sorry." Kit felt the man's obvious despondency. "If there is anything I can do ..."

"Can you bring Sammy back?" he snapped. Quickly he said, "I'm sorry. I have not slept. My mind is not in a hospitable temper."

"I well understand."

"Your name again?"

"Kathleen Shannon."

The man squinted. "Do I know you?"

"I don't believe so."

"I have heard your name, then."

"Perhaps. I practice law."

"You are that woman lawyer."

Kit nodded. "Perhaps I can be of some encouragement."

"Encouragement? How?"

"By offering a good word."

"There's no good that can be done now."

A voice from inside said, "Salem?" The man turned his head but did not answer. A woman in a plain yellow housedress joined him at the door. "Company?"

"This here is Miss Shannon, the lawyer."

The woman seemed surprised. "Well, let her in."

"She's here to see Winnie," the man said, not moving.

"Please, Salem." The woman moved past the large man and extended a hand to Kit. "I am Alice Laine, Winnie's sister. Won't you come in?"

The inside of the home was as simple and unpretentious as its exterior. A white vase on a small table held a clutch of daisies that were beginning to droop. A parakeet in a cage near a mirror was silent, seeming to sense the sorrow that filled the house. The only hopeful sign was the smell of bread baking in the kitchen. Kit had the feeling this must have been a house brimming over with laughter at one time.

Alice led her to a room at the end of the hall. The door was partly open. Alice pushed it farther and looked in. "Winnie? You have a visitor."

Kit heard no answer from inside the room. Alice motioned for her to come in anyway, and Kit followed.

Winnie Franklin was seated in a chair by the window. The tiny room held a bed and a dressing table, not much more. A child's stuffed bear lay on top of the bed. These were quite popular now, and people had started calling them "Teddy Bears" in honor of the rough-riding, big-game-hunting president of the United States.

"Who is it?" Winnie said. To Kit, Winnie appeared to have

lost her color. Her cheeks were almost translucent, her voice a thin reed.

"A Miss Shannon," Alice replied.

Winnie's face did not move. She was looking blankly at the window. "I don't believe I know a Miss Shannon."

"She was with you, dear, when ..."

Winnie turned and fixed her gaze on Kit's face. "Who are you?"

Before Kit could answer, Salem put a hand on her arm. "I don't think this is such a good notion. Winnie hasn't been herself."

"Perhaps this will help," Alice said. "Come, Salem, let us give it a chance."

"I don't like it."

"I want her to stay," Winnie said. "Please let her."

Salem hesitated, then with a brusque nod left the room. Alice smiled encouragingly at Kit and closed the door behind her.

Once they were alone, Winnie said, "You were the one who helped me yesterday."

Kit sat on the edge of the bed, very close to Winnie. "I happened to be driving by and saw the crowd."

"It is hazy to me now."

"Of course."

Winnie's eyes softened just a bit. "What was your name again?"

"Call me Kit."

Winnie nodded. "I like that. How did you come by the name?"

"My given name is Kathleen. My mother called me Kat once when I was little, but my father thought I was more like a kitten, and that's when I became Kit."

"Was there love in your family?"

"An abundance, yes."

Winnie looked away for a moment, sighing. "Do you have children of your own?"

"No."

"Do you hope to someday?"

"Yes."

"Got a fella?"

"His name is Ted Fox."

A slight smile stole across Winnie's face. "He must be clever, with a name like that."

Kit nodded. "He is quite good with machines. He is building an aeroplane."

"My Sammy was clever." Winnie Franklin's voice suddenly sounded distant, whispery. Kit took her hand and held it. Winnie gazed out the window as she spoke. "He liked to spell words with his blocks, you know. He could spell *dog* and *cat* and even *train*. He liked trains. I think he would have ..."

Her voice broke. Kit felt her stiffen. For a moment Winnie Franklin was a statue, a sculptured rendition of confused grief.

She then fell forward into Kit's chest, her wails as agonized as any Kit had ever heard.

"My boy, my boy, my boy ..."

Winnie's cries were muffled. Kit felt the hot breath on her blouse and the wetness of the woman's tears. She stroked Winnie's hair and held her close.

The door flew open, and Salem rushed into the room with Alice close behind.

"What is it?" Salem said, his eyes wide.

Kit shook her head at him, quieting him.

The man stared for a moment, confused about what to do next. He said, "You've upset her!"

Alice pulled at his arm. "No."

"She should go."

Winnie sat up, her face blotchy and wet. "I want her to stay! You go away!"

"Now, see here—" Salem took a step forward, but Alice held him back.

Winnie Franklin screamed.

"No, dear, no," Kit said gently, enfolding the woman in her arms, praying for God's peace to come.

She held her for a long time, then helped Alice get Winnie on the bed. Kit unlaced Winnie's shoes as Alice unbuttoned her dress.

Salem discreetly left the room.

The two women found him slumped in a wing chair, head in hand.

"She's so gentle and sweet," he said when he became aware of their presence. "And now I fear she's broken. Ruined."

Alice knelt by her husband.

"Mr. Laine," Kit said quietly, "your sister-in-law needs the attention of a doctor."

"That would cost ..." He stopped himself, embarrassed. He pointed to his head. "Her problems are here."

"Yes, and for that there is another kind of physician. Have you a church?" asked Kit.

Alice was the more eager to acknowledge this.

"Surround Winnie with prayer," Kit said. "I will join you in this."

Salem got up and walked toward a curtained window. "God should not have allowed this to happen. Taking a little boy!"

"Don't speak that way," Alice said, tender in her rebuke. "'Twas not God that hit him. It was an accident."

"Accident! Don't you believe what the Bible says? A sparrow shall not fall to the ground without the Father ... ? It was God's will, and I don't understand it."

"I do not believe God willed Sammy's death," Kit said.

"You claim to know God's mind?"

"Only what His Word says. And it says we are of more value than many sparrows."

"Value?" Salem waved his arms around the small chamber. "We are not people of great means, Miss Shannon. If Winnie is in need of medical care, how are we to provide that?"

"Have you a telephone?"

"That's another luxury we cannot afford."

"I will summon a doctor for you," Kit said, "and have him come round."

"But I told you that—"

"Do not concern yourself with the payment."

Resolute, Salem said, "I will not accept charity!"

"Allow one visit for the moment," said Kit. "And allow me to make an inquiry on your behalf."

"Inquiry? Of whom?"

"The trolley line, to start with."

The man's eyes blinked in bewilderment.

"I would hope," Kit said, "that they would be willing to help."

Chapter Five

"What do you know about the Los Angeles Electric Trolley Line?" Kit asked as she took a chair in Earl Rogers' office. Rogers, behind his desk, was dressed in his usual crisp, cream-colored suit. In addition to being the predominant trial lawyer in the country, Rogers was one of the most fashionably dressed men in Los Angeles. His devotion to clothes bordered on the obsessive.

"I know they are in breakneck competition with the Pacific Electric Line," Rogers said. "Henry Huntington has been a burr under the saddle of the L.A. Line since 1901."

"Huntington runs the Pacific?"

"A smart man, too. He saw that urban rail was going to be tied to real estate, so at the same time he expanded his line he was buying up tracts all over the San Gabriel Valley. He subdivides the tracts and sells them when rail transport is available there. He's making Los Angeles into a city of sub-urbanites."

"Who runs the Los Angeles Line?"

"That would be Stanton Eames. He's worried that Huntington's lines will cut into his freight business. For the last several years Eames has been currying favor with the politicians and buying up real estate himself, especially to the south—Gardena, Wilmington, even Long Beach. They say he isn't shy about handing out money under certain tables."

"I see. And what manner of man is this Eames?"

"I've met him once or twice, casually. He's a force to reckon with—no doubt about that. Plenty of power on his side. He's been putting politicians in his pocket for as long as he's been around."

"Anything else I should know about him?"

Rogers scowled. "Kit, what exactly have you got it in your head to do?"

"I thought I'd pay a call on Mr. Eames. It is always good to know as much as possible about those you are dealing with."

"Dealing? With Eames?"

"One of his trolley cars killed a little boy yesterday."

"Ah." Rogers nodded. "I read something in the newspaper about that."

"I just want to see if Mr. Eames might be amenable to seeing to the care of the mother, as a gesture of goodwill."

"Goodwill?" Rogers let go a robust laugh. "The only goodwill Stanton Eames is concerned with comes printed on United States currency."

"He has not yet heard my request. Perhaps he will be open to reason."

"Reason is what we lawyers use," Rogers said. "Mere mortals are not always so clear in their thinking."

"I shall take that into account."

"I take it you will be seeking out Mr. Eames soon?"

"Today."

"That's my Kit! Very well, if you're determined in this, you have my good wishes. But how about telling me all about it tonight at dinner?"

"Why, Mr. Rogers, are you asking me to dine with you?"

"Bring along that fiancé of yours, the flyer. I have someone I'd like you both to meet. A friend of mine you may have heard of. Mr. Jack London."

"The writer?"

"The very same."

"*The Call of the Wild* is a marvelous book."

"Yes, all about the return to nature and conquering by force. I'm glad you've read it. You will need plenty of force if you ever get tangled up with Stanton Eames."

Kit paused, rubbing her hands together.

"Something else on your mind?" Rogers said.

"Just wondering whether to take on a new client. I may have to turn this one over to another lawyer."

"Oh?" Rogers' eyes lit up with curiosity. "Why is that, Lawyer Shannon?"

"You know I will only represent those who I believe are innocent."

Rogers sighed and slapped his sides. "Yes, yes. And I find it hard to call you a defense lawyer!"

"I simply cannot—"

"You mean you simply *will* not. Kit! You are a professional now, a full-blooded member of the bar, a criminal defense lawyer. It is not your business to sort out guilt or innocence. That is for the jury. Your job is to try to beat the rap that the D.A. files."

Kit shook her head. How many times had they had this discussion? It was no secret that Earl Rogers reveled in beating the district attorney's office, no matter how strong the evidence against his clients. "I do not see it that way," she said.

Now Rogers' expression began to flare. "Who made you the all-seeing, all-knowing one? You cannot know who is guilty or innocent without a trial."

"What if a client all but confesses?"

"Sometimes a client is the worst judge of the facts. I've had people confess to things they never did, out of some other motive. Who is this poor soul you're thinking of turning down?"

"His name is Malloy."

"Tell me what you know."

If only to help get it clear in her own mind, Kit told Rogers what Mousy Malloy had related to her about his case.

When she was finished, Rogers did not hesitate. "You

don't know if this man is guilty any more than Davenport does. If he was drunk, maybe he didn't have the intent to kill."

Kit was not quite sure what he was getting at.

"Read the statutes, Kit. Attempted murder requires *intent.* But your man was drunk. And where did he get the gun? Maybe he's holding out on you, maybe he isn't. The least you owe this man is to investigate his case a little further."

"But a man who drinks himself into—"

"Wait! Are you sitting in judgment of this man now? Do you sit in judgment of me?" He said the last with a strong note of sadness.

"No, I just—"

"Wasn't it Jesus himself who was accused of being a winebibber, because of His associating with such sinners? Kit, as a defense lawyer you're going to have to get your hands dirty."

"Perhaps," Kit said, finding the logic compelling. Jesus would not turn away from those who sought help.

"No perhaps about it," said Rogers. "That is your job. Unless you want John Davenport and Clara Dalton Price to run this town, and for others of their ilk to run the country, we need to stand up and make them prove their cases."

"It appears I've got two cases going on at once."

"Ah! You sound like a real lawyer now."

The offices of the Los Angeles Electric Trolley Line were housed in one of the newest buildings in Los Angeles: the Rayburn, which boasted a sandstone, dressed brickwork exterior unmatched by anything in the city. As striking as it appeared on approach from the street, the truly remarkable part of the building was its interior, a virtual honeycomb of cast-iron grillwork over translucent windows. Shards of light crisscrossed the space inside, brightening the entire affair. In the center, two glazed elevators transported busy occupants throughout the ten floors of the building. The place reeked of motion and money, power and progress, and as Kit entered from Main Street, she thought she could smell America's future.

Kit exited the elevator at the tenth floor and immediately saw, at the end of the corridor, large double doors. Inscribed on the doors were the words *Los Angeles Electric Trolley Line.* A section of railroad track had been affixed above the door, reminding one and all that rail lines were worthy of enshrinement as art.

Swinging open the doors, Kit stepped into a spacious reception area. Behind a flamboyant balustrade sat a young woman dressed in modest business attire. Behind her desk the floor opened up to an array of more desks. Kit could hear the clatter of typing machines and the voices of switchboard operators—the music of modern industry.

The receptionist glanced at Kit and asked if she might be of assistance.

"My name is Kathleen Shannon. I am an attorney. Would it be possible for me to see Mr. Stanton Eames for a moment?"

The young woman, whose hair was tightly bound in a swirl atop her head, frowned. "Is Mr. Eames expecting you?"

"No, I have not made an appointment. I just thought he might happen to be available. It is a matter of some importance."

"I am sorry, but no one drops in on Mr. Eames. He is an extremely busy man."

"Of that I am sure. Perhaps if you announced me, he might find—"

"He sees no one without an appointment."

Kit leaned over the receptionist's desk. "I understand you are doing your duty. Please understand that I am also doing mine. Would you mind merely announcing that Kathleen Shannon, attorney, wishes to speak with him?"

With a huff the woman grabbed a handset that looked like a telephone but was connected to a wooden box with a set of switches. She flicked one of the switches upward and said into the mouthpiece, "A Miss Kathleen Shannon, who says she is an attorney, would like to see Mr. Eames . . . I have told her that . . . I beg your pardon? Yes. I will."

She replaced the handset, a look of astonishment on her

face. "I am told you are to wait a moment," she said to Kit. The astonishment did not decrease when a muffled buzzing sound came from the wooden box and the woman received a message. She looked at Kit. "If you'll follow me."

The receptionist led Kit down a corridor, past rows of cabinets and drawers and desks, to a large door. After a quick knock, a booming voice from inside called for their entry.

Stanton Eames' office was large enough to house a small family. A bank of windows looked out at the city's bustling downtown and provided a breathtaking view of the business district and the Santa Gabriel mountain range in the distance.

In the center of one of the windows, as if he might be a mountain peak himself, stood a man in a dark blue suit with a high starched collar and striped tie. A gold watch chain hung in a perfect loop across his vest. He had a bushy white mustache and a full head of white hair.

"Good day," he said. "I am Stanton Eames. They didn't tell me it would be a woman!"

Confused, Kit said, "I am sorry; I announced my name and thought—"

"Nothing of it, nothing of it." Eames strutted forward and extended his hand to greet her. "These are modern times, are they not, Miss... ?"

"Shannon." She shook his hand. His grip was firm and confident.

"Yes, modern times." Eames motioned for Kit to sit in a dark, burled-wood chair. "A woman in the law, why, that's a grand idea, I say. Dresses those dusty courtrooms up a bit. Like a flower in a cave, eh?" Eames clasped his hands together. "Now, what news from Frisco?"

"I beg your pardon?"

"Frisco!" Eames plopped into the chair behind his desk. "A little news from around the town before we get down to business."

Kit shook her head. "I am afraid I'm confused. I have never been to San Francisco."

Stanton Eames stiffened. "Aren't you the lawyer from the home office?"

"No, Mr. Eames. My office is here in Los Angeles."

Eames' eyes narrowed into an imposing scowl. "Then I am afraid I do not understand this intrusion."

"I have come with a simple request," Kit said, "and then I will be on my way. I am sure you are a busy man."

"Yes. Quite." Stanton Eames seemed suddenly ill at ease, like he could not figure out Kit's intentions. Kit wondered if he'd ever had a woman inside this office on a matter of business. It would not have surprised her if she was the first. The railroad and transportation enterprises were men's clubs, the same as virtually every other business in the country.

"Since you are here," said Eames, "I will give you five minutes. What is it that is on your mind?"

Better to get right to the point, Kit thought. "I am sure, Mr. Eames, that you are as saddened by the tragic events of yesterday as is the rest of the city."

For a moment it looked as though Eames did not have any idea what Kit was talking about. His stare was blank, or purposely obscure. Then, slowly, he nodded. "You mean the little boy?"

"Yes. Sammy Franklin by name."

"Tragic. Yes. Of course. Did you know him?"

"I happened to be motoring by just after the accident occurred."

"Motoring?"

"An auto."

Eames shook his head. "Go on, Miss Shannon."

"I was with the mother, Winifred Franklin, for some time immediately following the accident. I also visited her home earlier today. She is, as you will understand, devastated. She is a widow."

"Very sad indeed, yes." Eames cleared his throat. "Our sympathies."

"She is going to need medical attention."

"Medical? Was she injured? I heard nothing about that."

"The injury is to her mind and heart, from losing her only child. And this has affected her physically."

"Of course. Understandable. But tragedy is part of our lot

on this earth. We must learn to overcome the inevitable setbacks of life."

"I believe that, sir. With the help of God and our fellow man."

"Well said."

"That is why I have come to see you today. A gesture of goodwill to this woman, in the form of covering her medical expenses, would be of tremendous comfort and would also show the city that the Los Angeles Electric Trolley Line has its heart in the right place."

"We are a business enterprise, Miss Shannon."

"Of course. But businesses are part of society and they create effects. Sometimes those effects are not positive ones."

"People understand that, Miss Shannon. It is the price of progress. Without it, we would still be savages." Eames pointed to his right shoulder. "Do you know what I have here? A scar from a Cheyenne arrowhead. I was supervising the laying of track in Indian country and got taken right off my horse in a surprise raid. Two of my men died. But I accepted it. It was something I knew might happen to me someday. I took it in the name of progress."

"Surely progress has its limits."

Eames raised his eyebrows. "I don't see it that way."

"A business enterprise may be at fault for an accident that—"

"Ah! Now you come to it. Our trolley line has been active for over six years now. The people of the city know us now. We cannot be responsible for those who carelessly put themselves in danger."

A small fist began forming in Kit's stomach. "Mr. Eames, you do not mean to suggest that a four-year-old boy—"

"Was this boy in the care of his mother?"

"Yes, but—"

"There you are, then. We certainly sympathize with her loss, but if we were to recompense every injury, there would soon be no business. America would come to a standstill. Quite literally, in our case, as we are in the transportation business."

Kit knew the man had a point. The issue of fault had not

been fully settled. Kit didn't know any of the facts leading up to Sammy's death. She had assumed them, and that was dangerous for an attorney.

"I can appreciate your point, Mr. Eames. I wonder if you might allow me to make a few inquiries of your employees."

"To what purpose?"

"To better understand what happened yesterday. Perhaps we can prevent further accidents."

"I'm sorry, Miss Shannon, but that would prove to be distracting. If you will leave me the name and address of the mother, I will arrange to have flowers sent. Now, if you will excuse me."

Eames stood and made a grand gesture with his arm as if to sweep Kit out of the room.

The fist in Kit's stomach began to pound. "May we speak on the subject again sometime? Perhaps together we can—"

"Certainly not. As I said, I run a business here. Time and energy are of the essence. May I suggest you put your own time into something more productive."

Chapter Six

"You're as flushed as a tomato," Ted Fox said.

"You say the sweetest things," Kit replied.

It was late in the afternoon as they walked up Broadway toward the Imperial, where they were to meet Earl Rogers for dinner. Kit hardly noticed the crush of afternoon activity on the street—businessmen leaving their offices, women from Angeleno Heights and the Adams district finishing their busy shopping day. The clang of the trolleys was but a faraway irritant.

Her encounter with Stanton Eames had left her furious, and she felt powerless to do anything about it. The Los Angeles Electric Trolley Line and its large parent organization, Western Rail, were indifferent to the day-to-day lives of its constituency, the passengers and ordinary people who paid the fares each day. What could be done about this? If Eames' attitude was any indication, it would take more than an appeal to goodwill.

At least Ted was in an ebullient mood, and Kit was appreciative. He looked dashing in his evening clothes and stepped with a more confidant gait than ever. With the aid of a cane, he had mastered walking on his prosthetic leg, almost to the point of stylishness.

Kit felt in high style as well, dressed as she was in an evening gown, specially made by Mrs. Norris, of spangled lavender chiffon with a lofted hem. The dressmaker had expressed reluctance at the modification to the hem, but Kit insisted. Mrs. Norris had acceded to the request, but only if she could add a plaited belt of liberty satin. Kit was happy to agree.

"It is a pleasant day in Los Angeles," Ted reminded Kit, "and you're stewing about something."

"So now I am a stewed tomato?"

"Concentrate on the good news."

"Which is?"

"That we are together. How can it get any better than that?"

Kit held Ted's arm lightly but squeezed it as she said, "Are men born pigheaded, or is that a skill they develop over time?"

"Why, Miss Shannon, I am cut to the quick."

"Oh, I don't mean you."

"Then you must have had another of your famous confrontations today. Would you like to tell me about it? Although I am of the male sex, I shall endeavor not to be pigheaded."

Kit had to smile. "I shall be the judge." Her smile quickly faded as she told Ted of her meeting with Eames.

When she finished, Ted paused a moment before answering. They came to a stop at the corner of Broadway and Third. "You are not trusting in the Lord," he said.

The words were simple and spoken softly, yet they hit Kit like a hard gust of wind. "I beg your pardon?"

"Isn't that what you've tried to drum into my pig head since I've known you? Trust in the Lord with all my heart? Lean not unto my own understanding? In all my ways acknowledge Him? And then what happens?"

"He shall direct thy paths," Kit finished. "Proverbs, chapter three, verses five and six."

"Those are the anti-stew verses, are they not?"

Kit looked at him, and his blue eyes danced.

"If you trust Him," Ted said, "there is no need to get worked up. He will direct you if you'll lean on Him fully."

Kit gave him a kiss on the cheek. "How did you get to be so wise?"

"I found the right girl," Ted said, holding out his arm for Kit to take once again. "Shall we?"

Earl Rogers was waiting at his usual table. He stood to greet Ted and Kit and then introduced the man who was sitting with him. "May I present Mr. Jack London."

He was a stocky, handsome man with a shock of curly dark hair and wide, intelligent eyes. He seemed to have the latent energy of a coiled spring.

"I have heard much about you, Miss Shannon," London said. "I'd like to write a book about you sometime."

"Jack writes a book every month or so," Earl said.

"Perfect," Ted said. "Kit gets into trouble every month or so."

The shared laughter broke the ice, and a convivial meal commenced. The tongues of Earl and Jack London became increasingly loosened, Kit gauged, by the schooners of beer they drank.

"I am a socialist, Miss Shannon," London announced during the meal. He was on a lecture tour, and Kit had asked him about his subjects. "Not because I hate capitalism, but because I hate the capitalists who mangle the system as their machines mangle their workers."

Kit, thinking of Stanton Eames, was intrigued. "Please explain."

"The powerful businessman has the advantage of too much money," he said. "He can bribe legislatures, buy judges, control primaries, and hire a bunch of men to sit around him and tell him all day that he is right and proper to do it. After all, progress is the god here, money the sure sign that this god is rewarding them."

Jack London was speaking with animation, his hands motioning the air. Earl Rogers looked to be amused and content just to listen. Kit thought this man London would make quite an evangelist should he ever seek to promote the Gospel.

"And because he sees money as his reward," London continued, "he will refuse to use any of it to make the machines in his factory safer. So every year his machines batter and destroy thousands of working men, women, and children. He does not care to pay a decent wage, knowing that for every worker of his who dies of starvation or is thrown to the mercy of the streets, there are dozens waiting to take his place."

London's eyes became filled with outrage. "I met a woman in Chicago who works sixty hours per week sewing buttons on garments. Her weekly salary is ninety cents. She is a mere twenty-seven, but her hands are already those of an old woman. Does the average potentate of industry care? No! He will chatter endlessly about the good he is bringing to the marketplace, all while his adulterated commodities kill thousands of babies and children. Do you know what most workers in the country have to go through, Miss Shannon?"

"A little." She had seen a couple of sweatshops back in the 1890s while living with nuns in New York.

London paused and took a long drink of his beer. When he put the glass down he said, "A young fellow sent me his manuscript last year. His name is Upton Sinclair, and his book is going to send shock waves across America. It is called *The Jungle,* and it rips the cover off the meat-packing industry. I've written the introduction. I want you to read it."

"I shall."

"So I lecture. I write books. Others do the same. We must open the eyes of the public and make them care. If we cannot move the mountains of industry this way, we must use every other available means."

He paused a moment, until Rogers prompted him. "Such as?"

"Revolution," London said.

"You're going to get thrown in the pokey if you keep talking like that," Rogers commented. "Though I think that is your plan, am I right?"

"Maybe." London smiled and finished his drink. "Would Miss Shannon defend me?"

"I will certainly defend your right to freedom of speech," said Kit. "But I would counsel a clear head when doing so."

London looked at her with a wondering gaze.

Earl Rogers jumped in. "Miss Shannon is an advocate of the sober life, Jack. You'd better watch out or you'll be a teetotaler before you know it."

"Are you against ale?" Jack London asked.

"Only the abuse of it," Kit said.

Kit glanced at Earl and Ted. Both of them looked like happy spectators at a boxing match, in no hurry to jump into the scuffle.

"So you would take away a man's pleasures?"

"Man's right to pleasure," Kit said, "ends where it harms others. My father was shot and killed by a drunken man. I know of a man sitting in jail right now who is accused of attempted murder because he let alcohol rule his faculties."

"Are you an advocate of temperance, then?"

"More an advocate of men knowing their limits."

London turned silent.

"Would you like another beer, Jack?" Earl Rogers asked with a wink.

Jack London scowled, then looked at Kit. "Maybe I won't write that book after all."

Stanton Eames listened to the crackling of the phone line with both wonder and disgust. On the one hand, the ability to speak to a person hundreds of miles away over wires struck him as amazing. Eames could remember when the Morse telegraph was reached across the continent, even Europe. Folks thought that was something. But voice to voice was something much better.

On the other hand, it was inefficient and somewhat degrading for Eames to have to raise his voice over the crackling.

But this was necessary.

"Are you there, Sutter?" Eames bellowed.

"Here, Eames."

Stanton Eames ignored the slight. The San Francisco lawyers did not like taking direction from him, and he knew it. Even so, Western Rail had given Eames authority to communicate directly with the company's law firm, and he was not going to let even the senior partner of Sutter, Wingate & Finn get his goat.

"I want your best lawyer on this," Eames said. "Get him down here now."

"What is the problem?"

"The problem," Eames huffed, putting as much disdain in his voice as he could, "is a lawyer named Shannon. She's trouble on the hoof. I can smell it."

"Are you referring to Kathleen Shannon?"

"You know her?"

Sutter's voice was faint over the line, but Eames heard him say, "I've read about her. I hear she's pretty good."

"Maybe too good for Sutter, Wingate & Finn."

Silence. Sutter said something Eames couldn't make out, but no matter. "Just get one of your best lawyers down here, reporting to me. I want this woman stopped before she even gets started."

Then, with pleasure, Stanton Eames hung up the telephone.

Chapter Seven

"Your name is Doogan?" Kit asked.

"Here now, miss. What are you doing in my establishment?"

Doogan's was located on Fifth Street, within smelling distance of the Madison Livery on Main. The morning air was replete with the scent of horse and dirt, while the floor of the saloon was covered with sawdust. It must have been a fresh batch, as the day's trade had not yet mashed it down.

After last night's conversation with Jack London, Kit had been going over and over the story Mousy Malloy had told her about the charges against him. Booze was a large part of what had happened, and the scene of the crime was the place to start.

Kit took a look around at the dusky interior. "Are you the owner?"

"Proud owner, and what of it?"

"My name is Kathleen Shannon, and I am an attorney."

Doogan narrowed his gaze as he wiped his hands on the apron he wore over his ample frame. He had been cutting onions, and the pungent odor mixed with the equine smell from outside was unlike anything Kit had taken in before.

"I've heard about you," Doogan said.

"And what is it you have heard?"

He leaned forward. Kit saw he had massive forearms. He could have been a bricklayer as well as a bartender. "I have heard that women and law don't belong together. Nor, come to think of it, do women and my place."

Kit folded her arms. "This is a public establishment, is it not?"

"It's *my* establishment, and in here I have two rules."

Kit waited, figuring he wanted to lay the rules out for her.

"Rule number one: your money has to be on the table if you want to stay in my bar. Rule number two: only the money of men is any good around here. That means you are in violation of both of my rules." Doogan's bushy eyebrows narrowed as he nodded toward the door.

Kit did not move. "I also have two rules, Mr. Doogan."

The man's eyes widened. In a near whisper, but one coated with scorn, he said, "And what might those be?"

"Rule number one," said Kit, "I never let silly rules get in the way of legal business. Rule number two... ?"

Now it was Doogan who folded his arms across his chest. "Yeah?"

"I always give people a second chance to do the right thing."

"What if they don't?"

"Then I would be forced to use some other means."

Doogan smiled. "Other means? You talking about getting rough or something?"

Doogan couldn't know that she and Corazón had been taking jiu-jitsu training for nearly a year. The martial art, all the rage for many women these days, was intended to help them "get rough" with a potential attacker.

What she had in mind was much more effective. "I would have to use the power of subpoena," she said, "to summon you to court because you have information relevant to a legal action."

Doogan huffed and pulled himself to his full height, sucking in his stomach in the process. His chest thrust out like the bow of a ship. "Ask your questions, then, but make it fast."

With a quick nod of her head, Kit said, "Are you acquainted with a man named Mousy Malloy?"

"You representing Malloy?"

"I am."

Doogan scratched his chin. "He tried to kill a man, you know."

"So I've been told. That is why he needs representation. Now, were you a witness to the incident?"

"I was. That is to say, it happened right in front of me eyes."

"Would you like to tell me just what occurred?"

"If I tell you what happened, will you leave me be?"

"For the time being, yes."

"Lady lawyers! I'll be hanged! Fine. I remember Mousy Malloy coming in that day, like he does most days. He sat at that table right over there while my cook rustled him up some eggs. He was minding his own business when Ellis Dyke come in."

"Is Ellis Dyke a frequent patron?"

"He is, and I like it that way. He's free with his bits and likes to have a good time."

"Does Mr. Dyke also have a temper?"

Doogan shrugged. "No more than any other man."

"What happened after Dyke came in?"

"The usual, but then I see him and Mousy get into it a little, you know, with the banter. I think there's some bad blood there, but I don't know no details. Any which way, Ellis and Mousy make a bet about who can drink the most. Ellis put up the money and I poured the drinks."

"What a lovely contest." Kit was growing more disgusted by the second, suddenly wishing she was anywhere but in a local bar.

"Listen, I sell drinks. That's my business. What men do with their drinks is none of my affair."

"How many other witnesses were there?"

"I don't know for certain. Half a dozen maybe. Everybody

was laughing and joking and having a good time. Until Mousy lost his mind and grabbed the gun."

"Yes, I was coming to that. How did Mousy Malloy get a gun?"

"He took mine."

Kit shook her head at him. "You own the gun?"

"I keep it here under the bar," Doogan said, "just in case I have to break up a fight. Look up there." He pointed to the ceiling. "See, three bullet holes. Three times I fired the gun to quiet things down. Never fired at another man, though."

"How did Mousy know the gun was there?"

"I showed it to him once."

"So what did he do, come around the bar and get it? With you standing right there?"

"No, that's not it at all. In fact, he took it out of me hand."

"How's that?"

"I had it in mind to fire another bullet at the ceiling, to quiet Mousy up. He was yelling and screaming at Dyke. Next thing I know, he's got the gun in his hand and that's when he fired. I came around the bar and grabbed Mousy before he could do any more damage."

Kit tried to picture the scene. "You say you came around the bar?"

"That's right."

"Would you mind showing me?"

"Is this really—"

"Yes."

With a roll of his eyes, Doogan clomped down to the far end of the bar top. Kit followed along on the other side.

"See?" Doogan said when he was almost to the end. "I was here. I had the gun out like this." He put his hand over the counter. "The actual gun is in police hands now. Mousy was about where you're standing."

Kit marked it in her mind. "And he fired once?"

"Right."

"Which direction?"

Doogan indicated the other end of the bar. "There, where Ellis Dyke and his friends were standing."

Kit mimicked the action. "Then what did you do?"

"Like I said, I came around."

"Please."

Huffing, Doogan continued his trek around the bar top. Three, four steps more and he was next to Kit. "Here."

"And what did you do?"

"I grabbed him like ..." He put his arms out and almost wrapped them around Kit. "I mean, I got a bear hug around him and then took the gun away."

"And then?"

"Dyke says to me, `You hold him, Doogan, I'm gonna get a cop!' So that's what I did."

"No one was hit by Mr. Malloy's shot, is that right?"

"That's right. He missed."

"Might he have missed intentionally?"

Doogan had obviously never entertained such a notion. "But he was drunk."

"That's not what I asked. From your observation, couldn't that shot have been a warning of some kind?"

"A drunk ain't in control of such things. He tried to kill Ellis Dyke, simple as that."

"Isn't that just an assumption on your part? What leads you to believe that Mousy Malloy had any intention at all of killing Ellis Dyke?"

A smug smile crossed Doogan's face. "Because, just before he fired, he yelled out, `I'm gonna kill you, Ellis.'"

If this had been a cross-examination in court, no doubt the jury—and the judge and gallery—would have laughed and nodded with certainty. But this was only an interview with a witness. Yet something didn't feel quite right about Doogan's story.

"One more question, Mr. Doogan," Kit said.

"Last one."

"Who else was in this drinking party with Ellis Dyke?"

"I don't want to be giving out no names."

"These are witnesses, sir. I would like to get their stories."

"I don't know."

"Of course," said Kit, "I can always stay here and talk to your customers as they come in."

Doogan slapped the bar top. "All right! Talk if you want to. Talk to Sam Hartrampf and Billy Rye. They're friends of Ellis Dyke, so it's no secret."

"Anyone else?"

"I don't recollect. There were some others around, but—"

The saloon door banged open, and Kit was stunned to see the figure of a boy. He looked to be around ten years old and, from the appearance of his garments, not from a well-off family.

"Hello, Bobby," Doogan said with grand affection.

"Hi, Mr. Doogan." The boy cast an uncomfortable look at Kit as he approached the bar.

"You ready for your first delivery?" Doogan asked.

"Yes, sir."

The barkeep walked back around the bar and took up two pails with wire handles and began to fill them with beer from a tap. Kit watched the boy watching Doogan. When both pails were full, Doogan put them on top of the bar for the boy to pick them up.

"Mind your spillage," Doogan said. "Same place as yesterday. Same price. And keep yourself to only a sip or two."

"Right." The eager young man held the pails carefully as he walked out of the saloon.

Kit turned on Doogan. "You employ that boy to deliver beer?"

"That's right."

"He can't be more than ten!"

"Can't an enterprising lad make some money for himself?"

"You allow him to drink, too?"

"A man's got to learn to drink sometime. Might as well start with somebody who knows how."

A feeling like a summer storm came over Kit. "That is outrageous, Mr. Doogan."

She left him without awaiting a reply.

Kit caught the boy at the corner of Fifth and Main.

"Your name is Bobby?" she said.

From underneath his cap the boy eyed Kit warily. His look seemed far older, and more jaded, than his tender years should have allowed. His arms seemed tired already from holding the pails.

"What you want?"

"I want to know if you are in the constant employ of Mr. Doogan."

"What if I am?"

"Do you also drink that beer?"

Looking as if he was being accused of a crime, the boy stuck out his chin. "I'm allowed. Mr. Doogan says so."

"Yes, I'll bet he does. Where are you going?"

"To deliver."

"What does Mr. Doogan pay you?"

The young man set the two pails on the sidewalk and, crossing his arms over his chest, rubbed his shoulders. "Why are you askin' me all these questions?"

"You can trust me. I'm not going to bite your head off."

"What's your name?"

"Kit." She put out her hand. "Pleased to meet you, Bobby."

His hand was rough for a boy.

"Where is your home?" Kit asked.

Bobby motioned with his thumb toward the south side of the city but said nothing.

"Do you live with your mother and father?"

The boy shook his head, looked at his shoes. They were dirty lace-ups with fraying strings.

"Orphan?"

"I gotta go," Bobby said. "I'll be late." He bent down for the pails, when Kit touched his shoulder, stopping him.

"What if I offered to pay you double what you're getting from Mr. Doogan?"

The news seemed to interest and confuse the boy at the same time. "You got beer, too?"

"No, no beer. I will pay you to leave me the delivery you are now transporting."

"What? You gonna deliver?"

"In a manner of speaking."

The boy appeared to do some calculations in his head. "Doogan pays me a dime a delivery."

"Then I shall pay you a quarter for each job," Kit said. "If you want, I'll find other work for you to do. More quarters. All you have to promise me is no more beer."

Scowling, the boy said, "I like beer."

"No doubt you do, but it is not good for you."

"Says who?"

"You're just a boy."

"What do you care, anyway? You ain't my mother."

"No, but I'd like to be your friend."

The boy took off his cap so he could scratch his dirty blond hair. He calculated a moment, then put his cap back on with purpose. "Fifty cents," he said. "I'll give you the beer for fifty cents."

"A man of business, eh?" Kit said affectionately. "Sold." She took out two quarters from the pocket of her dress and put them in Bobby's outstretched hand. He seemed quite pleased with this transaction.

"You gonna deliver that now?" Bobby asked, indicating the pails on the ground. "I'll tell you where."

"No need." Kit picked up the first pail and, with one swoop, tossed the contents into the street. As the boy's jaw fell, she did the same with the second pail.

"Hey!" he cried. "You can't do that!"

"I just did."

"But you—"

"No buts. Are you hungry, Bobby?"

Slowly, the boy nodded.

"Then come along with me. I know a place that serves a hot dog almost as good as the ones at Coney Island."

Chapter Eight

Stanton Eames bellowed, "Where's our beer?"

The president of the Los Angeles Electric Trolley Line peered over his desk at Julius Rhetta and Tom Phelps, the reporter for the *Times.*

Rhetta blinked. "I ordered it from Doogan's, same as always."

Eames shook his head, let out a breath of aggrieved air, and grabbed the mouthpiece of the interoffice phone. "Helen! Give a telephone call to Doogan's and ask about our beer." He slammed the mouthpiece down. "Incompetence and inefficiency. Two things I cannot tolerate." He allowed his demeanor to soften. "Now then, gentlemen, until we wet our whistles, let's talk business, shall we?"

The two men across from Eames nodded. They were just where he wanted them, compliant and ready. In so many ways, business was like a game of chess, a pastime which Eames had mastered long ago.

"I am sick and tired," Eames began, "of reading about another land grab by Collis P. Huntington. I don't care if he is a blood relative of the Southern Pacific—he's getting prime property, and you know what he's going to do with it. It's not right that one man should be able to bring such leverage to the rail fight in this city. Don't you agree?"

Julius Rhetta pulled at his bow tie. "It is a free country, Stanton. The chamber of commerce encourages all citizens to—"

"Oh, stuff it, Julius." Eames rapped the desk with his fist. "You know what I'm talking about. I'm not supporting you and Tillinghast in your lofty positions for my health. I want you to get out there and stop Huntington from doing all this."

"But how?" Rhetta cleared his throat.

Eames shifted his attention to the reporter. "Have you ever taken a close look at Huntington's business practices?"

Tom Phelps, who looked to Eames like an eager traveling salesman as much as a reporter, shrugged. "Only when he makes news."

"A land grab is news, isn't it?"

"Maybe. But it's news when it comes from either side of the fence."

Eames wagged his finger at Phelps. "You are not here to look at both sides of the fence, young man. You are here to offer service."

"Haven't you heard about the freedom of the press?"

Impertinent tone, Eames thought. Hadn't Rhetta explained things to this man? Eames paused, leaned back, and sized Phelps up. A few seconds later Eames decided Phelps was just like any other red-blooded American on the move. Therefore, the same smell would have its effect on him. The smell, that is, of money.

"Look here," said Eames, "I've not asked you into this *sanctum sanctorum* to get a lecture on press freedoms. Julius here tells me you're a smart man. Ambitious. All I am suggesting is that you take an interest in the same things that interest me. Why? Because what interests Western Railroad, and the Los Angeles Electric, is of great significance to the future of this city."

"Mr. Eames plans to expand the border of Los Angeles," Julius Rhetta interjected with a little too much enthusiasm for Eames' taste.

"Which will be of benefit to all." Eames pulled back his coat slightly so Phelps could get a good look at his diamond stickpin. "I am quite prepared to reward such services to our agreed-upon goals and dreams."

"I won't be bought," Phelps said, but with a lot less mustard, Eames assessed, than the sentiment demanded.

"Of course not," Eames said. "No one is suggesting any such thing. But an additional income from taking an interest in certain things, things we discuss together over ..." Eames paused, then picked up the mouthpiece again. "Any word on our beer?"

The voice of his secretary was tinny and crackling over the wire. "Mr. Doogan said the delivery boy should have been here half an hour ago."

Eames shook his head disgustedly and put down the mouthpiece. "How can civilized men discuss matters of import without convivial drink between them?" Eames had acquired his taste for beer and talk while at Princeton, class of 1868. He'd latched on to it as a "man's drink"—this coupled with his drive for academic and athletic success. And although his capacity for drink had also added to his considerable girth, he accepted it because, to his way of thinking, men's tongues were unloosed by golden suds—something that often gave Eames the advantage in his business dealings.

"As I was saying, Mr. Phelps, I am prepared to reward what I see as a good journalistic effort. No one needs to know about this, of course. It will be our little arrangement and, I might suggest, a very lucrative one. Just to show you what I mean ..." Stanton Eames slid open his right-hand drawer and removed several paper bills. Placing the bills on the desk in front of Tom Phelps, he said, "That's one hundred dollars. More than you make in six months, I'll wager."

Phelps looked at the money.

"Go on, take it. A little reward."

"Reward?"

"On account. For the excellent job I know you're going to do."

Phelps hesitated, looked at Rhetta, then back at the money.

He licked his lips, and that's when Eames knew he'd hooked him like a trout.

"Go ahead," Eames prodded. "Are you against the American dream or something?"

The reporter's hand shot out and grabbed the bills. He shoved them in his pocket without counting them. "Just remember," Phelps said, "I am not going to be told what to write."

"Of course not," said Eames, letting out a little of the fishing line. "We both understand our positions and interests, eh?"

Phelps paused a moment, then nodded.

"Good," Eames said. "Now, there's one other little matter that came up. I understand you are acquainted with that lawyer Kathleen Shannon."

Hearing the name perked up Phelps's interest. "Kit? Yeah, I know her. Ever since she first came to Los Angeles."

"What manner of woman is she?"

"Ha! The highest and best kind. She's not for sale, either."

"No? My experience is that all lawyers have a price. That much is in their training."

"Not Kit."

"What makes her different?"

Phelps shook his head in admiration. "She's got a backbone of steel. She'll chew your hide if you get on the wrong side of the law with her."

"Well, then," Eames chuckled, "let's hope it never comes to that. I've been known to chew a little hide myself."

Kit paced back and forth about a hundred times before being shown into the mayor's office. The man who escorted her there, one Jones, was a bespectacled, owlish sort who kept clicking his fingernails together when he spoke.

"I hope you understand that the mayor is very busy," he said, "and the only reason he is seeing you is to stop your pestering letters and telephone calls. They have become quite a distraction, and you know the mayor has many important matters to take care of."

"I should think the mayor would be happy to hear from his concerned citizens," Kit said.

Jones stopped, turned, and grimaced. "Miss Shannon, the mayor is the mayor of all the people, not merely those who wish to stir up trouble. The fact that he is seeing you today shows he is a man of great generosity, and I hope you will appreciate that."

"I appreciate all attempts to use reason and judgment in the proper discharge of one's duties."

Jones opened his eyes wide. "You will have ten minutes," he said.

The mayor's office was a spacious, wood-paneled chamber stuffed with knickknacks and odd curios. A small rendition of an elephant, made entirely of walnuts, sat on the corner of his desk. The hard-shelled pachyderm looked skeptically at Kit through its painted eyes.

Kit had met with the mayor on one previous occasion. It had been a gathering at the Los Angeles Chamber of Commerce a year ago, in a meeting honoring the local bar association. Kit had not been on the original invitation list, but Earl Rogers insisted she come along as his guest. He wanted her inside "the belly of the beast," he'd said.

Mayor Tillinghast spoke for about an hour at that meeting, waxing eloquent on his view that municipal power should be centralized at city hall for a more efficient Los Angeles. Though he was prone to repeat himself—his message could have been delivered in half the time—Kit found him a skilled politician, who could wrap golden words around tin ideas.

After the talk, Earl Rogers brought her to Tillinghast and introduced them.

"Ah yes," Tillinghast had said, "the lady lawyer. Tell me, since a woman's work is cleaning up, are you here on a mission to sweep out our city?"

Biting her tongue, Kit only said, "If you hand me a broom, I should be happy to."

Tillinghast had not looked amused.

Now, standing in the mayor's office, the first thing Tillinghast said to her was, "Looking for that broom, are you?"

At least he's being direct, she thought. "In a manner of speaking, yes."

Tillinghast motioned for her to sit. He was a man slight of build, who liked to use outsized gestures to compensate. He did so now, motioning toward Kit with a grand gesture of his hand. "You appear to have a bee in your bonnet about the sale of alcohol in the city," he said.

"I have a concern, a grave concern."

"As do I, Miss Shannon. That is why I am in full support of all laws against public drunkenness."

"This is only part of the problem, sir. The trade in liquor is corrupting boys and young men. The saloon owners hire them. That is why I—"

"But there's nothing I can do about the way a man chooses to run a legal establishment. Nor would I wish to do so. The men who come here to build a new life for themselves, who sweat and strain to move our city forward as a metropolis of the twentieth century, deserve a certain license."

"License to harm boys?"

"Miss Shannon, you perhaps overstate matters."

"Is there any way you can justify this?"

"I am not a religious figurehead, Miss Shannon. I am the mayor, and the saloon owners as well as the church are my concern."

"This has nothing to do with the church. But I do not see that you should favor one constituency over another."

Tillinghast leaned back on his heels. "Are you accusing me of favoritism, Miss Shannon?"

"I am asking you a question. Will you give as much thought to the concerns of citizens who see alcohol as a problem for our youth as you will to those who see it as a way to make money?"

Tillinghast paused before answering, "I will take your suggestion under advisement."

"May we meet again in another week to discuss plans and ideas for a new strategy?"

"Suppose you leave that to me and my staff. These men are trained to look out for the best interests of the city."

"Surely the input of a woman would not be unwelcome," Kit said.

"If you wish to send me more letters, I shall give them considerable thought. Now if you'll excuse me ..." Tillinghast made a motion toward the door.

It was a smooth and elegant attempt to brush her off. Kit would have none of it. "It is a long time until November."

Tillinghast regarded her with a suspicious look. "Are you going to try to change that? Is that a veiled threat?"

"Only the voice of a concerned citizen, one who has yet to decide whom she will support for mayor. Perhaps your opponent will be more passionate about the issues that concern so many of us."

"That is the democratic way," said Tillinghast, opening his office door. "I bid you good day."

Without a single concession, Kit exited city hall, all the while feeling the eyes of Mr. Jones watching her go.

The Los Angeles Institute of the Bible had been established in 1899 by the Reverend Miller Macauley, a Scottish immigrant who was now Kit's own pastor. In its first few years the Institute struggled along, causing barely a ripple in a city of so many Catholic and Protestant churches.

Then, in 1904, Aunt Freddy left Kit her multimillion-dollar estate. Kit knew that Freddy, who had adopted the Christian faith before she died, would have been pleased with Kit's decision to turn over most of the estate to the Institute.

Kit was appointed to the board, whose members included G. Campbell Morgan, the English evangelist, and several other theologians and Christian business leaders.

The stated purpose of the Institute was the following:

> **We exist to champion the Word of God in our country and the world; to teach the fundamentals of the Christian faith to all people; and to do battle with those ideas which seek to keep men in bondage to sin.**

Not all the Christian clergy in Los Angeles had embraced the Institute, especially after Kit's gift catapulted it into greater influence. The most prominent critic, Dr. Edward Lazarus, had engaged Kit on occasion in debate over the accuracy of Scripture. It was Edward Lazarus who had first begun referring to the fellows of the Institute as "Fundamentalists."

Knowing Edward Lazarus as she did, Kit was not dismayed by the term. It was, in its way, a badge of honor. If the Christian faith had not fundamentals—strong foundation stones upon which to build—then it was just another philosophy in mankind's string of false pearls. Papa had taught her that.

The Institute had recently taken up residence in a new building on Main Street, between Second and Third—The Fairbank, named for Aunt Freddy. And it was into this building that Kit Shannon all but stormed.

Ted Fox looked up from the book in which he was making notations. He was the financial officer of the firm—utilizing his background in banking—when he wasn't trying to get his plane into the air.

"Kit!" Ted plopped the pencil and book down. "We weren't expecting you in today."

Kit swept through the swinging gate, similar to the ones found in the courts of law, and sat on the edge of Ted's rolltop desk.

Ted put out his hands. "What, no kiss for your intended?"

His smile was, as always, irresistible to her. She leaned over and kissed him on the cheek. "Aunt Freddy would be scandalized," she said. "Kissing in a place of work!"

"I think Freddy would be pleased that we are giving expression to our troth in the building she built."

"Perhaps. But she would not be pleased with what I just

discovered. I have just spent time with a ten-year-old boy of the street, who has been working for a saloon, delivering beer. And learning to drink!"

"Drink?"

"Yes. Encouraged by the men around him."

"Such as whom?"

"Such as Bill Doogan."

"The saloon owner? What were you doing there?"

Before Kit could answer, the Reverend Miller Macauley strode into the office. He was a man with kind, alert eyes and spoke with a burr chiseled from his ancestral home in the Scottish highlands. "Kit! How nice to see you! We all thought ye'd be in court." He gave the *r* in *court* his familiar little trill.

"Kit's just come from a saloon," Ted said with a twinkle in his eye.

Kit slapped Ted's hand. "Don't mind him, Pastor. He's giddy today."

"Only with the wine of love," Ted said.

"Be quiet," Kit said. Then to both of the men, "I want us to issue a statement regarding the saloons in this city that use boys in their establishments."

Macauley raised his eyebrows. "Take on the temples of alcohol, eh?"

"Exactly."

"Give her an ax," Ted said, "and we will have our own Carry Nation!"

Carry Nation, the most famous of alcohol abolitionists, was currently in Los Angeles for a series of lectures. She was an object of fun in the papers, which drew caricatures of her holding her famous hatchet. But that hatchet was no laughing matter to the numerous saloon owners who had seen what Mrs. Nation could do with it.

"Stop it, Ted," Kit protested. "I am not talking about the liquor trade, only its influence on children. There are no ordinances against this practice."

Macauley stroked his chin. "They're a powerful lot in this city. Would that be in keeping with our mission to spread the Word?"

"The fight is right. I want to see laws passed that would protect children from the reach of alcohol. If we do not take this cause as our own, I must go out and speak of it by myself."

Ted stood up and threw his arms around her. "How can we resist this force of nature?" He looked at Macauley. "Let me make this matter part of my talks in San Francisco."

Kit had nearly forgotten that Ted would be taking the train to San Francisco to deliver Bibles to a boys' home there. "Yes, that would be a start," she said.

"I will impress upon them that their minds are what separates them from the animals, and if they want to get ahead in this life, they must keep their minds clear. I'll tell them that's what God wants of them, too. And if they learn their Scriptures, I'll say, they may one day become a lawyer."

Kit put her hands on her hips, smiling. "I may marry you after all," she said.

The telephone on the wall jangled. Reverend Macauley answered it, then turned to Kit. "It is your assistant."

Kit took it. "Yes, Corazón?"

"There is a message that has come for you," Corazón told her. "The brother-in-law of Winnie Franklin."

"Salem Laine?"

"He would like to see you. He is at his house now."

"I'll go right over. Have you got a pencil?"

"Yes."

"I'd like you to see if you can locate three people for me. Ellis Dyke. Sam Hartrampf and—"

"Excuse?"

"I think that would be H-A-R-T-R-A-M-P-F."

"This is a name?"

"Also a Billy Rye. R-Y-E or some such. Have you got that?"

"I will do it."

"I knew you would. How is Raul?"

Raul Montoya was Corazón's beau, a handsome local who had once saved Corazón from an assault.

Corazón had sunshine in her voice. "He is going to ask me, I think."

"To marry you?"
"Sí!"
"It is about time!"

Chapter Nine

Salem Laine was waiting outside his house. Kit saw him pacing on the porch, his hands clasped behind his back. When he saw Kit approach, he practically jumped down the stairs.

"Thank you for coming," he said. "We've been frantic."

The look of concern in his eyes was deep and penetrating. "Is Winnie ill?"

"She's been asking for you, Miss Shannon. But it scares me."

"How so?"

"It is like she is possessed of something. She refuses to eat. She will not listen to reason. She ..."

"Take me to her."

Winnie was in her room, as before, in the same chair by the window. Only now she was rocking back and forth, her arms folded in front of her chest. Small moans emitted from her throat as she swayed.

She looked up and saw Kit, and her eyes grew wide. "Help them!" she cried.

Kit felt the shock of the words and the gaunt, wild aspect to Winnie's entire being.

"I don't know what she's talking about," Salem said. Alice stood by his side, looking equally worried. "She says she'll only talk to you, Miss Shannon."

"Help them, please," Winnie said.

Kit went to her, taking her hand while sitting on the edge of the bed. Winnie's hand was cold and dry, trembling. "I'm here, Winnie."

"Can you help them? Can you?"

"Who, Winnie?"

"It's Sammy. He is asking."

"Sammy?"

"He knows."

"Knows what?"

"You are the only one."

"Tell me more."

"Sammy came to me in a dream," Winnie said. "He told me things."

"Yes?"

"He told me that he loves me, that he is in a beautiful place and that I should not worry for him. But he told me he wants to save other children."

"Save them?"

"There are other children in danger. The thing that happened to him might happen to them! He needs your help to stop it!"

Winnie was starting to shake with some sort of inner desperation. Had her son really come to her in a dream? There were many instances in the Bible where God communicated in dreams. Yet Winnie was clearly in distress and could have created the experience herself—not uncommon in times of grief.

I trust in you, Lord, Kit prayed silently. *You are my guide in all things. Guide me now. Help me know what to do.*

Winnie's shaking hand reached up and took hold of Kit's blouse. "Please help. Can you?"

"Winnie," Kit heard herself say, "I will certainly try in any way I—"

"No." Winnie pulled Kit closer. "You must!"

"All right, Winnie. All right."

The woman's face immediately relaxed, and she released her grip on Kit. Her smile turned soft, signifying a comfort she had previously longed for but failed to attain.

Kit turned to Salem and Alice, not knowing what she was going to be able to do. Only one answer came readily to mind. "Will you join us in prayer?"

Salem hesitated. "I don't reckon I can." He rubbed his hands self-consciously on his shirt. "I haven't been on good terms with the Lord lately."

With watering eyes Alice Laine looked at Kit. She didn't need to say anything to communicate her anguish.

"May I ask," Kit said, "if you believe in Jesus?"

"'Course I do," Salem said.

"That is faith enough. Will you allow me to lead us?"

A short pause. Salem nodded. Winnie stood and embraced her brother-in-law. "Come, Salem," Winnie said. Taking his hand, she led him to the side of the bed, where she knelt. Salem joined her on his knees. Alice, tears running down her face, was next.

Finally, Kit knelt at the foot of the bed and began to pray.

Chapter Ten

Kit drove back to her office, the Ford bouncing down the street a little more loudly than she would have liked. A farmer with a horse cart shouted, in no uncertain terms, what he thought of her "rattletrap."

Maybe he had a point. Advances in technology were not always a benefit, were they? Not that living in huts was to be preferred, but science and inventions all had to be strained through the filter of wisdom and common sense.

Even as she pondered these things, Kit passed a huge web of steel girders on the corner of Fifth and Hill Streets. A new department store was going up, the most ambitious building project in the city. It would be directly across from the city's central park in the crowded business district. How long would the park itself last, Kit wondered. Commerce demanded its share of space and was always hungry.

At the office, Corazón anxiously awaited Kit. "I have found two of the three," she said.

"Good," Kit said, removing her hat and letting her auburn hair tumble freely over her shoulders. "Who have you got?"

"The man Ellis Dyke, he is listed in the Western Rail office. That is near the Plaza."

"Yes, I know the building. Who else?"

"The man Hartrampf. He has a home on Santee Street. He works at Pioneer Drugstore."

"Good work. That leaves Billy Rye."

"I did not find him. He is not in the directory."

"Perhaps he is an itinerant worker. My guess is he's with the railroad in some way, because of his friendship with Dyke. Meantime you can also check—"

There was a knock at the door. Corazón opened it. "Oh, you again." She turned around to Kit. "A boy asking for you."

It was Bobby, his hat in his hands.

"Come in," Kit said.

The boy did so cautiously, staring at Corazón.

Kit patted him on the back. "This is my assistant, Corazón. A good friend."

Bobby looked at the floor. "Hello."

"Hello to you, too," Corazón said.

"Bobby has accepted my offer for services," Kit said. "He can clean and file and run errands. He is a good worker, I can tell."

"This is a good thing," Corazón agreed.

The boy, still looking at the floor, shook his head. "I can't."

"What is it, Bobby?" Kit asked.

"Mr. Beasley says I can't."

"Beasley," said Kit. "Of the Beasley Home for Boys?"

Bobby nodded.

"I see." Kit knew about the home and its reputed good work, though now she wondered what this man Beasley could have against one of his charges doing respectable work.

"How about if I talk to him?" Kit said, noting the downcast look in Bobby's face.

"Oh no!" Bobby said. "He wouldn't like that."

"What harm is there in just talking?"

"I can't do it, that's all," Bobby said, planting his cap on his head. "I came to tell you. I have to go now." Bobby turned his back and ran out of the office.

"Wait—"

Kit almost went after him, but instead she turned to Corazón. "Why don't you see what you can find out about this Mr. Beasley."

"I will do it."

"While you're at it, I'll go have a chat with Mr. Ellis Dyke."

The Western Rail building, near the terminus at the old plaza, was within spitting distance of the Pico House, one of the oldest structures in Los Angeles. Western Rail had arrived in 1885, just in time for the first big population influx from the East and Midwest. However, it found a fight on its hands with the more established Southern Pacific Railroad.

The SP had two train stations in town, the biggest being Los Angeles Junction at Spring Street and Fifth. The other was a storefront brick building called River Station in Chinatown. And now it was at work on a new station located on Central Street.

In the midst of all this, another line—the Atchison, Topeka & Santa Fe Railroad—stuck its considerable nose into the fray. The great benefactors of the competition were the passengers. There was a time, in 1887, when a ticket from Kansas to L.A. was only a dollar.

Kit knew a little of the history and also knew a lot of money was tied up in the thousands of miles of track snaking in and out of the city. Money sometimes made men do desperate things. All that was in the back of her mind as she entered the Western Rail building.

Kit found a small, no-nonsense clerk inside the doors of the wood frame, furiously sticking small papers in a series of tidy boxes. The static of a telegraph crackled on a nearby desk. Undoubtedly this man was the human conduit of the messages that came through.

"Excuse me?" Kit said.

The man stopped short.

"Is Mr. Ellis Dyke in?" Kit asked.

"Mr. Dyke?"

"Yes."

"I do believe he is, yes."

"Would you mind asking if—"

With a flustered look, the man waved his hands and said, "Wait here." He spun like a top and was gone.

"But—"

A door slamming was her answer.

A little too nervous, she thought. If this man's actions were any indication, something was going on of great import to the enterprise. That or Western Rail had hired the most nervous clerk in the region.

In less than a minute the clerk scurried back into the reception area and told Kit to follow him. He led her, without comment, to an inner office. He opened the door and practically shoved her inside before skirting back to his post.

"Well helloooo," the man in the office said. He had black hair slicked down and parted on the side and a beard trimmed short in high-society style. His shirt sleeves were rolled up. White teeth gleamed in the leering smile he shot her way. "I am Ellis Dyke. My man said there was an attractive young lady to see me, but I couldn't have known she would be absolutely gorgeous."

The commodious office had a single window that gave a view of the platform where the Western Rail trains pulled in and out. The smell of coal dust permeated everything here, even with an electric ceiling fan stirring the air.

"Mr. Dyke, I am Kathleen Shannon, an attorney."

"Attorney? You?" He looked her up and down. "What sort of law do you practice?"

"At the moment, criminal."

"Well, I'll be a donkey's daddy." Dyke slid a chair out for Kit and one for himself. He sat with the back of the chair facing outward, leaning as if over a fence between neighbors. "I've seen lawyers most of my life, but they've all been prune-faced old geezers with whiskers. You do not fit that description, Miss Shannon. Criminal, you say?"

"That's right."

"You mean, prosecuting mean old defendants?"

"I am a defense attorney."

Ellis Dyke shook his head in wonderment. "Do you want to know something?"

"What?"

"That's about the most incredible thing I've ever heard a pretty lady say. Yessiree." He smiled again and raised his eyebrows. "But I don't get why a criminal attorney, man or woman, would be wanting to talk to me."

"It concerns the incident with Mousy Malloy."

Ellis Dyke's eyes, to this point gleaming with lechery, suddenly darkened. "What have you got to do with Mousy?"

"He is my client."

"Is he, now?" Dyke gripped the sides of his chair a little harder. "That no-good tried to shoot me! That's all you need to know. If he hadn't been drunk, he might have hit me for sure."

"That's what I'd like to talk to you about."

"What more is there to say?"

"A great deal," Kit said. "One thing a lawyer learns is that one side of a story is never enough to get at the truth."

"If you want my side, you'll get the truth. Mousy Malloy's been after my hide for a long time, ever since I dusted him in a fight. He's been talking about me behind my back for a year. Now that they've got him, he deserves time behind bars. He's a menace."

"You say that you bested him in a fight?"

Dyke nodded.

"How did you happen to get into a fight with Mr. Malloy?"

"That's a tale in itself. You want the long version?" Dyke showed his teeth again. "Because for you, miss, I've got all day."

"This is not a social call," Kit said, not liking at all the way he looked at her.

"We can change that. I know some fancy places in town. We could have something to drink and—"

"No, thank you. If we can just—"

"Don't be so quick, Miss Shannon. I'm a gentleman, and I know how to show a lady a good time."

"Mr. Dyke, I am engaged to be married."

If Kit thought that would stop Ellis Dyke in his lascivious tracks, she was mistaken. It seemed only to enliven his interest. "This is 1906, Miss Shannon. You need not take such an old-fashioned view of matters. Now, the French, they—"

"If you please, Mr. Dyke, I would like to conduct this interview in a businesslike fashion. I am not interested in anything else."

"We'll see." Dyke relaxed his gaze. "So you want to know about Mousy and me? Here it is. I came down from the home office to do some work on the line. My father thought it would be good for me to learn the business from the bottom up, the way he did."

"Your father is Addison Dyke, is he not?"

Ellis Dyke's face grew cloudy. "The name's been hung around my neck, yes."

"It is a burden to you?"

"I got no complaints, I suppose. Pretty soon he'll see ..." Dyke became sunny again, the charmer. "So it was while working the rails outside of Oxnard that I ran into Mousy the first time. He set off to get on my bad side right away."

"Why would he do that?"

Dyke shrugged. "Mad about the world, I suppose. I had money. He didn't. He accused me of slumming. He put the needle to me whenever he could. Worse when he had a few drinks in him."

"Did he ever threaten you?"

"Sure. Talked big all the time."

"For instance?"

"I can't remember all that. And why should I? He did what he did and that's that."

A brick wall suddenly sprang up in the middle of the room between them. Once Earl Rogers had told her you could often get more out of a witness by entering through the side door rather than the front. She decided to give it a try.

"Will you be taking over the railroad someday?" she asked.

Ellis Dyke stuck his chest out a little, like a proud little boy. "Of course. That's what I'm doing here in this desert."

"Desert?"

"Los Angeles, dear girl. Another part of Father's plan. I'm to do another year in this office and then I can go back to civilization. San Francisco."

"Do you have many friends here?"

"Not as many as I'd like." He raised and lowered his eyebrows at her again.

"Other men?"

"Oh, sure. Of course."

Kit waited for him to continue. But he stopped abruptly and stood up.

"I know what you're up to," he said. "You're a clever little thing, aren't you?"

"I beg your pardon?"

"You want me to give you names so you can go around and give the grill to them. Well, not me, missy."

"Billy Rye? Sam Hartrampf?"

Dyke froze in place. "How did you—"

"How long have you known them?"

"You can take your leave now."

Kit got to her feet. "I am only searching for the truth, Mr. Dyke."

"Well, search for it on your own. You won't get any more help from me. Unless it's over a nice bottle of wine."

"Good day, Mr. Dyke."

He stepped in front of the door. "Just remember one thing, Miss Shannon. We railroaders are a pretty tough bunch. You go where you're not wanted and you're liable to get hurt."

"May I pass, please?"

Ellis Dyke did not move. He gave Kit another lingering look, then smiled as if nothing had just happened between them.

Slowly, he opened the door.

Chapter Eleven

"You are ignoring your work!" Gus Willingham said.

"This is my work, too." Ted stuck a few more Bibles in the trunk. He and Gus were in the rear of the Institute, where a new supply of Bibles had come in from a printer out East.

Gus prepared to let out tobacco juice but saw there was no spittoon anywhere. Frowning, he went to the door, opened it, spit, and stepped back inside. "But what about the plane?" he said.

"I will be back soon," Ted said calmly. "I'll only be gone a week."

"That's a week lost on the plane."

"No, it's a week doing God's work. If I am faithful in that, God will be faithful in blessing the plane."

"You made a deal with Him?"

Ted held up a new leather-bound Bible. "The deal is in here. I want you to read about it when I'm gone."

Gus folded his arms. "When you come back, you're gonna get married. You'll have God and a wife—two things that'll take your mind off flying."

"I'll also have you." Ted clapped him on the shoulder. "That should even things out nicely."

Despite Gus's crusty nature, Ted loved his old friend. Ted knew that his conversion to Christianity had been something of a blow to Gus. The mechanic was not a God-fearing man and so did not have much understanding for Ted's work with the Institute. Still, Ted sensed his friend was waiting to see if his faith was genuine, if it would crack under the strains of life. Ted was determined to bring Gus, even if it took wild horses, into the Kingdom.

Ted put the last of the Bibles into the trunk and latched it. "Now, try to behave yourself while I'm away."

Gus shook his head. "I don't need no lessons from you."

"This Sunday, why don't you go to church?"

"I'll go to church when God drops by for a visit and invites me personally."

"I'll see what I can arrange." Ted shook Gus's hand. "Take care of the plane," he said.

The Beasley Home for Boys was a brooding, spare building on the south side of the garment district, just below Eleventh Street. It looked a little like the county jail, Kit thought as she approached. It had stone columns and bleak windows—a place Charles Dickens might have described in one of his books.

Inside, the place smelled of neglect. Dust and dirt were evident on the floor and the walls. The only light in the foyer filtered through musty curtains covering the window at the top of a staircase. No one appeared to be about the place. The silence was eerie, as though all signs of life had been permanently discarded.

Then Kit heard a door open, followed by the sound of feet on the hardwood floor. A shuffling line of boys, different heights but all seeming to be dressed in the same drab fashion, filed into the foyer. Behind them came a bony man in a severe black suit. He carried a large rod in his hand, waving it as one might when swatting at flies.

Seeing Kit standing there, the boys looked either confused or delighted. There was a stranger in their midst. Kit smiled at them.

The man with the stick did not look pleased. He hit the floor with the wooden rod, a quick succession of clacking sounds.

"On, on!" he ordered the boys, who responded by scurrying past Kit without a word.

Kit saw Bobby in the line. He gave her a worried look, appearing fearful about her presence here. He turned his head away from her as the line disappeared through a door on the opposite side of the foyer.

The man stayed and faced Kit. "May I inquire as to your business here?"

Kit felt the chill of his disapproval. He was perhaps fifty years old, with a large forehead and receding hairline. He would have made a perfect ghost for a place like this.

"I would like to speak to Mr. Beasley," Kit answered.

"I am Chester R. Beasley," the man said. "And you are...?"

"Kathleen Shannon."

Beasley's eyebrows shot upward. "So you are the one."

"I beg your pardon?"

"The one who has meddled with my work. Young woman, I must ask you to attend to your own affairs and leave the direction of these boys to me."

"You are referring to Bobby ... I don't know his last name."

"That is no concern of yours."

"Are you aware, sir, that Bobby has been delivering beer for a saloon?"

Beasley paused, squinting at Kit with jaundiced reflection. "Then he shall be justly punished."

"Are you saying you were not aware of this?"

"Who are you to be questioning me?"

"I am a concerned citizen."

"Hadn't you best leave your concerns at home, where they belong?"

"I don't understand what you mean."

Beasley sighed with frustration. "You are a woman. You are not equipped to know what is in the best interest of boys who must grow into men. Instead, you ought to be caring for your own children. Have you children?"

"Mr. Beasley—"

"Ah. Husband?"

"Sir, I wish to—"

"I see. What, then, occupies your time?"

"I practice law."

Beasley's eyes widened.

"But I am not here in my capacity as a lawyer. I am here because I do not believe boys should be working in bars."

"Miss Shannon, we house, educate, and feed over forty boys here. When we can, we send them out for gainful employment or to be apprenticed. If that privilege is abused on occasion, we cannot always find that out. If we do, the boy is punished."

"If employment is desirable, why then would you forbid Bobby to work for me?"

"I do not know you, miss."

"Do you know a Mr. Doogan?"

Beasley shook his head slowly. "I cannot say that I do."

"He is a saloonkeeper who is only one of many who use boys in his employ. What I was offering to your young man was good, honest work for more money than he was earning from Mr. Doogan. So I ask if you would consider allowing our arrangement to continue."

"I am sorry, Miss Shannon, but I am the one who must decide what is in the best interest of these boys."

"Isn't a good, healthy job in their best interest?"

"Some, perhaps. Not this one."

"Bobby?"

"He has been here four years and is a constant problem."

"I think I can help."

"Thank you, but no. Now if you will excuse—"

"Would you consider visiting my office? I can show you—"

"No, I thank you. I must attend to my charges now. Pardon me if I do not see you to the door."

Earl Rogers stopped Kit as she charged up the stairs.

"Ho there!" he said. "You're going to mow somebody down."

"Earl!" Kit was breathing hard. "I'm glad you're here. I wanted to see you."

"Here I am."

"I want to ask your advice."

"On... ?"

"Using the law as a weapon."

The famous trial lawyer smiled. "You'd better step inside my office."

Once inside, with the door securely closed, Kit let her feelings spill out, about the Beasley home, saloons, the exploitation of children, the trolley lines. "If we don't do something," she said, "these abuses will only continue."

"We defend people accused of crimes," Earl said patiently. "Isn't that enough for you?"

"Why should it be? The law should be an instrument of good. I haven't been able to stop thinking about Jack London's talk of revolution. Can't the law be used rather than violence?"

"Give me an example of what you have in mind."

"To get the attention of the rail companies, for one thing. Isn't there a way?"

"Perhaps," Rogers said. "What do you remember of your law of torts?"

Kit thought a moment. "Well, it wasn't until the 1830s, I believe, that accidents by machinery were recognized under the rubric of negligence."

"Very good. Primarily it was the railroads. When the trains kept coming, killing cows and sheep and people and all other manner of being, the law began to take notice. Negligence finally and firmly became the basis for tort liability. Tell me, what is required for recovery?"

Kit heard the voice of her law professor, Melle Stanleyetta Titus, at the Women's Legal Education program, University of

New York. "First, a duty recognized by law. The party must be obligated to obey a standard of conduct."

"In the case of, say, the railroad, does such a duty exist?"

"Of course," Kit said emphatically. "It is an enterprise that is dangerous to the public if not properly maintained."

"Continue." Earl nodded at her, ever the law professor. Indeed, he would have made a good one at some prestigious law school. He never forgot anything he read.

"A failure to conform to the required standard," Kit answered.

"And?"

"A connection between the conduct and the injury. The conduct must have caused the injury in a way the law will recognize."

"Very good. What else?"

"Damages."

"You'll make a lawyer yet!" Rogers said with a happy gleam.

"Thank you so much."

"Now to business. If you want to take on the rails, where should we begin our analysis?"

"With the damages."

"Quite right, for without damages a cause of action is pointless. Now, here we have a problem. A boy is dead. For the moment we'll assume the trolley line is at fault, though this is by no means established. If suit is brought by the mother, what will her claim for damages be?"

Kit pondered the question and was troubled when nothing came to mind. "Services?" she suggested.

Rogers nodded. "You are heading in the right direction. The common law did see the loss of a child as the loss of a type of servant but only with relation to the father. For, as you know, the wife was also seen as a type of servant. Therefore, a wife could not claim servant damages for the loss of a child."

"But that is unjust! A widow would then be denied damages even though she is both father and mother to the child, even though she might be working to make ends meet!"

"You don't have to convince me, Kit. Only a court. But I

believe you are the one who can do it. There may be a better way."

"What way is that?"

Rogers stood and moved about the office. This was his way of thinking aloud. Numerous times Kit had been dazzled by his legal ideas, thrown out almost at random, as he paced the floor. "What is more important than services, especially to a mother?"

"Why, the loss of companionship of her own child."

"Precisely. The affection of the child. This is, it seems to me, in no way different in kind from the loss of companionship between a husband and wife, which has recognition in the law. It is called consortium."

"Does the law recognize this same thing with regard to a child?"

"No. I seem to recall a case from 1825 or so. *Hall v. Hollander*, I think. It held against a recovery in the death of a small child."

Kit clenched her teeth. "I suppose the judges didn't realize children who stay alive tend to grow up."

With his engaging smile, Rogers said, "It would have been wonderful to hear you make the argument."

"What I want is an argument I can make now."

"You would be blazing a new trail. But then, you've done that before. I'd love to try this one with you. Your client, her name is ..."

"I don't have a client yet."

"You mean we've just been speculating here?"

"The mother, Winnie Franklin, has no idea I am thinking about this."

Rogers slapped his sides. "You mean to tell me you haven't even been put on a retainer?"

Kit shook her head. "Nor would I ask for one. These people are not well-off."

"No money! No client! But a cause of action! Kit, you are turning this profession on its head."

"Perhaps for the good."

"Just what does that mean, my idealistic Irish rose?"

The thoughts came out, jumbled at first, but flowing from some deep part of Kit that had been considering these ideas for some time. "The law, it seems to me, is more than just a vehicle for settling disputes between two parties. It should do its best to make social relations more just."

"Social relations?"

"Cities are on the rise in this country, and with them have come things like trolleys and trains and gas-powered automobiles. These things are bound to hurt people, maim, or kill them, as with the little boy. Something should be done to make such accidents less frequent."

"Then let it be done."

"If the powers behind the industry wish them to be done. But what if they do not? The law must be used to force them. You remember what happened in that sweatshop in New York? A fire broke out and dozens of children—children!—were burned to death. So Congress is considering child labor laws. That's a good thing."

"But it takes Congress to fight those interests. One lawyer is not enough."

Kit shook her head. "I cannot believe my ears. Is this the great Earl Rogers talking?"

"I am just looking out for you, Kit. I don't want to see you get hurt."

"Who would try to hurt me?"

"The machine, for one."

"What machine?"

"The political machine, of course. The one that's running Mayor Tillinghast's reelection campaign."

"I thought Tillinghast ran things in this town."

"Tillinghast is an old cog in a political machine that has been around ever since the city started wearing long pants," Rogers explained. "Political power in Los Angeles resides not in the parties but in the wards. Even though municipal authority is vested in the mayor and the municipal council, who are supposed to be an independent executive and legislature, the fact is the machine runs this city."

"Who manages this machine?"

"Local bosses. Their power and influence changes, just like the changes of power among the Tongs or the Black Hand."

"Can't anyone bring about reform?"

"There have been attempts," Rogers said. "In the 1880s a group known as the Board of Freeholders drafted a new charter that would have weakened the machine politics in Los Angeles, but the defenders of the status quo poured a lot of money into an opposition campaign, and local voters turned down the document. A similar campaign was defeated around the turn of the century."

"Are no progressives attempting opposition?"

"Yes. Now we have the Direct Legislation League founded by John R. Haynes. They are attempting to run a candidate against Tillinghast. One of the things they want to do is break the connection between private enterprise and governmental authority. That would reduce the machine's principal source of funds. They also want to reduce the cozy relationship between the mayor's office, the police, and various agencies—including the D.A.'s office—who find it beneficial to cooperate with each other, even if such cooperation extends beyond the boundaries of the law."

"You think there's a chance that Tillinghast will be defeated?"

"I think they are running scared. They need money, and the rumor is they're getting a lot from the local prostitution trade."

"What about the saloons?"

"No doubt they're kicking in money to Tillinghast, too."

"One big, happy family," Kit mused.

"With a dangerous reach," Earl Rogers said. "So be careful whose eye you poke."

Chapter Twelve

"Watch out for Gus, will you?"

Ted embraced Kit on the platform at the Western Rail depot. Scattered around were various passengers saying their morning good-byes.

Kit felt a shudder in her body. Ted was leaving her again. "Please be careful," she urged. "The last time you left town, you were arrested as a German spy. You seem to find creative ways to get into trouble."

He kissed her on the cheek. "How can anyone get into trouble in San Francisco?"

Kit shook her head. "This is no laughing matter. You still intend to try to get to Addison Dyke?"

"I told you I do."

"Well, that can lead to trouble."

"Don't you trust me, Kit?"

"It is not a matter of trust."

Ted stroked her cheek. "Yea though I go through the valley of the shadow of death, or up to the top of Nob Hill, the Shepherd is with me." He ran his finger tenderly across her lips. "And so are you."

The soft warmth of his touch filled Kit with inexpressible comfort and longing.

"See me on the train?"

Coming down from the clouds, Kit said, "I'm afraid I'll be late for court."

Ted scowled. In jest, Kit hoped. She could not read his voice when he said, "I can see what our married life is going to be like."

"Then see this instead and take it with you." In a most un-Freddy-like fashion, Kit took Ted's shirt in her hands and pulled him to her, kissing him fully, passionately, as the steam from the train hissed behind them.

"Please tell the court, Mr. Doogan, how Abner Malloy, also known as Mousy, attempted to shoot Mr. Ellis Dyke."

Clara Dalton Price almost beamed with the asking of the question. Kit caught her smirk, directed toward her without a doubt.

They were facing off in a courtroom under the eye of Judge Alton Trent. Today, at the preliminary hearing, there would be only the merest evidence offered by the prosecution, enough for the judge to bind over Mousy for trial. All Clara Dalton Price needed was Doogan and perhaps a follow-up witness or two.

Doogan, looking out of sorts in a suit and tie, his hair slicked down on his head like an oil stain, cleared his throat. He proceeded to tell his story in about the same words as he had to Kit. It took but five minutes.

With the confidence of a gambler holding four aces, Mrs. Price turned to Kit. "Your witness."

Kit patted Mousy on the arm, then stood up. "Good morning, Mr. Doogan."

Apparently shocked at such a cordial greeting, Doogan squinted. "Morning."

"Do you recall, sir, the day I came into your establishment?"

"I won't soon forget it. You drove away some customers."

Laughter from the gallery seemed to cheer Doogan, who smiled widely. Kit let him bask in momentary glory. A little overconfidence in a witness always helped.

"And when I did, you told me that Mr. Malloy knew you kept a gun under the bar counter, isn't that right?"

"Right you are."

"You also told me you have had occasion to fire shots into the ceiling, three times, I believe."

"Had to break up some situations, that's what I did."

"You even showed me the bullet holes, didn't you?"

"That I did."

"There were two bullet holes you didn't show me."

Doogan looked confused, then slowly shook his head.

"I'm talking about the bullets Mr. Malloy allegedly fired at Ellis Dyke."

With a shrug, Doogan said, "Funny, I never thought to look for 'em."

"Yes, isn't that funny?" Kit paced a moment in front of the witness. "The bullets' locations might tell us where Mr. Malloy was aiming, isn't that correct?"

"He was aiming at Ellis Dyke."

"You assume he was."

"Where else would he be aiming, saying he was going to kill him?"

"Maybe he just wanted to scare him."

"That don't make sense."

"Does it make sense, Mr. Doogan, for you to fire your gun into a ceiling to scare people into silence?"

Looking like he'd been clipped on the jaw, Doogan sat back and scowled. "That's different."

"How is it different, Mr. Doogan?"

"Malloy was drunk."

"Ah yes. Let's examine that for a moment."

Clara Dalton Price objected. "Your Honor, Mr. Doogan is not here as an expert on drunkenness."

"Who could be more expert than a saloon owner?" Kit offered to the judge.

"Overruled," Judge Trent said with a smile and wink. "You may continue, Miss Shannon."

Kit did not know what the judge was so jovial about, but at least he wasn't adversarial. In her short career in the courts of L.A., she'd had her share of judges who viewed her with suspicion if not outright hostility.

She turned back to Doogan. "You say he was drunk, sir?"

"Very drunk. He was trying to beat Mr. Dyke in a bout of drinking."

"A contest?"

"That's right."

"You served the drinks, did you not?"

"That's my job. So long as they have the money, I pour."

A few people laughed at that. Kit got the impression it was the reporters, most of whom would understand Doogan quite clearly. As a class of people, they were some of the greatest habitués of the city's watering holes.

"How many drinks did you serve to Mr. Malloy?"

Doogan looked at the ceiling. "Oh, maybe six, seven. There was a little bet going on, you see."

"Yes, in this little contest you spoke about. It was a bet to see who could hold their liquor best, Ellis Dyke or Mr. Malloy, correct?"

"That's the way it was."

"And apparently Mr. Malloy lost that bet."

"He sure did."

"No doubt in your mind that he was drunk?"

"No doubt at all."

"You could tell by looking at him?"

"Sure. The way he moved, the way his speech got thick. His eyes were as red as a rooster's comb. I've seen it a million times."

Kit paused, then asked, "How many others were present during this contest?"

Doogan shrugged. "A whole group was there, cheering them on."

"About how many would you say?"

"I don't know, six maybe."

"All friends of Ellis Dyke?"

"Some of them were. I knew that."

"Do you know their names?"

"A few."

"Please tell the court who else you saw there."

Again Clara Dalton Price objected. "Your Honor, some of these men may be witnesses for the prosecution. I would request at this time that their names not be mentioned in open court."

"I don't see any reason why that information should be kept confidential," the judge said. "The witness will answer."

"Sam Hartrampf was one," Doogan said. "Billy Rye. Some others whose names I don't know."

"Was a police officer present?"

The question seemed to jolt Doogan. He cleared his throat. "I don't recall."

"You don't recall if a police officer, in uniform, was present?"

"I'm not paid to remember things."

"Just take money and pour, is that it?"

"A man's got a right to operate his business, don't he?"

"And employ young boys?"

There was a sudden silence in the courtroom then. Kit knew the question was irrelevant, but it had slipped out anyway on wings of outrage.

"I will withdraw that last question," Kit told the judge. "The matter of this city allowing boys to be exploited as cheap labor in the saloons will be addressed at another place and time." She glowered at Doogan. "You can count on it." With a quick turn, her skirt swirling, Kit returned to her table and sat next to Mousy.

Clara Dalton Price stood. "Your Honor, the prosecution submits the matter to you. We have only to present enough evidence for you to find it probable that a crime may have been committed. We request now that you bind Abner Malloy over for trial on the charge of attempted murder."

"Miss Shannon?" the judge inquired. "Have you anything to say to that?"

"I do, Your Honor." Kit picked up the volume of the penal code that was on the counsel table. "I direct the court's attention to Section 20, which says, `In every crime or public offense there must exist a union or joint operation of act and intent.' This is the foundation for all criminal law. As Blackstone stated in his commentary on the common law, to constitute a crime against human laws there must be a `vicious will' coupled with a `forbidden act.' The prosecution has charged my client with a crime that requires an intent to kill. I submit to the court that the prosecution has failed in its burden of proof on intent. There is therefore no *corpus delicti*. The case must be dismissed."

The judge looked stunned, but in a pleasant way, as if this were a fine puzzle for the prosecution to solve. He looked at Clara Dalton Price and said, "What says the deputy district attorney?"

Mrs. Price had no pleasant look on her face. "Your Honor, I am mystified at the assertion of the defense. We have an eyewitness to the crime. The fact that the defendant fired a gun at Mr. Dyke, after expressing his intention to kill, is evidence of the state of mind necessary for the crime."

"That same eyewitness," Kit said, "testified that my client was drunk. No evidence to the contrary was introduced; therefore the court must accept it as true for purposes of this hearing. May I read to the court from *People v. Roberts*?"

The judge nodded.

Kit looked at her notes and read, "`If a defendant's mental faculties were so overwhelmed by intoxication that he was not conscious of what he was doing; or if he did know what he was doing but did not know why he was doing it, then he had not sufficient capacity to entertain the intent, and in that event we cannot infer the intent from his acts.'"

Clara Dalton Price returned Kit's volley immediately. "If Miss Shannon will also read Section 22 of the penal code, she will see that drunkenness is no excuse for crime."

Kit returned to the code. "And if Mrs. Price would read the entire section, she will see that it states, `But whenever the actual existence of any particular purpose, motive, or intent is a necessary element to constitute any particular degree or species of crime, that fact may be taken into consideration in determining the purpose, motive, or intent with which he committed the act.' So while drunkenness is no excuse for a crime, it can be introduced to show the lack of any necessary element, including intent."

"Facts," Mrs. Price shot back, "are for a jury. I would remind Miss Shannon that the law does not look favorably upon a defendant who becomes *voluntarily* intoxicated."

That was quite right. If Kit had entertained any hope that this point of law would skirt by Mrs. Price, it was dashed by this exchange. She knew the law as well as Kit—and both, Kit was sure, knew it better than the judge.

"I find this very curious indeed," Judge Trent said. "Fine arguments from both sides. I will take this matter under submission. I would like to see both of you in my chambers."

Kit, somewhat mystified, joined Mrs. Price in the judge's office. He was sitting with his hands laced behind his head, a smile on his face. "We have a very close matter here," he said.

Mrs. Price did not hold back. "This is only a preliminary hearing! How can you even be thinking of dismissal?"

The smile melted from the judge's face. "Does the prosecutor think I am some sort of puppet, beholden to the whims of your office?"

"Whims! It is a matter of evidence."

"I expect a higher level of presentation from Davenport's minions," the judge said sharply.

Kit saw Mrs. Price's neck turning an angry shade of red. She did not blame her. Being dressed down by a judge, in front of the opposing lawyer, had to be particularly galling.

"Nevertheless," Judge Trent added, "I think this is a case that ought to go to a jury. The issue of mental state is one they must decide. But let me tell you, Mrs. Price, I'll be watching your evidence closely."

The angry red became a nearly purple rage. Without a word, but with the language of her body unmistakable in its outrage, Clara Dalton Price charged out of the judge's chambers.

Chapter Thirteen

At two in the afternoon, the coroner's inquest into the death of Sammy Franklin was held in the hearing room on the first floor of the city morgue. Kit, appearing on behalf of Winnie, was present with Salem and Alice. Winnie did not want to come, expressing that it would be too much for her. She had promised, however, to pray for the truth.

Kit also had, courtesy of Corazón, a small item to present to the coroner at the proper time. To make sure this item had its full effect, she had invited Tom Phelps of the *Times* and his counterpart with the *Examiner* to be there. She gave them each the promise of fireworks in the otherwise dull process of an inquest.

The coroner, Raymond J. Smith, was well-known to Kit from several past trials. He was a smallish man, who sometimes seemed uncomfortable on the witness stand. But inquests were his bailiwick. Like a judge in a courtroom, he ruled his roost—and was not shy about clucking. Procedure dictated that the family of the deceased be allowed to attend the hearing and be represented by counsel if they so wished.

Sometimes, if the death occurred under questionable

circumstances, a coroner's jury would be called. But in the case of deaths caused by trolley or horse, Smith alone usually heard the evidence and rendered a decision himself.

To begin, he called to the witness chair one Silas Timmons, a man of about forty, with small, ferret-like eyes. He might have been a model for Ichabod Crane, Kit thought.

After he was sworn in, Smith began questioning him, staying seated at all times behind a wooden desk.

"What is your occupation, Mr. Timmons?"

"I am employed by Hudson's Mercantile, where I oversee the inventory."

"How long have you worked there?"

"Three years."

"And how do you get to your place of employment?"

"I take the trolley from my home in Whittier. A nice home, in a new development there. I—"

"Thank you. Now, Mr. Timmons, you were a passenger aboard the trolley that killed Samuel Franklin?"

"Yes, sir."

"Did you have occasion to witness what happened before the unfortunate accident?"

"Yes, oh indeed. I am an observant man, Mr. Coroner, which is what one has to be in inventory. As I was—"

"Just tell us, please, in your own words—and only the words necessary—what you saw concerning the accident."

Timmons cleared his throat. "I was sitting on the front bench, which I like to do to feel the air in my face. It wakes me up in the morning, you see. Mrs. Timmons sometimes doesn't wake up in time to make my coffee; she has a condition. It keeps her—"

"Mr. Timmons, if you please. Put yourself back on the trolley. Concentrate."

"Concentrate. Oh yes. In the front, as I said. It was a pleasant morning, as I recall, somewhat hot. But very pleasant when the wind hit your face, which is what I prefer, you see."

"Please, Mr. Timmons, to the events in question."

"Yes, yes. As I say, we were going down the street as usual. I take the Broadway line. My office of employment is near the end of the line, which is very convenient for me. And so, as we were on our way, as usual, I saw something out of the corner of my eye. As I said, I am an observant man, which is why I am a valued employee at the Mercantile—"

"Go on!"

"Yes, yes. I saw that it was a small lad."

Kit felt Salem tensing next to her.

"The boy dashed out, you see, and then appeared to stop right on the rails. I cannot say why. I turned to the motorman immediately and called out to him to stop, there was a boy out there."

"What did the motorman do?"

"Why, he immediately pulled the brake. But alas, it was too late. Too late." Timmons shook his head woefully.

"Thank you, Mr. Timmons," Smith said. "You may step down now."

"My observations are quite clear in my head, you see, which is why I—"

"You may step down!"

"Excuse me," Kit objected, getting to her feet. "I have some questions for the witness."

With a sour expression, Smith said, "The coroner recognizes Miss Shannon. You are representing the family of the decedent?"

"I am."

Smith waved his hand toward Timmons. "Proceed. But please bear in mind, I would like this wrapped up before the lunch hour."

Kit faced Timmons. "Sir, how far away was the boy when you first saw him, as you say, out of the corner of your eye?"

"How far?"

"Yes, as best you can estimate."

"Well now, Mrs. Timmons tells me I am quite good at estimating. I can look at a room full of boxes from a shipment and tell you, within five or six, how many there are."

Smith slapped the desk with an open hand. "Just answer the question!"

Timmons cleared his throat. "Yes, yes." He pulled at his tie. "What was the question?"

Kit remained patient. "I asked you how far away the boy was when you first saw him."

"Ah. Yes. In my estimation, he was, oh, let me see—" Timmons made several motions with his fingers—"I would have to say, and this is in retrospect, that the distance was approximately fifty feet."

"And you say you watched this boy as he ran to the track?"

"Yes, I did say that."

"How long did it take him from the time you first saw him to the time he reached the track?"

"Oh, well, let me see. Yes. It was very soon. He was fast, the boy was."

"Would you say a matter of seconds?"

"Seconds? Oh yes, seconds."

"How many seconds?"

"Now let me see." Again Timmons wiggled his fingers. "I would have to say three seconds, no more than that."

"I see." Kit tried to imagine the scene. "Now, how much time elapsed between the time you saw the boy on the track and your turning around to the motorman?"

"That I did instantly, of course."

"You say you called out to the motorman?"

"Yes."

"What words did you use?"

"Words? I believe I said, `There's a boy on the tracks!'"

"And in response the motorman pulled on the brake?"

"Oh yes. That is what he did."

"But it was too late, wasn't it?"

"Too late, I am afraid."

"Which means, does it not, that the motorman was not looking down the track when Sammy ran onto it?"

Silence descended on the room like a heavy cloak. Timmons looked nonplussed, his head shaking slightly.

Then Dr. Smith's voice rang out, "That question is not for Mr. Timmons!"

Kit looked the coroner in the eye. "Do you intend to call the motorman?"

"There is no need to call the motorman."

"No need?"

"I have the testimony of this witness. This appears to be an accident, caused by circumstances out of anyone's control. No blame can be attached to it."

The words triggered Kit, who did not answer but instead walked to her chair in the gallery. She opened her briefcase slowly, making sure the reporters and Dr. Smith watched her every move. She took out three pieces of paper.

She handed one to Tom Phelps, one to the *Examiner* reporter, and the last she placed in front of Raymond Smith.

"This is a listing of trolley fatalities in the last year," she said, "taken from the official inquest transcripts of this office, which rendered sixty-seven verdicts. As you can see, the wording changes very little. It is a variant of `No blame can be attached.' I will read them.

"`January 31, Anton Klobas. We attach no blame.'

"`February 13, George T. Hamilton. We affix no blame.'

"`February 18, Gardner Brooks Cotton. No blame attached.'"

Kit looked up. Smith's face had changed colors, from placid white to a dangerous hue of reddish pink.

"What is the meaning of this?" he managed to stammer.

"The facts, sir," said Kit. "Not one death was held to be the responsibility of the rail lines. This information is now in the hands of this city's two leading newspapers. Once again, I demand that the motorman be called as a witness. I have some questions for that man."

With beads of sweat popping out on his forehead, Raymond J. Smith called the proceedings to a halt so he could take the request under submission. And then, as quickly as he could, before the two reporters could get to him, he left the room by way of a side door.

Kit had barely had time to move when she noticed a man approaching her from the back of the room. There was no doubt that his intention was to talk to her. His eyes were fixed on her like a tiger stalking prey. The other spectators, now milling about him, might as well have been invisible. He wore a dark suit that fit him splendidly. He was trim, near forty, and his hair was expertly clipped, slicked, and combed in the most popular fashion, parted on the side.

When he reached Kit, he bowed slightly. "Allow me to introduce myself. I am Walter Mill, and like you I am an attorney."

Kit regarded him, found his formality a bit forced, but nodded politely. "I am pleased to meet you."

"Your presentation a moment ago was, if I may, a thing of absolute beauty. I am an admirer of the fine legal argument, the skewering of a point. And to hear it come from one as young and pretty as you was a particular delight."

"Thank you."

"I wonder if I might have just a moment of your time, one lawyer to another."

"You wish to discuss a legal matter with me?"

"Along those lines, yes. You see, I am from San Francisco."

Kit wondered what he meant. "I have not yet had a chance to visit your city."

"Oh, you must, truly." Mill indicated the rear door of the chamber. "Shall we?"

"May I inquire, sir, what this is concerning?"

Mill smiled. "Possibly your entire legal career."

San Francisco lay shrouded in mist, a city under a wet gray canopy. From Market Street to the wharf, from the business district up over Nob Hill, the city by the bay was dim and cool, seemingly in wait for something exciting to happen.

The sight of it, and the accompanying feelings, were not new to Ted Fox. He had been here several times before, in his banking days. He was quite familiar with the moan of the foghorns, which sounded like mournful sea lions, as he was with the clanging bells of the cable cars.

Having trollied in from the train station, Ted caught a cable car on California Street, taking a seat on the outside bench. The business district was in full swing, with suited men hurrying along sidewalks, mixing with the occasional seaman wandering the streets looking for fortune or a lady or a good stiff drink.

Men were not so very different here, Ted thought, though they seemed more pushed together than in Los Angeles. Down south there was more elbowroom. Up here, everyone was jabbing each other with elbows and umbrellas.

With a swaggering clang of its bell, the cable car began its steep ascent up Nob Hill. It paused only once, at Dupont Street, where Ted could make out the pagodas and colors of Chinatown. He saw a couple of silk hats and single braids on men crossing the street. An old shaman with a long beard sat on a brick overhang, peacefully smoking his pipe.

The view did not last long. With a sudden jerk, the gripper pulled on the lever that took hold of the underground cable, and the car continued upward into a thick fog. Ted had to grab the handrail to keep from sliding off the bench. No fancy ceremony here. The cable cars went about their business and that was that.

Finally the car reached the apex of Nob Hill. Ted knew this part of the city from his society days. He recognized the stately mansion of Leland Stanford, peering out of the fog like a gothic guardian, and the even more imposing home next door built by Mark Hopkins. From here, both these powerful men could view the city below as if it were their personal fiefdom.

Another mansion, farther along California Street and larger than the other two, was also familiar to Ted. The castle of Addison Dyke, patriarch of the Dyke railroad dynasty and president of Western Rail. Ted nodded knowingly. He would enter the place at some point, very soon. He only wondered how he would be received.

The cable line ended at Van Ness Avenue. Ted began the short walk to 1801 Van Ness, the residence of the Reverend Harlow Hayes.

It was a well-appointed home in the Queen Anne style, with a porch that looked out upon the street and a pathway lined with heliotrope bushes. The lawn sloped majestically down to the street, a lush green carpet. This was the abode of a citizen of significant standing in the city, though certainly not in the same stratosphere as the Stanford, Hopkins, and Dyke residences. Such placement was only for the gods of industry and commerce in progressive America.

A swift knock on the front door brought a stout woman to greet him. Her face was flushed, but she seemed relieved when she saw Ted. She wore a housedress, quite copious, with a white apron across the front.

"Mr. Fox!" the woman said.

Ted bowed. "At your service."

"Please come in!" The woman waved with a sort of desperation for Ted to follow her, almost as if something in the kitchen was on fire. "I am Mrs. Hayes. The Reverend has been expecting you. Oh, you have come at the right time."

She waddled quickly toward the parlor, Ted following. Inside was a man who might have been the woman's twin—plump, graying, friendly under other circumstances. He sat in a chair with his head in his hands.

Mrs. Hayes swayed to the man. "Harlow, Mr. Fox is here."

Harlow Hayes looked up, a swift relief in his eyes. "Mr. Fox, how good of you to come." He rose and extended a hand.

"I shall have tea prepared," Mrs. Hayes said, hurrying out of the room. She had not stopped moving from the moment Ted had first laid eyes on her.

"I am grateful for your hospitality," Ted said.

"Nothing of it, nothing of it." Reverend Hayes and Ted sat near the fireplace, where a small fire crackled and gave off warmth. The chilliness of the outside mist was all but forgotten.

"Your donation of Bibles is much appreciated," Reverend Hayes said, "though now I don't know where they will go."

"I don't understand. Aren't they for your boys' home?"

"There may be no boys' home. A foreclosure has been threatened."

"By whom?"

"Western Rail."

Ted shook his head. "Isn't that interesting? They have their tentacles out in a number of places."

"Yes, they own the property and wish to build a new rail station there, for an urban trolley system."

"You have a lease agreement?"

"Ten years, but it is about to expire. The company does not wish to extend."

"Surely you have other locations to choose from."

"We had one, on Market Street, except it has since been withdrawn."

"Won't the railroad give you an extension of a few months?"

Reverend Hayes shook his head. "The company won't budge. I received this just before you arrived." He held up a letter.

Ted took it from him. It was from a lawyer, Walter Mill, informing the reverend that there would be no extensions on the lease. The boys' home had two months remaining on the lease, and Western Rail expected them to be gone by then.

"Perhaps while I am here," Ted said, "I can fulfill the proverb about two birds and one stone."

Hayes looked at him curiously.

"Addison Dyke is the head of Western Rail."

"Yes," the clergyman said, "but no one gets to see him."

"There may be a way."

"But how?"

Ted smiled and took out a newspaper clipping. "There is to be a banquet on Nob Hill tomorrow night. According to my hometown social column, Mr. Dyke will be present."

"But such an affair would require an invitation."

"I am from Los Angeles," Ted said. "We try not to let custom stop us from anything. All I need is a tuxedo. And guess what? I seem to have packed one."

Hayes gave Ted a knowing stare. "I am beginning to think there is more to you than meets the eye."

Chapter Fourteen

The sun shone bright, assaulting Kit's eyes. Spring was in full bloom in the City of Angels, the scent of laurel and magnolia in the air, a stark contrast to the gloom and cheerlessness of the inquest room she had just left.

Walter Mill pulled a cigar from his coat pocket and a gold clipper from the pocket of his vest. He snipped the cigar end. "I represent Western Rail," he said as he struck a match. "I came down for the inquest. Frankly, I thought it might have gone a bit more smoothly."

"More smoothly?"

"Yes. Not much here that is so difficult. These types of accidents are unavoidable. Tragic, of course, but part of life today. We must accept that."

"I do not believe we have to accept an *avoidable* death."

"My point, Miss Shannon, is that death is not always avoidable. People died because of the cotton gin, but that did not make Eli Whitney a villain."

"Mr. Mill, I believe Sammy Franklin's death might have been prevented. My concern is only to find out the truth about what happened."

Mill eyed her with suspicion. "And make a big fat name for yourself?"

Kit felt her skin prickle at the insult. "Sir, I am not practicing law to make a name," she said calmly.

"Don't kid me. We both know how this works."

"Do you have anything else to say to me?" Kit was prepared to turn her back on this man immediately. She had work to attend to and did not think any good was going to come of further conversation.

"Hold on there." Mill puffed on his cigar with a leisurely air. "I have an offer for you and your client. Maybe you'd like to hear it. Could save us a lot of trouble down the line."

"I'm listening."

"Good. I will get right to the point. If you will cease any more comment on this matter, I can arrange to have a sum of money deposited in your account, half of which you may keep for yourself. The sum is four thousand dollars. That is not a bad take for a few hours' work."

"I am not interested in, nor am I in need of, your money."

Through a gray plume of smoke, Walter Mill's eyes became hostile slits. "Are you expecting more than that?"

"No. I am telling you the truth. I do not want your money. I want a fair amount for Winnie Franklin, but both of us desire one thing above all else."

"And what would that be?"

"Safety guards on the front of all trolleys in the city, a lower speed limit, and minimum requirements in training for all motormen."

Mill looked like he'd been shot in the leg. "Surely you are joking."

"No, sir. That is what we want."

"What *you* want? What gives you the right to demand anything?"

"The death of a child by trolley, for one."

"It was an accident!"

"It did not have to happen."

"So you say."

"Would you rather a jury decide?"

With a frown Walter Mill said, "What makes you tick, Miss Shannon? What is it you're really after?"

"That is an insulting thing to say, Mr. Mill."

"You don't want to answer?"

"Why should I?"

Mill shrugged. "Let's say to satisfy my curiosity."

"Should it come as such a shock that I believe in my client?"

"Come now, Miss Shannon, surely you don't think that is enough."

"What else is there?"

"The exchanging of money and power. I am a legal realist. I know that decisions are made every day in court that have nothing to do with what's right, because who can really know? Rather, it is about who will pay. That's why you are destined to lose your cause. It may be just, but it will not pay."

"I do not hold to that definition of the law. There is a higher justice for those who practice law."

"You sound like a preacher now."

"I've been called much worse."

Mill squinted through smoke, then broke into a hearty laugh. "By golly, you are quite a specimen!"

Kit cleared her throat self-consciously. "Will there be anything else, Mr. Mill?"

"Simply this," the lawyer said, his smile fading. "Drop this lawsuit and accept our offer, or I will make your life a living ... misery."

Kit stalked back to her office with scarcely any awareness of the pedestrians around her. The streets of Los Angeles remained their usual hubbub of activity, yet she cut through the crowd like a ship through brine.

Keep your temper in check, she reminded herself. With a deep breath she tried to envision the still waters of the Twenty-third Psalm. She needed peace.

It did not work. The thought of Walter Mill and Western Rail going after her if she dared step into court against them was too much.

She got back to her office and met Corazón there. Her assistant immediately knew there was something amiss.

"Your cheeks are red," she observed.

"I was walking."

"No, it is the angry kind."

Kit had to laugh. "I can't slip anything by you anymore. I admit it. I've been threatened by the lawyer for Western Rail."

"What did he say?"

"He said something about making my life a living misery. You know, the way we lawyers make small talk."

Corazón smiled and shook her head. "I am told that Mrs. Price is madder than, how do you say, the wet hen?"

Kit cocked her head. "Do tell."

"Around the courthouse some lawyers are saying that Mrs. Price is tired of losing to Kit Shannon and is going to fight to the finish."

"Judge Trent dressed her down a little in my presence," Kit mused. "Knowing Mrs. Price, that probably did not sit well. Any news on witnesses?"

Corazón nodded and looked at the paper in her hand. "Still I cannot find Billy Rye. It seems that he is no longer here."

"You think he's been taken out of town?"

"I do not know."

"I wouldn't put it past Davenport. He's tried to hide witnesses before." During the Hanratty murder trial, a key witness had been put up in a hotel in the San Fernando Valley. Finding him had been a breakthrough in the case.

"But I did find Hartrampf," Corazón said.

"Tell me."

"I wait for him to leave his house on Santee Street, as in the city directory. I follow him to his place of work. He works for Pioneer Drugstore on Main."

"I know the place."

"I went inside and said I would like to talk with him. He

asked me what it was about, and I tell him it is a legal matter. He laughed. He said he had nothing to say to a Mex."

"I'm sorry, Corazón."

"It is no matter. I am used to it. Besides, we are women, and sometimes the men will not talk business to us."

"Then we must persuade them. I think I'll go down to the drugstore and pick up some, oh, soap. I will ask for Mr. Hartrampf's help and then I'll ask him a few simple questions. No harm in that, is there?"

"No harm at all."

"Now we must prepare for Western Rail. Let us take up the law of torts."

For the next two hours Kit and Corazón went over the law together, took notes, asked each other questions, and talked about strategy. Any case against a railroad was going to be tough. They had deep pockets and the best lawyers. But Kit and Corazón had the David spirit as they looked for Goliath's weaknesses, and the time flew by until interrupted by the jangle of the telephone. Kit picked it up.

"Shannon?" The man's voice was low and scratchy over the phone line.

"Yes, this is Kathleen Shannon."

"You think you know things?"

"Who is this?"

A long pause on the line. "You don't know nothin'." The voice made no attempt to mask a tone of threat.

"What is this about?" Kit demanded.

"I know about you, Lawyer Shannon. I know you are made out of money."

"Sir, I am not interested in playing games over the wire—"

"You interested in Mousy Malloy?"

Kit pressed the earpiece closer. "I want to know the meaning of this call."

"Hold your horsehairs, lady. You got a friend you don't know you got."

"Start with your name."

"You don't need to know that. What you do need to

know is some things about what happened the day Mousy shot at Ellis Dyke."

Kit took a wild stab in the dark. "So this is Billy Rye." She saw Corazón's eyes light up next to her. Kit could almost feel the chill over the phone line. The long silence told her she was right.

"Pretty smart, aren't you?" the voice said.

"If you have something to say to me, Mr. Rye, you best say it."

"Let's start with how much?"

"How much what?"

"Money! I thought you were smart."

"I will not pay you anything."

Static on the line, then, "You must be crazy. I ain't gonna offer what I know for free."

"Money in exchange for testimony is a felony in this state, Mr. Rye."

"I'm not testifying in court if that's what you're thinking."

"If your information is useful to my client, you may have to."

"I can cut this telephone call right now, and you will end up with nothing."

Kit thought quickly. Just keep him talking. He probably did know something important or wouldn't have bothered to call. There was a chance he was bluffing, but she needed more time to find out.

"Something tells me, Mr. Rye, that what you want to say to me comes from other motives. Something against Ellis Dyke, perhaps. In that case, I would view your information as suspect."

Billy Rye snorted into the phone. "I'm startin' not to like you."

"I hardly see the relevance of that. But if you should have any information you would like to convey to me, information that can be corroborated, you will receive something more important than money."

"What's more important than money?"

"The chance to do what is right."

"No," Rye said. "If you want what I've got, you have to give me something in return."

"I already told you, I—"

"Ah, keep your money. You're a lawyer. Give me some law work."

"You have a legal problem?"

"Not now. But I will. We have a deal?"

"I cannot offer you anything until I hear what you have to say."

"No deal."

"Good-bye, Mr.—"

"Wait! I'll give you some of it. Once you hear what I have to say, you'll want the whole thing."

Kit thought a moment. "I will be in my office until five o'clock."

"No, I don't want to be seen going in there. You meet me. Do you know the depot in Glendale?"

"Yes."

"Be there at nine tonight. There's a dirt road on the east side. Walk down that road till you reach the trees; it's not too far."

"This is too much."

"I want to be sure you're alone."

"Why should I trust you, Mr. Rye?"

Rye laughed. "I guess you'll have to have a little faith. You're a godly woman, they say. And if what I have means your client gets off the hook, I have a hunch you'll exercise some faith in me."

The connection cut off.

"No," Corazón said when Kit told her about the conversation. "I do not want you to go alone."

"Don't worry," said Kit. "He means me no harm. He is desperate for some sort of deal, wants to give me something. It might be useful, it might not be. It could even be false evidence, like a decoy. But I won't know that until I talk to him."

"You will take a gun?"

Kit owned a derringer, given to her by Earl Rogers.

Certain parts of Los Angeles, at certain times of night, were not always hospitable to a woman alone.

"I will," Kit promised.

Corazón nodded her approval.

"Meanwhile, I would like you and Raul to follow Ellis Dyke from his office. Let's see where else he likes to spend his time."

Chapter Fifteen

The depot at Glendale was little more than a station house, a wood-slatted platform, and a telegraph pole with a single wire. At one time it was thought this might have been the best place for a railroad terminus, but the Los Angeles interests prevailed and now Glendale was poised for an uncertain future. Would it become a vibrant community of its own? Or would it be gobbled up by private industry for various purposes? Oil was rumored to lie beneath the sun-soaked soil.

Kit was the only passenger on the trolley this night. The motorman told her the last run would be in an hour and if she wanted to get back to Los Angeles, she best not miss it.

She did not intend to.

The path that Rye told her about was a thin ribbon in the moonlight. Kit saw it disappear into a grove of ghostly trees. She began walking.

All of this was probably a mistake, she thought. Billy Rye was not going to be here. *You're a fool, Kit Shannon.*

A breeze touched the leaves of the birch and eucalyptus trees not far from her. It was like the whispering of the world, advising caution. Kit patted the derringer in her pocket. Armed with that, and prayer, Kit was not so much worried about a meeting with Billy Rye as she was anxious to get on with it.

But there was no sign of life.

A dark cloud passed over the moon, a gloved hand in front of a magic lantern. Then Kit heard the crunch of dry brush within the trees.

"Mr. Rye?" she called.

No answer. The sound stopped. She wondered if the sound had come from a deer or, perhaps, a coyote. Or a California black bear. Every once in a while bears would make their way down from the hills, though usually this was around the ranches scattered about the valley. They came for food, not lawyers.

Kit stood still, listening. The air became cooler by the minute. Kit pulled the light shawl tighter around her shoulders.

She thought of Ted then, wondering what he was doing tonight. Thinking of her? Longing to get back to Los Angeles and her embrace? Once he did, she was not going to let him go.

A doubt shot into her mind, a small but palpable speck of uncertainty. What if for some reason he did not return? What if something happened? An accident? Unnamed calamities filled her thoughts.

She shook her head. *No, Lord, it won't happen. You will watch over him ... you will ...*

"I'm surprised you showed." The voice spun her around.

From the darkness of the trees a shadowy form moved toward her. Kit stood her ground, her hand on the pistol in her pocket. "Billy Rye?" she said.

The dark figure got closer, and now Kit could see a few facial details in the moonlight. His eyes seemed to take in light and kill it, leaving them black and inscrutable.

"I didn't figure you wanted to deal with me," he said. He stopped a yard away from her. He had nothing in his hands, yet they looked to be ready for the opportunity to grab something.

Kit went over her jiu-jitsu in her mind. All the training with Mr. Hancock may have to come into play. She pictured, for a split second, Billy Rye on the ground after an over-the-hip move.

"To tell you the truth, Mr. Rye," she said, "I do not want to deal with you."

Billy Rye frowned.

"But I am obligated to follow up anything that might be of help to my client. So here I am. I'm listening."

Rye smiled in the moonlight, turned his head, and spit. "You think you know what happened at Doogan's?"

"I know what my client told me. I know what Doogan claims."

"Then you don't know anything."

"Why don't you tell me, Mr. Rye?"

"I'd rather hear your version of it."

"Mr. Rye, you might be called upon to testify at the trial. It would be improper of me to affect your testimony in any way. I've come a long way tonight at your request. Tell me what you want to tell me."

"You going to give me something in return?"

"Legal help?"

"That's right."

"I cannot say. But you can trust me. If you know anything about me, you know that much. I will help you if I think I can. I want to know first why you brought me out here."

Billy Rye was quiet for a long moment, then gave her a quick nod. "You think Ellis and Malloy got into a drinking match, don't you?"

"Go on."

"And Malloy can't hold his liquor as good as Ellis, right?"

"I'm still listening."

"Well, then, I got news for you. Ellis Dyke couldn't hold a single beer without falling all over himself."

"What?"

Billy Rye smiled again. Kit noticed he was missing a tooth. "Interested now, aren't you?"

"How do you know this about Ellis Dyke?" Kit asked.

"I been drinking with Ellis for a year. He's a lousy drunk. I also seen Mousy drink, and there's a man who can stand his ground against the demon rum."

"Are you saying Mousy Malloy could not have lost a drinking contest with Ellis Dyke?"

"That's what I'm saying."

"If what you say is true," Kit said slowly, "then Ellis Dyke wasn't really drinking that morning."

"Oh, he was drinking all right. I was standing at his elbow. Only he wasn't drinking beer."

"What was it?"

"Apple cider."

"Doogan was serving cider to Dyke?"

Billy Rye nodded. "And boiling Malloy's drinks."

"Boiling?"

"A shot of whiskey in the beer. A horseshoe, we call it."

The picture was becoming clear. "So Ellis Dyke arranged this little contest with Doogan, but it was not equal from the start. They both meant to get Mousy drunk."

"That's it."

"But why?"

"You'll have to ask Ellis about that."

"Is there more you want to tell me?"

"Did your client tell you why Ellis Dyke was always after him?"

"Yes."

"What did he say?"

"What do you think he said?"

Rye nodded. "He told you he got in a fight with Ellis and whipped him, and that's what Ellis has been mad about all this time."

"Continue."

"Well, that ain't the half of it."

"Are you going to tell me the other half?"

"Now, that's where you have a choice to make." Billy Rye looked at the sky. "Nice night."

"What are you driving at, Mr. Rye?"

"There's more to my story, Miss Shannon. I thought I'd

give you this much to show you I got a lot to say. But now I need something from you."

"Are you in some sort of legal trouble?"

"Nope. Just want something."

"What?"

"A place to call my own. A little spread. Got my eye on a lot over near the foothills."

"You want me to help you in a real-estate venture?"

"Something like that."

"I can't say as I see any difference between that and my paying you money for—"

"Hang it all! Do you want to find out the truth or not?"

This time Kit sensed desperation in his voice. Something else seemed to be going on beneath the surface of this man. Was he truly in trouble? Or was he trouble himself?

"I will offer you legal advice," Kit said, "as I would any other prospective client. If I think I can help you, I will. It must all be legitimate and aboveboard."

Billy Rye heaved a long sigh, and it sounded a little like the breeze blowing up dust in the Glendale burg. "Good. More to come. Will you meet me again?"

"Why can't we settle this now?"

"You have to do this my way."

"Must it be in such a remote spot?"

"Oh yeah," he said. "I don't want to end up dead. That's not such an unreasonable thing, is it?"

Chapter Sixteen

The following morning, at the breakfast table with Corazón, Kit opened to the *Los Angeles Times* editorial page. She wanted to keep her finger on the pulse of the city because it helped her when selecting jurors for the Malloy case. The men who were called to serve did not operate without preconceptions. Part of her job as a defense lawyer was to make sure there were no hidden prejudices against her clients.

And, on occasion, she would find something of personal interest, such as the times she herself wound up mentioned by name. The idea of a woman trying cases in court was not greeted with universal enthusiasm.

That battle had seemingly been won, however. The name Kit Shannon was no longer whispered with conspiratorial derision, her standing as a lawyer no longer challenged.

So it was with a mixture of shock and surprise that she found herself in an editorial once more—not by name, but by implication. For the editorial was written by none other than Chester R. Beasley! It carried the title "The Scourge of the New Woman."

There is about in our cities today a type of "new woman." Where there should be a beating heart, there is only the cold calculation of ambition. Thus, this new woman is an abomination—one of the greatest, in my opinion, of this age—because a woman without a heart is not a woman.

There are three types of this abomination:

The first is the woman with children, a husband, and a home who neglects all three of them for the sake of the club and the drawing room.

The wider liberty of this age grants men and women a certain license, but it saps the real liberty and makes one a slave to home-destroying influences. Our own city is not free from this evil.

The second type is a distinct menace to society. She is the childless wife. She is too often seen in the well-fed, tastefully gowned, and handsomely brought up dame who cannot bear the burden of looking after children, as such an occupation would interfere with her own privileges. Such a type is only too common in our large cities.

The third class is that of the woman, single or married, who neglects her home duties to emphasize to the world "women's rights." This type is a distinct menace to society. She would blot and destroy God's most glorious picture. She would seek to wear the uniform of the professional man, do battle in the arena where men are the stronger sex. She becomes strident and unattractive.

I have dealt with such a woman on a recent occasion. She sought to tell me my business in the very halls of my establishment. Without experience, without compassion, without any of the saving graces of womanhood, this "new woman" brought her scourge into a functioning world.

God save us from this curse before it becomes an epidemic.

"Miss Kit?"

Corazón's voice seemed to come from across a distant sea, calling Kit back to shore. Kit's face felt flushed. "I'm sorry, Corazón. But listen." She read the opinion piece to her assistant.

Corazón shook her head when Kit finished. "People will see this is only one man's thinking, yes?"

Kit slapped the newspaper and showed the page to Corazón. "But look at this!"

At the bottom of the page was printed a four-paneled cartoon. The first panel showed a woman asking her husband, huddled over sheets of paper, if he would like to read her his speech. He says no, and she is insulted. In panel two she says, "Oh, so you do not think I have any brains?" The man agrees to read it. In the third panel, he begins, "Gentlemen, I appeal to your intelligence as citizens." The wife, sitting in a chair, is smiling. But in the last panel, she has fallen asleep, and the cartoon strip ended with, "Isn't that just like a woman?"

Corazón looked at Kit with a hand over her mouth.

"I would like to show them Jael," Kit said, "from the Book of Judges, who smote an enemy of God with a tent nail pounded through the temples. Isn't that just like a woman?"

Corazón broke into peals of laughter. As she did, her mother, Angelita, Kit's housekeeper and cook, walked into the dining room with a letter. "This is from a messenger," she said.

"Thank you, Angelita." The envelope had the coroner's office address stamped on it. Kit ripped it open.

"News?" Corazón asked.

"A verdict in the inquest," Kit said. "According to our coroner, Raymond J. Smith, in the matter of the death of Sammy Franklin in a trolley accident, he finds no blame."

Corazón sighed. "That is just like before."

"Exactly like before," Kit said. "This is all a sham. Are you ready to get to the bottom of this?"

"All the time!"

As they were finishing their breakfast of *huevos rancheros* and corn tortillas, formulating plans for their investigation, the telephone in the hallway rang. Angelita answered and told Kit it was someone from the county hospital.

Kit went to the phone.

"Are you the representative of Abner Malloy?" a woman's voice said.

Kit tensed. "I am."

"He has been brought here from the jail. You'd better come."

Winnie let Alice take her arm.

"It will be just fine," Alice said, patting Winnie's hand. "You need to get back into daily life, dear."

Winnie knew this was true, yet was it simply a matter of stepping through a door? Alice had talked her into a shopping visit to the Broadway Department Store. But it seemed like only yesterday that Winnie had been taking Sammy in to buy him a suit of clothes. She was afraid she might faint at the sight of fabric.

On the other hand, she had been grasping hard after God. Kit Shannon was a big reason why, having spent two evenings with her reading the Bible and praying. Winnie knew that a step through the door was a step of faith, and she willed herself to take it.

Inside the store, the bustle of afternoon shoppers was a pleasant distraction, its own little world spinning around, and the troubles of the outside seemed all but forgotten. So many choices! A chemise for fifty cents caught her eye, a silk petticoat for five dollars, and a lovely beaded purse, advertised to be on sale for fifty-nine cents. On a nearby table lay a line of corsets, starting from forty cents.

Winnie began to feel a sense of life returning, if only as a tiny spark, and she was thankful for it. For the first time since Sammy's death there was a sliver of hope inside her.

She spent fifteen minutes haggling over gingham fabric, which was going for twelve-and-a-half cents a yard. When the floor manager approved knocking off the half cent, Winnie actually became elated and bought five yards. She would get back to her sewing, and time would once again heal.

But then it happened, as starkly as if some demon had waited for the perfect moment to rip any happiness from her breast. Loaded down with boxes and bags, Alice and Winnie had turned to leave the store, talking about taking lunch, when Winnie heard the boy's voice.

It was so very much like Sammy's. Winnie knew at once

the boy would look like him. And even though his hair color was different and he was perhaps a year older, the boy was still shockingly like her own dead son—dressed in a new suit, the tags still upon the sleeve, with his doting mother standing by him.

"Mummy," the boy chirped, "I look just like Daddy, don't I?"

Hot wires twisted and gnarled in Winnie's chest. Her arms fell to her sides, the boxes she held plopping on the floor.

"Winnie?"

She heard Alice's voice while the little boy in the new suit looked at her. His eyes were blue, innocent and pure, and the hot twisting shot up into Winnie's head. White light exploded in her head and she fell to the floor.

"Delirium tremens," the doctor said.

"How severe?" Kit asked.

"It is always severe. Mr. Malloy was screaming in his cell. Apparently he was under the delusion that giant insects were attacking him."

"How is he now?"

"We've managed to sedate him and so he's quiet. He's been asking for you. I must warn you, he is not coherent."

"Let me go to him."

"And he is still a prisoner."

"I understand that."

"Then you will understand that he is not alone."

"What?"

"Follow me."

The doctor led her down a long, dark corridor to a room at the end. Stepping inside, Kit saw her client bound to a bed with leather straps and guarded by the hovering presence of Detective Mike McGinty. Next to McGinty stood the most shocking presence of all—Chief of Police Horace Allen.

"What is going on here?" Kit said immediately. She

hurried to the bed, where Mousy turned his head toward her, his eyes sunken and tired.

"Hold up there," McGinty said. "We're trying to get a word in here."

"No! My client is in no condition to speak to you, and even if he were, this would not be proper."

Chief Allen, wearing a copper policeman's badge on the coat of his brown suit, pointed his finger at Kit. He was a bull of a man and no one to trifle with. "We are not in a courtroom now."

"Location is of no consequence," Kit said. "My client's rights under the Constitution are—"

"You can forget about the Constitution!" Allen bellowed.

Kit turned to the doctor, who seemed a calm man. "I would like you to be a witness to this conversation and note what the chief just said."

That made the waters of rage break through any dam of civility the chief had left. He walked out of the room with his face reddening, grunting at Kit as he passed by.

McGinty seemed a bit amused as he followed his boss. He stopped in front of Kit before he left the room. "You have a way of getting people steamed, don't you?"

"You know me," Kit said.

"People usually don't talk to the chief that way."

"No one has the right to trample the Constitution, and no one's going to do it to one of my clients."

"Fair enough. Oh, we're posting a man outside the room, just to be safe. You know, I don't think the chief trusts you very much." Then with a wink and a nod McGinty was gone.

"May I have a moment with my client?" Kit asked the doctor.

"Not very long."

"Five minutes."

The doctor nodded his approval and took his leave.

"Mousy?" Kit looked into a pair of rheumy eyes that seemed tired of life. They had not even bothered to gown him; he still wore the old clothes he'd had on in jail.

"Hello, Miss Shannon." Mousy Malloy's voice sounded rough and whispery.

"How are you?"

"I feel like I been put through a coffee grinder."

"Mousy, I have to ask you a question."

"Yes?"

"What were the police asking you about?"

Mousy thought about the question but didn't answer. Kit could smell the remnants of alcohol seeping through his pores, mixed with the ammonia scent from the scrubbed floor.

"Did you hear me?" Kit pressed.

"I don't know what they wanted."

Kit shook her head. "I don't think you're being entirely honest with me."

"No?"

"I'm your lawyer. I'm doing everything I can on your behalf. But if you hold back information from me, I can't help you."

"It's not anything about the trial, Miss Shannon."

"Why would the police be questioning you?"

Mousy looked down at his bound body. "Would you loosen the strap for me, Miss Shannon? A man's got to be able to scratch his head."

"I don't know. I'd better ask the doctor."

"No!" Mousy's eyes darted around the room. "He won't let me! He's a devil, he's—"

"Now, Mousy, don't—"

"Please, Miss Shannon. I promise I won't do anything bad. I just don't like being tied up like an animal."

With a sigh Kit decided to loosen one of the restraints. After Mousy's right arm was free, he rubbed his eyes with his hand. "Ah, that's good."

"Please, tell me what the police chief and Detective McGinty wanted from you."

"They wanted to know where they could find Billy Rye."

The name spilled out like a dark secret. "They think you know where he is?"

"I reckon. But I don't. He was one of the ones in Doogan's who—"

"I know who he is, Mousy. I spoke with him last night."

With his free hand Mousy reached for Kit's sleeve. "You talked to Billy?"

"Yes. What I want to know is your connection to him."

"Where did you see him? Did he come to your office?" Mousy's voice was anxious, quick.

"No, we met somewhere else. At night. Why would he want to meet with me?"

Mousy let go of Kit's arm. "It's not important."

"Why don't you let me be the judge of that?"

"I don't know why the cops are so interested. Is it because he's a witness?"

"You just said it wasn't about the trial. Mousy, what is going on?"

He shook his head slowly. "I don't really know, Miss Shannon. Honest."

"How far back do you go with Mr. Rye?"

"A couple years. He worked the rails with me."

"Do you want to know what he told me about the morning at Doogan's?"

Mousy's face, pale and unshaven, lit up with interest.

"According to Billy Rye, Doogan was boiling your beers."

"A shot of whiskey?"

"That's what Billy said. At the same time he was giving Ellis Dyke apple cider. You were not going to win that drinking contest, Mousy."

She watched as her client's face underwent several permutations of emotion—anger, torment, confusion. With a grunt he raised himself off the bed. It was a pitiable effort. His left wrist was still bound to a rail on the side, and a large leather strap constricted his middle.

Kit gently pressed him back on the bed. "Don't, Mousy."

"I'll kill him!"

"Be quiet! Do you want someone to hear?"

"They'll never get it. Never."

Kit leaned down a little, alerted by Mousy's desperate tone. "Get what?"

At that moment the doctor, looking less patient and kind

than a few moments before, stormed into the room. "What is the meaning of this?"

"Doctor, if I may have a few more minutes."

"This has gone on long enough."

"When may I return?"

"I suppose around four o'clock. By then he may be in a better condition to speak to you. Now I must ask you to leave."

"I'll be back," Kit said to her client. "In the meantime, don't talk to anyone, not even the chief of police."

Chapter Seventeen

With fresh questions for Doogan roiling in her mind, Kit drove her Ford straightaway to his saloon on Fifth Street. She estimated at one point that she was doing at least ten miles per hour and so slowed herself down to a more civilized speed.

Doogan was a clever one; her approach would have to be clever, as well. She did not think the tavern owner would give up any information easily.

So she expected a bit of a duel with Doogan. What she did not expect to see, however, was a crowd gathered on the sidewalk outside the saloon. Upon approach she saw it was someone giving a street-corner talk, as often occurred in Los Angeles—preachers, salesmen, con artists with the latest two-dollar fad. The last one Kit had seen was peddling a wristband that supposedly harnessed the power of the sun. "Giving new life to blood vessels, my friends."

Such mountebanks were not uncommon on the city's streets. But there was something different about this speaker. For one thing, she was a woman.

A tall, broad-shouldered woman with clipped gray hair was speaking with fire in her eyes and a raging thunder in her voice.

Her fists pumped up and down in the air, and as soon as Kit heard the words issuing from the woman's mouth, she knew exactly who it was—the scourge of saloon owners everywhere in America—Carry Amelia Moore Nation.

Since 1900, Carry Nation had been on the warpath against alcohol and the establishments that sold it. The newspapers had gleefully reported her arrests on several occasions, due primarily to her penchant for taking a hatchet into liquor dens and chopping up the places. Usually she was accompanied by her followers, who also carried clubs and hand axes.

With her celebrity on the rise, Mrs. Nation was making lecture tours now. She supplemented her income by selling little toy hatchets as souvenirs. There was no mistaking her passion for her cause.

Kit stepped up to the back of the crowd and listened.

"God is a politician!" Carry Nation cried. "So is the devil! God's politics are to protect and defend mankind, bringing to them the highest good and finally heaven. The devil's politics are to deceive, degrade, and make miserable, finally ending in hell. The Bible fully explains this. The two kinds of seed started out from Abel and Cain, then Ishmael and Isaac, Esau and Jacob. There are but these two kinds of people: God's crowd and the devil's crowd. Which are you?"

Carry Nation's eyes bore into the mostly male listeners, though Kit noted a small band of women who were standing close to Mrs. Nation and dressed eerily like her—long black dresses with white linen frill around the collar. She also noticed, just on the other side of Carry Nation, Jack London, who appeared to be taking notes. Kit was not surprised. London was constantly writing news dispatches for various papers, and Carry Nation was news.

"The first law given and broken in Eden was a prohibition law," Carry Nation declared. "God said, 'Thou shalt not.' The devil tempted and persuaded the first pair to disobey. We are here to bring prohibition back to where it belongs."

"Go back to Kansas!" a man shouted.

Mrs. Nation did not flinch at this but pointed her finger at the offender and rebuked, "No rum-soaked, whiskey-swilling rummy is going to tell me what to do! You can take the matter up with the Lord Jesus Christ! I am but a bulldog running along at the feet of Jesus, barking at what He doesn't like—and He hates whiskey!"

"Well, I like it!" another man shouted, drawing some cheers from the other bystanders.

"Soon you won't be able to get it!" Carry Nation responded. "The saloon is going! God reigns and His people will awake. And as the saloon lies dying at last amongst its bags of gold, we will stand over it and say, down, down to hell, and say we sent thee there!"

Kit glanced at the swinging doors and saw the anxious face of Doogan peering out. Good. If Carry Nation could put the fear of God into the man—and it appeared she was doing just that—it was a step in the right direction. It might teach him not to exploit boys or dipsos like Mousy Malloy.

Mrs. Nation reached down for something. When she stood up Kit saw a hatchet in her right hand. The sun glinted off its blade. A few men near her took backward steps.

"And now, ladies," Carry Nation cried. "Smash!"

The armed woman stepped off the crate and was immediately joined by her sisters in weaponry. From under their dresses they produced clubs and axes and, in one woman's hand, a small whip.

Doogan's eyes nearly popped out of his head. He looked at Kit. "Miss Shannon, do something!"

The small crowd parted, giving Carry Nation and her entourage a path toward the entrance to Doogan's.

"Please!" the saloonkeeper pleaded.

An odd turn of events indeed! Kit almost laughed. Here was a man, a liar, booze merchant, and false witness, asking a Christian lawyer for help to protect his liquor!

But then, Kit thought, not so odd after all. She was a representative of the law and, with no policeman in sight, the only one present who could possibly do anything for Doogan and his predicament. Despite what he stood for, he was still a business owner with certain rights.

Mrs. Nation was almost to Doogan's door, much to the

delight of the crowd. Their faces carried signs of eagerness for the show about to take place. Jack London was among the most anxious, fighting his way to the forefront, pencil and paper in hand.

Kit pushed through the doors just before the squad of joint smashers.

Doogan had taken refuge behind the counter. In front of him, like soldiers on a rampart, stood a line of bottles, whiskey of various kinds. Why they were displayed like that Kit did not know. But they made a prime target for the ax-wielding Mrs. Nation and her cohorts.

Carry Nation burst through and sized up the place, no doubt looking for the best target to begin the mayhem.

"Now, see here!" Doogan's frantic voice cried out. "You have no right!"

"God is the author of right!" Carry Nation shouted. "And the demon liquor is not right! There can be no right of sin! The beginning of right begins with `Thou shalt not!'"

"*Thou shalt not* chop up other people's property!" Doogan exclaimed.

Mrs. Nation only squinted at him, then immediately returned to her purpose. With a mighty *thwack* she brought her hatchet down on the backside of a wooden chair, sending splinters flying.

Carry Nation looked to her assemblage. "Smash, ladies, smash!"

The others fanned out inside the saloon, hatchets and clubs at the ready.

And then a shot cracked the air.

Doogan held his gun pointed at the ceiling. "You can stop right there!" he shouted.

The ladies froze for an uncertain moment. Carry Nation marched to the bar. "I fear not the hand of man!" she said, swinging the hatchet on a line in front of her like a scythe, clearly aiming for the liquor bottles.

Doogan, his bluff called, took a shaky step back.

Kit lunged toward the bar, but Carry Nation stopped her approach. "Young woman, what are you about?"

"I understand your zeal, Mrs. Nation," Kit said. "I know your concern is for the souls of men and the evil that can often flow from places like this."

"Then stand aside and let me at my mission!"

"Except there are laws, and we must respect the law. This establishment is legal. Let us rather work together on the changing of the laws so we can honor both God and man."

"I see no honor here!" The robust woman raised her hatchet high into the air.

"Mrs. Nation, you are a Christian woman, as I am. I admire your determination. Please, will you dine with me tonight, to discuss this further? We will break bread and decide what is best."

Carry Nation lowered the hatchet. "What is your name, young woman?"

"Kathleen Shannon, attorney-at-law."

"Attorney?" The news seemed to please her.

"Yes, I—"

Kit stopped as a boy of ten or so, one whom she had not seen before, scurried into the middle of the maelstrom. When all eyes turned to him, he looked around as if a cornered rabbit.

"I ... I ..." the boy stammered, then looked up at Doogan. "I got here as fast as I could."

Kit eyed the boy, who looked dirty and confused, and wondered if he was another escapee from the Beasley home. And then, eyes flashing, she turned on Doogan.

He recoiled from Kit's glare as he might have from the hatchet in Carry Nation's hand. "Now, be reasonable," he said.

Kit motioned to the bottles on the bar top and said to the boy, "Are you here to deliver these for Mr. Doogan?"

Momentarily frozen, the boy finally nodded his head.

"May I have that?" Kit said to Carry Nation, indicating the hatchet. Mrs. Nation, appearing now as stunned as the boy, handed the weapon to Kit.

Kit took the hatchet and proceeded to smash every bottle of liquor on the bar.

Over the sound of crashing glass and exploding liquid, Doogan yelled, "No! No! You can't!"

So intent was Kit on the task at hand that she did not take note of the flashing powder that meant a newspaper photographer was taking pictures of the scene. When the job was done, Kit admired the hatchet in her hand. "Very efficient," she said and handed it back to Mrs. Nation. Then to Doogan, loud enough for all to hear, Kit said, "Send me the bill for the damages. But if I ever catch you hiring another boy again for your trade, you will not want to see what I do to this place."

"Well spoken!" Carry Nation said. "Let us dine together indeed."

The last pair of eyes Kit saw as she left Doogan's belonged to Jack London. He smiled widely, then scribbled something on his pad.

Chapter Eighteen

The Rickman Hotel was one of the oldest, and finest, in the city of San Francisco. A Nob Hill landmark, it had been host to presidents and men of industry. It was said to be steel baron Andrew Carnegie's favorite abode when visiting the city, and Teddy Roosevelt had once spent an eventful night here on his way to the Hawaiian Islands during his first term as president. The night was eventful because an assassin had been stopped in the lobby when a sharp-eyed house detective noted a particular "stink" about the man.

No one who smelled that way belonged in the Rickman, he reasoned, and it was well that he did. The man was an anarchist from Stockton, with a gun in his jacket and an anti-American note in his pocket.

Tonight, however, would not be an evening for anarchy. The elite of San Francisco society gathered outside the hotel with another scent in the air—old money. The occasion was a dinner to honor Addison Dyke for his many years of service, and donations, to the city.

Ted Fox knew, from his years in the high-society social scene in Los Angeles, that the rich carried themselves in a certain fashion. Anyone who did not have this air about them was likely to be spotted as easily as that anarchist from Stockton. Ted thought of it as a certain attitude of mind, a mien of absolute confidence, snobbishness, and *savoir faire*. He had seen it over and over again in his life.

Even though he was now a Christian, his memory of the old days worked wonders as he walked through the doors of the Rickman in his tuxedo and fresh boutonniere as if he owned the place.

He smiled with absolute confidence while strolling through the lobby, his cane a fancy stick borrowed from the Reverend Harlow Hayes, given as a gift to him from a wealthy benefactor of the boys' home. Ted nodded at several of the well-heeled couples, who smiled and returned the acknowledgement. They did not know who he was, of course, but would never let on. In this set, one acknowledged others on the chance they were someone important.

Near the entrance to the grand ballroom, Ted paused. Two attendants in black tie, tails, and white gloves were taking invitations from those who entered.

A minor detail, Ted thought. He was prepared. He put his nose up slightly, sniffed once to get into character, and walked toward the doors.

One of the attendants nodded politely and held out his gloved hand.

Ted shook it. "Thank you, wonderful to be here." He let go of the hand and took a step toward the open doors.

"Excuse me, sir," the attendant said somewhat sheepishly. "Your invitation?"

"Invitation!" Ted snorted. "Sir," he said, leaning in close, "do you know who I am?"

"I ... I am afraid not."

Ted rebuked him with a stare, let him dangle for a moment like a carp on a hook. Then, with a jaunty smile, Ted clapped him on the shoulder. "No matter, my good man. I will let it go this time. *This* time." Ted gave the attendant a curt nod and then entered the ballroom with no further trouble.

He felt transported back in time. Social gatherings like this had once been a major part of his life. Before Kit, before coming to know the Savior, Ted had been in banking and was on the upward spiral of success. All of these memories came flooding back as he made his way through San Francisco society.

In the middle of the exquisite room, which held one of the largest chandeliers Ted had ever seen, was a large table covered in fine, embroidered linen. A feast fit for Solomon covered the length of the table. Shrimp and salmon, caviar and oysters created a seagoing theme for the elegantly dressed men and women who looked over the repast.

As a string quartet played in the corner, the aristocracy of San Francisco mingled and posed, glided and bowed, in a ritual of affluent cross-pollination. No one would be thinking about social problems this night.

Not yet, Ted thought.

Carry Nation said, "Today the country is ringing with the cry of political bribery, boodle, and official corruption, from the highest to the lowest. The rum traffic is the principal factor in demoralizing and destroying the dignity, honor, and integrity of civic life!"

"Yes, we have many challenges," Kit agreed. They were seated in a booth at the Imperial. Kit thought the change would do Carry Nation good, though when offered a drink by the waiter, Mrs. Nation almost turned the table over.

"The demon rum is the insidious foe that is hatching and nursing crime," Mrs. Nation shouted at the befuddled servant. "This demon, this Moloch of perdition, must be destroyed!"

"We shall just have water," Kit told the waiter, who went away in relief.

"I am more concerned with the effect of the liquor trade on our children," Kit said. "Boys are being taught to drink as a rite of manhood even as the saloonkeepers use them to make their deliveries."

Carry Nation's face reddened. "I have seen this time and again! And why isn't anything done about it? Because the liquor men and joint keepers subscribe large sums to political campaigns with the understanding of immunity from prosecution and punishment on the part of candidates and officials. This has been going from bad to worse for twenty years!"

"Political corruption is not unknown in this city, Mrs. Nation. Los Angeles is still trying to find its soul."

"What, then, is to be done here?"

"We must change the law."

"Blackstone says, `Law commands that which is right and prohibits that which is wrong.'"

"You know Blackstone?" Kit was impressed. His treatise on the law was the standard reference for lawyers and a volume she studied constantly.

"Of course," Mrs. Nation said. "But the law moves too slowly for my taste. That is why I carry a hatchet."

"I am afraid I was not the best example today. When I saw that boy in Doogan's—"

"Miss Shannon, you were glorious!"

Kit had to laugh and, for once, Mrs. Nation laughed along with her.

Their laughter was interrupted by a shadow falling over the table. Kit looked up and saw two looming figures staring down at her. She sat back with a start. What was Chief of Police Horace Allen doing here, and with one of his uniformed cops?

"Kathleen Shannon." The chief's voice came out thunderous and caused all conversation to cease within the place. Kit felt the silence, sensed the social opprobrium flowing her way from the genteel patrons. A pleasant evening was being rudely interrupted, which was not why people came to the Imperial.

"Good evening, Chief." Kit gave him a raffish nod.

"Not so good for you, Miss Shannon. Where is he?"

"Where is who?"

"Your client. Malloy."

"He's in the county hospital."

Allen shook his head.

A chill shot through Kit. "He's gone?"

"And you know where he is."

Kit slipped out of the booth and stood to face the police chief. "I do not know where he is, but maybe he will try to contact me. I must get back to—"

"Not so fast," Allen said.

"What do you mean?"

"I mean, Miss Shannon, that you are under arrest. You too, Mrs. Nation."

The woman was tall, matronly, and bedecked in jewels, her hair done up with strings of baby pearls, offset by a sprout of white ostrich feathers that burst forth like flowers blooming in the spring.

She was also alone, which was why Ted approached her. She would, he hoped, provide his introduction to Addison Dyke.

"Good evening," he said. "I don't believe we've met."

The woman nodded. "How do you do? I am Mrs. Harrison Bosworth Elkington."

Ted took a wild stab and asked, "Of the San Francisco Elkingtons?"

"Of course! Are there any others?"

"Not of any significance," Ted said, bowing. "Very pleased to make your acquaintance. I'm afraid I'm rather new in the city—don't know many people as yet. Theodore Fox at your service."

"Fox. Would that be the Virginia Foxes?"

"I'm afraid not. Los Angeles."

Mrs. Elkington sniffed. "Well, you seem like a nice young man, regardless. What is it that you do in"—she wrinkled her nose in mock disgust—"Loss Angeleese?"

"I am in the burgeoning aviation business."

"How quaint. I understand flying is a hobby but hardly the stuff of industry."

"I plan to test that very thing, Mrs. Elkington. You see, I think there is a great future in flight. Can you imagine one day traveling through the air? Why, you could be in New York the same day you leave San Francisco."

"No!"

"It is true! And if I could have a word about this with Mr. Dyke ..."

"Do you really think it is possible?"

"Having a word with Mr. Dyke?"

"No, silly boy, flying in the air! Like a bird."

Ted smiled politely. "Quite possible."

"You are a dreamer, aren't you?" she said with a coquettish curve of the lips and bob of the eyebrows.

Oh dear, Ted thought.

"You would like to meet Addison?"

A *whoosh* of relief escaped Ted's mouth. "Yes!" he replied.

"Would you like me to introduce you?"

Ted pulled at his collar. "Mrs. Elkington, I would be much obliged to you."

"Nothing of it." She smiled, turned, and said, "Take my arm."

With some trepidation, Ted did as he was told. The matron walked him across the floor, as she might have a prized poodle, toward a shiny oaken bar. There, surrounded by tendrils of cigar smoke, two older gentlemen conversed.

Without a second thought, Mrs. Elkington tapped one of the men with her fan. He looked around quickly, eyes glowering under bushy white eyebrows.

"Elvira!" he spouted. "I am in the middle of—"

"Tut tut," Mrs. Elkington said. "I want you to meet this fine young man. Mr. Theodore Fox, may I introduce Mr. Addison Dyke."

The man gave Ted a cursory look and extended his hand. "Pleased to meet you."

"Likewise," Ted said. Dyke appeared taken aback by the informality.

Mrs. Elkington beamed. "Mr. Fox runs an aeronautic

enterprise, something that should interest you, Addison. Competition for travel and all that."

Dyke grunted.

Elvira Elkington ignored him. "Mr. Fox, will you dine at our table?"

"I would be honored," Ted said.

"Very well. I'll leave you two to talk." She took the other man by the arm and conveniently walked him away, chattering about the dreamer who hoped to fly.

Addison Dyke shook his head. "A busybody. Did you say your name is Fox?"

"I did."

"Of the Chicago Foxes?"

"Afraid not, sir. Los Angeles."

"Foxes in Los Angeles? I can't say as I know any. I thought all you had was coyotes! Eh!" Addison Dyke expelled a hearty laugh, giving Ted an elbow to the ribs.

"Very clever, sir," Ted said. "If I may—"

"Aviation you say? Tell me, son, do you honestly think air will ever become a preferred mode of travel?"

"I do not see why not."

"But the rails, man, the rails! America was built by rail. How can you even think of competing with that?"

"The two may coexist, I believe."

"Nonsense."

"That's what was said of the gasoline-powered automobile a few years ago. But it is quickly becoming the preferred mode of urban travel."

"Ah, that's nonsense as well. The trolley lines are what people need. If the streets get filled with these tin monstrosities, we'll have more noise and smoke in the air than we can handle." Dyke took a lingering puff on his cigar, eyeing Ted closely. "What brings you up to our city, young man?"

"I am here primarily at the behest of the home for boys on Jackson Street."

There was a momentary blankness in Dyke's eyes. "I believe I know it."

"Oh, you do, Mr. Dyke. The property is owned by Western Rail."

"Ah yes. Aren't we building something there?"

"That is the plan, I understand. Which brings me to a question, sir." Ted cleared his throat. "I wonder if you might reconsider."

"Well, I don't look into the day-to-day of things. I have plenty of people to handle that."

"Surely you are interested in the future of boys who, for one reason or another, have no home of their own?"

"Of course, young man. But that is all in the hands of the lawyers. Everything will be worked out for the good."

"Would that apply, sir, to all of your enterprises?"

Dyke squinted. "What is your implication, sir? I get the distinct feeling that you have something more on your mind than orphaned boys."

"Are you aware of the trouble concerning the Los Angeles Electric Trolley?"

There was a long pause before Dyke spoke again. The lilting strains of the string orchestra seemed absurdly out of place now as tension gripped Dyke's face.

"To what are you referring, sir?" Dyke asked pointedly.

"An accident where a young boy was killed."

Without so much as a twitch, Dyke said, "Such things happen. Naturally it is a tragic occurrence, but we cannot eliminate tragedy from the world."

"Perhaps, Mr. Dyke, there are steps that can be taken in order to make tragedy less frequent. Surely one thing—"

"See here, what is your game?" Dyke was suddenly not the gentleman anymore but the rugged, two-fisted ex-soldier who built a huge company by force of will.

"I assure you, Mr. Dyke, I have no self-interest here. But I have not given you the full story. Allow me."

"I'm listening."

"I am the fiancé of Kit ... Kathleen Shannon, a Los Angeles attorney. She is—"

"Wait!" Dyke raised his hand. "I know all about her. Are you her representative here?"

"Only on an informal basis. I thought if we had the chance to talk—"

"I told you, these matters are handled by my lawyers."

"Mr. Dyke, you have a chance in this case to do something great for the people you serve. That's all I am asking you to consider."

"Talk to the lawyers. I believe a Mr. Mill is handling the matter."

"Won't you consider—"

"Enough, young man. I am beginning to have a bit of an acid stomach. Tonight is supposed to be about good spirits, and you are upsetting mine. If you will excuse me."

Dyke bowed quickly and walked away. Yet Ted could not help feeling there was something else going on beneath the surface of Dyke's overly formal demeanor.

And he meant to find it out.

Chapter Nineteen

"You busted up private property," Horace Allen said.

Kit sat on the rough wooden chair in the chief's office, not normally a place for a criminal suspect to be interrogated. Usually they were grilled in one of the windowless rooms on the first floor. This was some sort of privilege, but Kit was not impressed by the honor.

She looked at the chief of police. "Are you saying that Doogan has sworn out a complaint against me?"

"I'm not saying anything." Chief Allen put his thumbs in his vest pockets. "Yet."

"Then why am I here? You placed me under arrest."

"Had to get you here, didn't I?"

Kit jumped to her feet. "You mean this was a ruse?"

Allen pointed a finger at her. "Sit down."

"I most certainly will not. Am I under arrest?"

"That's up to you."

"Where is Mrs. Nation?"

"In the hoosegow. Along with her other cohorts."

"All of them?"

"We'll spring 'em in a little while. I want them to know

they can't go around chopping up licensed saloons in this city. They'll be invited to leave town."

"I repeat—am I being charged with something?"

"Let's just calm ourselves, shall we?" Horace Allen sat himself in a squeaky swivel chair. Behind his desk, yellowing windowpanes obscured the glow of the new electric lights on Main Street. "I am not an unreasonable man."

Suspicious, and knowing Allen had something he wasn't telling her, Kit sat once again, watching his face. "What is there to be reasonable about?"

"One thing you get to know pretty quick in the modern city is that there are little matters and larger matters. As chief, I have to look at all of that and decide what needs my attention. It's not an easy thing, being chief. I have to make these decisions every day."

"So you decided to arrest me, even though you knew you wouldn't be filing a charge?"

"I needed to talk to you."

"You could have done so by calling at my office."

"I also needed your attention."

"Why? Because Mousy Malloy is at large?"

Allen sighed. "That's a problem, yes. But not the big one."

"What is the big one, then?"

"You."

Kit shook her head. "Explain, please."

"You make trouble. In my town, I don't like trouble."

"If you mean breaking up Doogan's bar, I have already said I will pay for the damages."

"I'm not talking about your little fit in Doogan's! I'm talking about your high-hat ways, throwing your weight around where it isn't wanted."

"I still do not know what you mean."

"You think it's your job to save the world. You have a holier-than-thou way about you."

"What is it you are really upset about, Chief?"

"Your crusade against the trolley line, for one thing. It's all over the newspapers."

Kit frowned, trying to understand Allen's connection. "That is a civil matter."

"But it affects my town. Pretty soon you'll start a riot and I'll have to clean it up."

"Chief," Kit said calmly, "the law is a many-faceted thing. When it comes to criminal law, I defend people I think have been wrongly charged."

"Like Malloy?"

"Yes. There is more to that case than you know."

"Maybe. And maybe there's more than *you* know."

"Chief, please level with me. What is this meeting about?"

Allen cleared his throat. "Miss Shannon, I am willing to let the little incident at Doogan's pass. You saying you'll make good on the damage, that's good enough for me. The D.A. will go along with it."

"You've already spoken to Davenport about this?"

"We talked, yes."

"What do you want in return?"

"Drop your interest in the trolley matter."

"Why should that be of any concern to you?"

"Just call it a favor."

Favor? He was not being forthright, and she knew he had no intention of letting more out of the bag. Still, he was in dead earnest about her dropping the trolley case.

"And if I refuse?"

Allen glared through narrowed eyes. "I shall be quite disappointed."

Kit got to her feet again. "No, Chief. I will do what I think is in the best interest of my client."

"Unwise," Allen said, his voice filled with threat.

"If you want to charge me with something, do it. Let Davenport try to get a conviction."

"You really are trouble, aren't you?"

"A regular thorn in the flesh."

For a long moment Horace Allen stared at Kit. She thought his eyes reflected a little hesitation along with his intended menace.

Finally he said, "Go. But don't say I didn't warn you."

"I will warn you right now, Chief. Release Mrs. Nation or I'll slap you with a *habeas corpus*."

Kit drove back to the office, her hands squeezing the steering wheel of the Ford so hard her knuckles whitened. Corazón was waiting for her with an anxious expression. "I thought you were in jail!"

"Almost." Kit untied the satin ribbon under her chin and removed her hat. It was lightened with dust from the drive through midtown Los Angeles. "We have a greater problem now. Our client has flown the coop."

"The mouse?"

"I suppose I should say he has scurried away. From the hospital."

"How?"

"I may have helped him."

Corazón put her hand over her mouth.

"Not intentionally." Kit pushed some strands of hair back into place. "But that does not change the fact that he is an escaped prisoner, and we need to find him. I'd like you and Raul to check the local saloons."

"We will do it."

"Start with Doogan's and work outward from there. Unfortunately, this city has more saloons than churches, so your job will not be easy."

"I do not like the easy ones," Corazón said with a smile.

Early the next morning, Kit drove to the Pioneer Drugstore on Main. She needed to get something favorable from an eyewitness, and soon. With Billy Rye playing games, Sam Hartrampf was the only good prospect at the moment. But would he talk?

Kit parked the Ford next to a hitching post, where a nag hauling a wagon stood resting. The horse gave her a sidelong glance, none too approving.

"I don't blame you," Kit said, giving his nose a pat.

The Pioneer was the largest drugstore in the city and boasted twice the floor space of its rival, the Owl. As Kit entered, she saw large displays for the latest nostrums and palliatives the store offered eager customers: Koenig's Nerve Tonic, Casler's Oriental Paste, Chamberlain's Colic & Diarrhea Cure, and Heinzman's Freckle Salve. In the middle of the store sat a small pyramid made of boxes of Violet Breath Perfume. Kit knew several lawyers in town who could use the whole lot.

The offerings, for everything from a woman's "monthly regulator" to a man's "masculine energy," made Kit think of a line of sideshow barkers. The shelves were a mirror of the fakes who offered wacky spiritual answers, from palm reading to the interpretation of head shapes. Los Angeles was a city that increasingly attracted the odd and the disreputable—because they could make a living here.

Kit wandered the aisles for a moment, then stopped a young clerk in a white apron and asked for Sam Hartrampf. The clerk nodded toward the back where a man, also aproned, stood on a ladder, stocking a shelf. He was sandy-haired and seemed bored with his task.

"Mr. Hartrampf?"

The man looked down at her, surprised at the call of his name. His face looked like the Before picture in a Heinzman's Freckle Salve advertisement. He was in his twenties, and when he spoke, Kit noticed a wide gap between his front teeth.

"What can I do for you?" he said.

"My name is Kathleen Shannon. May I have a word with you?"

Hartrampf paused, holding a tin canister in his hand. It said *Damschinsky's Liquid Hair Dye.* "The lawyer?"

"I understand you are a witness to the events in Doogan's Saloon?"

Hartrampf shoved the tin onto a shelf. "I was there, yeah."

"Would you mind if I asked you some questions about it?"

Hartrampf rearranged a couple of the canisters, then stepped down off the ladder. "I don't know if I should say anything to you."

"Mr. Hartrampf, I have this conversation a great deal with

witnesses. You have nothing to fear if you tell the truth. That's what you will do if called to the witness stand by the prosecution or the defense. I just want to know what happened."

"Who else have you talked to?"

"Mr. Doogan," Kit said. "And Billy Rye."

Hartrampf's eyes almost bugged out. "You talked to Billy?"

"Is that a shock to you?"

"No, I ... how is old Billy?"

"In good health."

"Is he, now? Where'd you meet him?"

"Is Billy Rye a friend of yours?"

"Sure he is."

"But you haven't been in touch?"

Hartrampf stuck out his jaw. "You think you're smart?"

"I just want to know what happened at Doogan's. Were you a witness to the drinking contest?"

"You know about that?"

"Yes."

"I saw what happened, sure."

"Describe it for me, will you?"

Hartrampf took a string of shoelaces from twin pegs and began twisting them into a braid. "It was something between Ellis and Malloy. All in good fun."

"Did you see Doogan pouring the drinks?"

"Sure I did. I was standing right next to Ellis."

"Did you notice anything strange about it?"

Sam Hartrampf looked long and hard at Kit. "I'm supposed to be working here. I ain't got time to answer all this."

"Is there a more convenient time?"

"No."

"How about if I meet you after work?"

"How about you leave me be?"

"What is it you aren't telling me?"

Hartrampf gave Kit a gap-toothed smile. "If I told you, then it wouldn't be a secret, would it?"

"There will be no secrets if you are put on the stand in a trial, Mr. Hartrampf."

"I'll take my chances."

Kit drove back to her office by way of the wholesale market on Central and Second. She wanted to pick up fruit for Angelita, especially fresh oranges. She sputtered past a long line of horses and carts lining Central. Most of the carts were owned by the farmers who brought the produce in from all over the outlying areas of the city.

On foot, Kit wound her way through the different stands, buying much more than she'd planned. It was difficult to turn down the package of crisp red apples for twenty-five cents, the oranges that went for fifteen cents a dozen, and the dried apricots at ten cents a pound.

Shopping was also a way to relax as thoughts of her thin defense of Mousy Malloy continued to churn in her mind. Would she ever be able to get to the bottom of the case?

It proved to be a pleasant diversion when a stocky man with a large handlebar mustache talked her into four cans of tomatoes by knocking a penny off the normal price of twenty cents a can.

Kit had about all she could hold in paper sacks and was heading back to her auto when she stopped cold.

A boy was stealing an apple from a cart. Not just any boy.

Bobby.

Before the proprietor of the apple cart turned around, Bobby had already disappeared into the crowd.

Kit put her bags down. Anticipating the boy's course, she darted to a spot in the muddle of people.

Bobby almost knocked her down. She caught his shoulders.

"Lemme go!" he shouted.

"Bobby, it's me."

He looked up at her and his mouth fell open. "Miss Shannon!"

"What are you doing out here?"

Bobby looked down toward his shoes, scuffing the ground with his feet. "I run away."

"From Beasley?"

He nodded.

"That's not right," Kit said.

"Don't make me go back, Miss Shannon. I got a whuppin' but good."

He lifted up his shirt, and Kit recoiled at the sight. Across the boy's back was a series of red crisscrossing welts. Kit yanked the shirt down.

"No, no," she said. "You're not going back. You're coming with me."

"Where?"

"First, we're going back to the apple cart. You are going to pay the man."

"But I—"

"I'll front you a nickel, which you can work off. Fair enough?"

After the transaction with the wide-eyed apple merchant, Kit found her groceries and plopped the bags and Bobby into the Ford.

A half hour later they were standing in front of Judge Wiley Ganges in his private chambers. Ganges was the judge who had presided over the Ted Fox murder trial and who had sworn Kit in as a member of the bar. After a bit of initial uneasiness with her, Ganges had become quite friendly. He looked at the petition Kit handed him.

"You want this boy as your ward?" he asked.

"Yes." Kit had her arm around Bobby, who trembled slightly.

"On an *ex parte* order?"

"This is an emergency, Your Honor. What happened to this lad shouldn't happen to a dog. Look."

She showed the judge the ugly welts on Bobby's back.

"You know that's not illegal," Judge Ganges said. "Law gives overseers like Beasley discretion to keep discipline."

"Not like this!"

"I got horsewhipped when I was a boy."

"Judge, I have spoken with Mr. Beasley. I am not impressed with his views on child rearing."

"What about you, Kit? You don't have children of your own."

"No, sir, but—"

"Yet you want me to take this boy away from a duly licensed home and hand him over to you? Without so much as hearing from Beasley?"

"Yes."

Judge Ganges shook his head slowly. "I just can't do it, Kit. Wouldn't be right."

"But I—"

"The law's the law. Now, if we were to have a full-fledged hearing in court, I could then consider evidence from both sides. Then I could hear just what this Beasley character is doing and render a fully enforceable decision. Why don't we try to do that?"

Kit felt only a small relief. "In the meantime, what about the boy?"

Judge Ganges winked and looked around the chambers. "What boy? I don't see any boy. Maybe he's back at your house, Kit. Why don't you get out of here and go check?"

Billy Rye grunted and poured himself another drink. It was just rotgut whiskey, bought directly from a two-bit drummer about to board the train at the Glendale station, but it got the job done and would do until his ship came in, which wouldn't be long.

If he played his cards right, and right now he was holding aces.

The little shack wouldn't be his home for much longer, either. No, for him it would be a nice big ranch in the San Gabriel Valley. He'd have the biggest house for miles, and cattle, and a whole bunch of *vaqueros* working for him. Then he'd show those railroad buttercups, like Ellis Dyke, what he was made of. Wouldn't be taking their guff anymore.

He started wondering about that Shannon woman again. Was she as smart as they said? If she was, she'd rise to the bait and help make things happen. What did he have to lose?

The next time he saw her, he'd give her the whole of it, make a deal with her. She was a clear-thinking woman, a lawyer, after all. Lawyers looked at things like money and power and who was in the strongest position. She'd see what was best for her and Mousy.

Mousy. The only joker in the deck.

Billy was prepared to deal with Mousy. If he got off on the charge, like he was supposed to—like Shannon was supposed to make happen once Billy gave her the inside story—then Mousy would know who to be grateful to. Billy Rye. Savior and friend. They could then strike up that partnership he told Mousy all about.

Which would last up to the time Billy could figure the best way to kill him.

But if Mousy got convicted and Ellis had his way, Billy knew he'd then have to go to the other plan, the one involving blood—Ellis Dyke's. This plan was not as elegant, but it would work all the same. No one was going to stop him from getting his spread.

He poured himself another drink. It was hot in his throat, fire in his stomach. Outside it was getting dark, almost time to track down to the depot and call Shannon to set up the meeting.

He heard a scuffing sound outside the shack. Or was it on the roof? They had raccoons out here, and possums. Billy thought about grabbing his rifle and hunting himself up some food, except the whiskey had made him lazy.

Maybe he'd go grab a bowl of red at the little café near the depot. He had exactly twenty-five cents left, enough for a bowl and a beer. Then he'd make the call. Let Shannon wait a little longer. Women grew curious the longer they had to wait.

He heard the sound again, only this time it was louder and more insistent, like a heavy-footed man who meant business.

Billy got up and snatched his rifle. Maybe it wouldn't be food he shot. Maybe it'd be somebody sticking his nose where it oughtn't to be.

Billy staggered a bit, the whiskey misting his mind. Give it a moment, he told himself, then go see who's out there.

Who could it be except maybe some stranger with no business snooping around? Had to be a stranger, because nobody knew he was here.

Except Mousy, of course.

Only Mousy was in jail, waiting for his trial.

The sound stopped. Just outside the door. Billy Rye listened intently, hearing only his own breath. Some boards creaked. Someone was out there all right.

Billy Rye checked the rifle, making sure he had it loaded. He did. One shot was all he could get out of it, but if need be, that would be enough.

He paused, took one more shot straight from the whiskey bottle.

No sound now outside, and Billy almost decided to let it go. But some instinct in him told him not to. That instinct had served him well in Manila, back in '98, when he and the other grunts helped Dewey's swabs take the city. Then, Billy had taken out a Spanish sniper no one else could pinpoint.

That day had been the high point of his life, and he had never lost the heightened sense that he could kill any man if he needed to.

Now maybe he needed to.

Billy stepped slowly to the window and used the barrel of the rifle to pull back the curtain—just a swatch of old, checkered fabric. He took a peek through the dirty glass.

No sign of anyone. He looked in the other direction, toward the skinny birches that surrounded his shack like hungry troops. Still nothing.

He strained to listen for more sounds, putting his ear close to the glass.

That was his last act on earth.

Glass shattered, and Billy Rye felt the shock—the stunning, exploding shock—of his head being split in two.

Part Two

Chapter Twenty

"If you're going to work for me," Kit told Bobby, "you need to keep your eyes peeled. Do you understand what that means?"

"Watch things. Listen."

Kit tousled his hair. "Then come along."

They walked from the courthouse down Broadway to catch the trolley at First Street.

"But what about your automobile?" Bobby suggested.

"We'll come back for it. This is business. Are you ready to watch and listen?"

"Ready."

They waited a few minutes at the corner of Broadway and First. A horse-drawn wagon carrying large wooden casks ambled by, and Kit saw the word *Beer* stamped on its sides. Good thing she didn't have one of Mrs. Nation's hatchets now, for Kit would have been tempted to hack holes in the barrels of brew.

Bobby held her hand tighter. "Will I have to go back to Beasley?"

"Not if I can help it."

"Please don't let him take me."

"We will fight him together."

The boy nodded eagerly as the trolley clanged toward them.

Corazón had discovered that the motormen who worked for Los Angeles Electric had regular routes and schedules. Day shift motormen logged two hours on duty, took an hour off, then worked a three-hour shift. Another hour-long break followed and then a final two-hour stint at the controls. Night shift motormen worked a somewhat different schedule until the line shut down at ten.

The less-experienced motormen took to the levers during the break times to learn the ropes.

Kit knew her plan was a bit of a shot in the dark, but the cost was only a nickel, and it was the only way she was going to get a chance to talk to the motorman who was at the controls when Sammy Franklin was hit.

The Broadway line began running at eight in the morning. By Kit's calculation, the full-shift motorman would be driving now. He was, according to the coroner's finding, an "experienced motorman" who would not have been "careless" enough to cause the accident. A whitewash if ever there was one.

Kit took Bobby toward the front of the trolley, near the motorman's post. He nodded to them as Kit paid their fares. She saw that he was a portly gentleman with a salt-and-pepper mustache that drooped over the sides of his mouth.

The trolley proceeded down Broadway. Kit watched a moment, noting the speed and the traffic as they went. The street was full of activity, especially with pedestrians crossing back and forth, trying to avoid the jumble of horses, autos, and trolleys.

She studied the motorman as he alternately clanged his bell and applied his brake. At the corner of Third Street he stopped to allow more riders to hop aboard.

"A hot day for you," Kit remarked, taking advantage of the lull.

"Indeed it is, ma'am," the motorman replied.

He was jovial, and Kit wondered if she had the right man after all. She continued with her plan to find out. "The street appears busy today."

"No more'n usual at this time, I'd wager."

"Do you find more care must be taken with the automobiles about?"

The motorman snorted. "They better take more care with me! We get the right-of-way, and if one of them gas coaches gets in my path, well, I am sorry for it." He pulled on the bell line, clanging his intention to continue.

Kit patted Bobby's knee. The boy was looking on intently.

"Are you the regular motorman for this route?" Kit asked.

"Indeed. I look at it like a Mississippi riverboat captain looks at the river. It's mine, and I know all the bumps."

"My name is Kathleen Shannon, and this young man is Bobby Whitlove."

The motorman touched the brim of his cap. "Pleased to meet you. My name's Bittaker. Norman Bittaker."

"May I ask you a question, Mr. Bittaker?"

"By all means."

"With all the pedestrians, and the city increasing in size, is there not a heightened risk of injury these days?"

The motorman's eyes wallowed in a dark gaze. "Accidents will happen," he said.

"Do you think the speed of the trolley has anything to do with it?"

Bittaker shook his head. "People need to watch, that's all."

"Wasn't it on this very street that the little boy ..." Kit let her voice trail off, studying the man's reaction.

It was instantaneous. His cheeks turned a mottled red, and his lips trembled a little. "An accident," he said in a voice so low Kit barely heard him.

And suddenly she had a reaction she was not prepared for. Pity. This was the one, the motorman who hit Sammy. She was sure of it. He had been at the helm when a little boy had been killed. Though he was a potential hostile witness, one she might have to skewer in court sometime soon, he was first and foremost a man, and it was clear he was filled with a deep spring of emotion.

How could she have been so heartless? Whoever this man was, whatever his fault, he had to be torn apart at having been at the lever when a small boy was killed.

Kit felt the lawyer part of her fall off like a loose coat.

"I am sorry," she said. "I did not mean to bring you ..." She stopped herself. "No, I did mean to get you to talk about it. Sir, I am a lawyer."

The motorman braked the trolley. Kit was not sure if this was a regular stop or not. Riders hopped aboard, but the motorman did not give them a glance.

"Lawyer?"

"The woman whose son was killed ... I am her representative. I wanted to find out what happened. I should have told you from the start."

"Get off." His voice was hard, menacing.

"Sir, I do not mean to do you any damage. My concern is with the company. If you—"

"I said *get off.*"

Kit noticed the other riders looking at them now—they were the center of attention. Most had impatient looks on their faces that expressed this little episode was holding them up from important business.

"I am truly sorry," Kit said, "but this matter is not going to go away. You can help me to resolve—"

"I'm not gonna help you resolve anything." His blotchy face now turned ruddy with anger.

"Please, allow me to help you."

"Get off, now!" He made a small step toward her, his hands in front of him.

Kit didn't move.

A man shouted, "Hey, lady, quit the troublemaking!"

Standing, Kit took Bobby's hand. "If you ever wish to speak with me," she told the motorman, "please call the office of Kathleen Shannon."

"I'll not talk to you, ever. And stay off my car."

Kit walked Bobby off the trolley, which started up the very second their feet touched the street. A runabout automobile sputtered toward them, and the driver, in goggles and gloves, squeezed his horn. With a quick pull, Kit leaped out of harm's way with the boy.

"That was close!" Bobby said once they were safely on the sidewalk.

"Are you all right?"

Nodding, he said, "Miss Shannon?"

"Yes?"

"Are you against that motorman?"

"I am not against him personally. How do I explain this? He may have done something that his company must take responsibility for."

"Miss Shannon?"

Kit looked at the boy.

"He looked kind of nervous," Bobby said.

Kit nodded and patted his head. "I have that effect on some people, don't I?"

"Boys, I'm here to tell you about Jesus and dreams."

Ted took in the faces of the boys, who sat obediently on wood benches in the boys' home. There were about thirty of them, ranging in age from seven to eighteen.

The older ones seemed a bit skeptical. Half a dozen had their arms folded. It was understandable. Dreaming was difficult in a place like this. But with God, anything was possible. That was the message Ted most wanted them to hear.

"You all have dreams, don't you? Maybe you have 'em and don't talk about 'em for fear of having some of the others laugh at you. Well, I want to tell you that Jesus wants you to have dreams. He made you that way. Shall I tell you my dream?"

The younger boys nodded enthusiastically. The older ones were at least listening.

"My dream is to fly aeroplanes." Ted pointed upward. "Some folks say that flying is only an idler's hobby, that man will never be able to fly more than a few hundred yards at a stretch. But they're wrong, just as they were when they told Columbus he'd sail off the edge of the earth.

"Now, every dreamer's going to have setbacks. That's what life is like. You get knocked down, but you don't have to stay down. You can get right back up again. So don't ever let any setback or problem stop you from actively pursuing your dreams. Sure, you're in here. You haven't got a home of your own, and that's a bad break. But it doesn't have to stop you."

A few of the older boys had unfolded their arms and were leaning forward.

"You remember this always. Jesus gives you dreams, and you place them in His capable hands. You pray every day. You do the duty of each moment to the best of your ability. Make yourself equal to every situation by the vigorous application of your best effort. As you master small things, that will pave the way toward larger achievements.

"Whatever you do, do well. Good work is its own reward. Ask Jesus to tell you your supreme talent, then get to work on your supreme task."

Ted paused and scanned the faces. "So, what is the immediate task at hand? I believe it is lunch."

The boys cheered and began falling over themselves running to the lunchroom. Ted had arranged for roast beef sandwiches and a big chocolate cake to be delivered for the boys, a welcome change from the soup that was usually the midday meal.

Reverend Hayes clapped Ted on the back. "Will you join us? The boys would like that, I'm sure."

Ted shook his head. "Thank you, but no. I also have a task today."

"Oh?"

"To get closer to the truth. I have a feeling Western Rail is hiding something up here that can be of use down there."

"Where?"

"Los Angeles, of course."

The guest piece in the *Examiner* was under the name of Jack London. Kit read it at her office desk. It ended thus:

> The Carry Nations of this world, in both thought and practice, seek to hack away at the delights of man. They think that with the swipe of a blade they can dictate what experiences will be allowed to grow in society's garden. It will not be a pleasure garden, I am quite sure of that!
>
> I drink, not unto drunkenness, but unto good fellowship. Many are the times of heightened cheerfulness I can trace back to a cold beer or a shot of good whiskey. True, I have seen the dark side of drink, but blame not the alcohol. That would make as much sense as blaming the gun that kills a man. If a man cannot drink, he oughtn't. The dipsomaniac must be cured of his need and walk away from John Barleycorn once and for all.
>
> But for those who are not physically dependent upon drink, there is no harm and much pleasure to be derived, especially for the male of the species. A man who can walk straight while pleasantly jingled, who does not stagger or fall, who bubbles with wit and expands with good comradeship, this is a man worth knowing.
>
> A man with a drink is my immediate friend, until he proves otherwise.
>
> Meanwhile, leave the law alone. If a man, drunken or not, breaks the law, arrest him. Try him. Dump him in the clink. But don't punish law-abiding citizens by forcing temperance down our dry throats.
>
> *Leave those of us who enjoy a bit of sunny liquor to our conviviality. As for Mrs. Nation and her band of hatchet bearers, there are plenty of trees that need cutting down. I suggest she start with these.*

Kit lowered the paper and shook her head. Didn't Jack London have better things to do than extol the virtues of drink?

She made a mental note to talk to London about this. With

all his literary fame and power, might he not be able to be a force for reform on the employment of children in bars? Surely he would. But it would take some convincing. She thought about laying it out as a courtroom argument, using her own powers of persuasion.

The telephone bell rang. On the other end of the line was the person Kit least expected to hear from—District Attorney John Davenport.

"Miss Shannon, I want to know where Malloy is." The voice was accusatory as well as demanding.

"So do I, Mr. Davenport."

"I think you know where he is."

"I do not."

"Further, I think you know what he's done."

"Done?"

"They found one of our key witnesses, Billy Rye, murdered."

Kit squeezed the earpiece. "When?"

"About an hour ago. Hatchet to the head."

"Where?"

"At an old shack in Glendale. Bloody mess, so they tell me. We think your client may have done it."

Kit could not believe it, but then again, under the spell of drink anything was possible. "Do you have any proof?"

"We have motive, and we have the weapon."

"You found it at the scene?"

"No, the killer threw it as far as he could into the trees. But it wasn't hard to find. It got stuck in a tree trunk. Lucky, I guess. Except for you."

"What are you implying?"

"We seized those weapons from Mrs. Nation and her band, remember? The hatchets all have ash handles. We don't make that kind out here. It was an ash-handled ax that killed Rye."

Kit's head started to buzz. "That still does not implicate my client."

"Chief Allen tells me you were down at the jail when they let those women out. That true?"

"Yes."

"Got their property back?"

"Of course."

"So all of this comes together. You had the hatchets in hand. Your client is gone. Billy Rye ends up dead, killed by one of those same weapons."

With a catch in her throat, Kit said, "Are you trying to say I gave one of those weapons to Mousy Malloy? Are you calling me an accessory before the fact?"

"Maybe even after the fact if you know where Malloy is."

"I already told you I don't."

"As of this moment, I am not taking anything you say at face value."

Kit felt like she was going to burst, like an old dam falling before raging waters. "I have never in my life told you, or anyone else in our system of justice, anything less than the absolute truth."

"There is always a first time," Davenport said.

Chapter Twenty-One

John Davenport was actually accusing her of lying! And providing her client with a weapon used in a murder. It was so outrageous, almost comical. But she wasn't laughing.

She tried hard to contain her anger, for Bobby's sake. She had promised him a ride up Angels Flight and a hot dog at the top. After paying two cents for both their fares, Kit sat with Bobby in the car called Olivet for the one-minute ride up Bunker Hill.

"Are there really such things as angels?" Bobby asked as soon as the funicular began its ascent.

"Oh yes," Kit assured him.

"What is God like?"

"Don't they teach you the Bible at the Beasley Home?"

Bobby shook his head.

"How does Beasley expect to turn boys into good men?"

The boy shrugged. The creaking of the cables cut through the late afternoon air. "He does it with a stick," said Bobby.

Kit shook her head. "You never knew your father?"

"Uh-uh."

"God is a father. Did you know there is a word for that? *Abba*."

"Abba?"

"Yes. Sounds like *Papa,* doesn't it? It's a very old word, from the language of the Jewish people long ago. It was often the first word a Jewish child learned to say, and it was a term of endearment for the father for the rest of their lives."

Bobby pondered that. His face gradually began to beam.

"The Word of God says that when someone is adopted into God's family, God is Abba to him. Wanting to give him all good things."

A little frown came to the boy's forehead. "I want good things."

"You'll have them. Shall we read the Bible together sometime?"

"I'm not too good at reading."

"I'll help you. Ah, here we are."

They got out, and Kit led Bobby to the food stand near an outdoor café. She bought him a hot dog with plenty of mustard and lemonade to go with it. They sat on a wooden bench looking down on the city.

"Miss Shannon, do you miss your fiancé?"

"Very much."

"I don't think I'll get married."

The firmness of the boy's opinion startled Kit. "You have something against marriage?"

"No, just girls. Except you, Miss Shannon. You're the best girl there is in Los Angeles, I'd say."

Smiling at the most sincere compliment she'd received in a long time, Kit said, "Thank you."

"You're about perfect," added Bobby.

"I wouldn't go quite that far. I have a bit of a temper, you know."

"You talking about what you did to Mr. Doogan's liquor?"

"That was a bit of an overreaction, now, wasn't it? Unlawful, too."

"But he was wrong."

"Sometimes the law says a person has a right to be wrong."

"A right to be wrong?"

"I know it sounds confusing, but Mr. Doogan has the right to sell liquor. And I did not have the right to destroy it."

Bobby smiled. "But it sure must have been a corker to watch!"

Back at the office, Kit and Bobby walked in on Mousy Malloy. He was slumped in a chair, his hair a tangled mess. Corazón was dabbing his forehead with a cloth. Raul Montoya rose from his chair.

"Good afternoon, Miss Shannon," Raul said. "We found him at a bar on Tenth Street."

"He is very drunk," Corazón said.

Mousy's eyes rolled back in his head a little. The smell of sweat and whiskey filled the office. Bobby let go of Kit's hand and held his nose.

"Can he speak?" Kit asked.

"I do not think so," Corazón answered, gently wiping Mousy's forehead.

"Here," Kit said, "maybe this will help." She grabbed the carafe of water sitting on her desk and threw the contents at Mousy's face.

Startled, Corazón stepped back. Raul and Bobby shared a laugh.

"I think you did it, Miss Shannon," Raul said.

Mousy was sputtering now, shaking his head and sending spray to the floor and on Kit.

"Wake up, Mousy," Kit ordered.

"What?"

Kit slapped his face, not hard but enough to make a nice smacking sound and get his attention.

"Hey!" Mousy put his hand to his cheek. Good. He was responding.

"Where have you been, Mousy?" Kit said.

"How's that?"

"Where. Have. You. Been?"

His bloodshot eyes joggled in their sockets. "I dunno."

"You're drunk."

"So I am."

"You ran off from the hospital. Do you remember that?"

Mousy squinted. It appeared difficult for him to think. "Sure could use a drink," he said.

"Coffee."

"No!"

"Bobby," Kit said, fishing in her pocket for a nickel. "Go get a coffee from the drugstore. Make sure it's strong and black."

The eager boy nodded and scampered out of the office.

"Now look at me, Mousy." Kit pulled his chin around with one hand. "Look at me. I want you to tell me where you were yesterday."

"Where I was?"

"You ran away from the hospital. Where did you go? You are in very big trouble. Escaping from custody like that."

"You'll help me, won't you?"

"Where did you go after you ran out of the hospital?"

"Let's see now." Mousy sat up a little straighter. "I think I walked for miles."

"Which direction?"

"I don't know."

"Did you see anyone? Talk to anyone?"

"I think I was out of my head. There was a dog...."

"A dog?"

"A talking dog. I don't think he could really talk, though." Again Mousy smiled.

"This is not getting us anywhere!" Kit took a deep breath. "You are going back to jail, Mousy. I have to turn you in."

"You're my own lawyer!"

"I am an officer of the court. You are an escaped prisoner. And you need to be protected from yourself."

"Please, Miss Shannon, I can't go back! I need to drink. I'll get them DT's again."

Kit grabbed his shoulders. "Listen to me. We've got a trial

to win. The sooner we do, the sooner you'll be free. As for your drinking, I have no sympathy for you. Your body must get rid of the need, and if it takes putting you in a cell, so be it."

Mousy looked at her like a scared cat. "You don't mean it."

"I do."

Mousy tried to stand up. Raul pushed him back onto the chair.

Chapter Twenty-Two

As night deepened over Los Angeles and the scent of orange blossoms gave way to evening mist, Kit and Corazón shared tea in the library of the house. This was a room where Kit had spent considerable time with her aunt and received many a lecture on the art of being womanly.

Tonight, though, she needed the consolation of her friend.

"Was I too hard on our client today?" Kit asked.

Corazón thought about it. Kit had told her always to be honest with her, not sparing her feelings. Corazón was sharp in her observations, and that was the important thing.

"No, I do not think so," Corazón said. "There are times for the tough talking."

"It broke my heart to see him taken by the police, even though it was Big Ed Hanratty we got to do it. But I had to."

"Sí. It had to be."

Kit looked deeply into her soft brown eyes. "You know, you are my closest friend in the world."

"Is true for me, too."

Kit took Corazón's hand. "I want us to stay that way, even after we each marry."

"Yes. Nothing is to change."

Kit sat back with a heavy sigh. "I wonder, do you think I should continue to practice law?"

"But yes! You are the best that there is!"

"Earl might not agree with you."

"I know better, I think."

The two friends laughed in the low light of the evening. "I am in earnest," Kit added. "I know Ted would allow it. But I wonder if he would truly accept it. A woman who works while unwed is one thing. It is almost unheard of for a husband to allow his wife to work outside the home. I would become that terrible `new woman' Beasley was writing about."

Corazón shook her head. "We should not listen to that man."

"Ah, but that's just it. He is a man. That is how men think."

"Not Mr. Fox. He is better than that."

"I don't know. I was in the bookshop looking at a book on modern marriage. The writer—a doctor, I might add—said that men want a girl who has not rubbed off the peach blossom of innocence by exposure to a rough world. I don't want to be an old peach for Ted."

"You are no peach."

"What am I, then?"

"A pepper?"

Kit laughed again. "What is that supposed to mean, my good friend?"

"Hot," Corazón said. "Too hot for the district attorney, I think."

"We will see. Tomorrow the trial begins, and I feel strongly that there are facts hidden from us. People know more than they are saying."

"You will find out on the cross-examination, yes?"

"I believe what Earl has said, that cross-examination is the best engine for truth we have yet devised. But I must know where to start. I must know how to expose—" She stopped, the wheels turning in her head. "Publicity."

"Excuse?"

"I want to lay open the perils of drink. We need publicity for that. I have an idea. Come along."

She led Corazón to the phone box and cranked it. "Bush 1336," she told the operator.

A moment later a girl's voice chirruped, "Rogers' residence."

"Adela?"

"Kit?"

"How are you, dear?"

"Very well, thank you for asking."

Kit smiled at the impeccable manners of Earl's eleven-year-old daughter. "Is your father's guest at home?"

"You mean Mr. London?"

"Yes."

"He and Daddy are swapping stories in the parlor." Adela's voice softened into a whisper. "But I think they are getting soused."

It was funny hearing *soused* come from a little girl, and tragic at the same time because it was her father. Earl's drinking had become a burden on his wife and child. "Would you ask Mr. London to come to the phone, please?"

"I will."

Kit heard the sound of the child's feet on the floor, scampering away. Presently the strong, now somewhat thick, voice of Jack London took the phone.

"What a pleasure this is," the writer said.

"Good evening, Mr. London."

"Jack. Please call me Jack."

"I would like to ask you to—"

"Have you read any of my books?"

"Yes."

"Did you like 'em?"

"*The Call of the Wild* is quite good. The law of raw nature." Kit paused a moment. "One might be able to say the same of men under the spell of liquor."

London said, "You have something on your mind, Miss Shannon. I believe you may have read my contribution to the *Examiner*."

"I did indeed."

"And didn't like it?"

"As I say, there are many things you could choose to which you could direct your pen. It is a talented pen."

"High praise from you, miss."

"Are you quite aware of the harm that is done by the saloons being open at all hours? By the young boys who are hired by tavern owners to deliver drink and imbibe themselves?"

"I was one of those boys."

"That is where you learned to drink?"

"Where I learned to be a man."

"It is not drink that makes the man."

"But it is a man who can hold his drink. As I wrote, if a man cannot do that, he should not drink."

"What of the example? You, Mr. London, are a hero to many a boy and young man. If you would put your talent to some social good, you could write a story that shows the horror of dipsomania. You might save some young lives in the process."

"My, but you are a persuasive one. I believe Earl when he says you weave spells in the courtroom."

"But to my point?"

"I will think on it, Miss Shannon. However, I do not take to the idea of armed harridans subjecting honest, hardworking men to fear and destruction. Don't you women have other social ills to attend to? Like getting the vote or raising good children?"

"How can good children come out of bad saloons?"

"I turned out a strapping enough man."

"You're one of the blessed ones, then. You have a responsibility—"

"I believe man is responsible for his own salvation."

"Man does not make a very good god."

There was a long pause before London said, "Surely you did not call to engage me on theology, did you?"

"I have a request for you. Would you be willing to take on another journalistic effort?"

"What would that be?"

"Attend the Malloy trial, which begins tomorrow. There is going to be publicity. You, I think, will be able to understand my client's story. Perhaps you can write a book about it."

London was silent for a long moment. "I have a trip planned to Catalina Island. I want to—"

"I can promise you fireworks."

"But I—"

"Big ones."

There was a brief pause. Then London said, "I think I'll cancel that trip."

So Jack London was present the next day, along with a full house of spectators, reporters, and curiosity seekers. The courtroom of Judge Trent buzzed with anticipation of another epic battle between Kit Shannon and the office of the district attorney, represented by Clara Dalton Price. Everyone in town knew—if the whispers were any indication—that Mrs. Price wanted to put Kit in her place this time. The "Dragon Lady," as Mrs. Price was now being called in certain circles, did not like to lose.

Jury selection took an hour, with Kit exercising two challenges: one against a Methodist clergyman who seemed about as merciful as Attila the Hun; the other a schoolmaster who announced that men who drink anything stronger than lemonade were "spawn of the devil."

For her part, Mrs. Price also kicked off two men, one whose only sin seemed to be that he smiled at Kit Shannon.

Once the jury was sworn in, Clara Dalton Price delivered her opening statement.

"This is what we call an open-and-shut case, gentlemen. The defendant, Abner Malloy, in front of several eyewitnesses, who will be presented to you, got into a drinking contest with Mr. Ellis Dyke on the morning of Friday, March 30, in an establishment known as Doogan's Saloon. Growing angry at his inability to keep up with Ellis Dyke, Malloy proceeded to make a spectacle of himself, causing Mr. Doogan to warn the defendant by showing him a handgun. Malloy managed to snatch the gun away and then proceeded to fire two shots at Ellis Dyke. Fortunately, the bullets missed. But the intent was clear. The defendant wanted Ellis dead.

"The witnesses will testify that Malloy shouted 'I am going to kill you!' at Ellis Dyke. He then attempted to do just that by firing the gun. The charge here is attempted murder, gentlemen, and the People of the State of California are confident that after you hear all of the evidence in this case, you will return a verdict of guilty."

The Dragon Lady swept back to her chair.

"Does the defense wish to make an opening statement?" Judge Trent asked.

Kit stood. "We will reserve our statement until the close of the prosecution's case."

"Very well. Mrs. Price, call your first witness."

"One moment, Your Honor," Kit said. "Before the prosecutor begins, we request that all other prosecution witnesses be excluded from the courtroom."

"I object to that, Your Honor," Mrs. Price said.

"Either party has the right to move for exclusion," Kit explained, "so witnesses cannot be altering their stories depending upon the testimony they hear."

"All of our witnesses will speak the truth!" Mrs. Price fired back.

"Then let them do it out of their own recollections," Kit said, "and not according to a script."

Judge Trent tapped his gavel on the bench. "That will be enough, counselors. Miss Shannon is within her rights to make the request. All witnesses summoned by the prosecution will please leave the courtroom."

After some scuffling of chairs, two men got up and walked, grumbling, out the doors. Kit recognized only one of the men—Bill Doogan.

"Continue," said the judge.

"The prosecution calls Samuel Hartrampf," Clara Dalton Price said.

The rather cocky clerk whom Kit had met at the Pioneer Drugstore strutted forward. He wore a cheap suit of mustard yellow, the kind a man from the country might wear trying to impress a city girl. All he lacked was a wilting bouquet of flowers in his hands.

After he was sworn, Mrs. Price asked him about his age and work. Hartrampf explained about his position at the drugstore but that he was planning on becoming a "man of business" someday.

"On the morning of March 30," Mrs. Price said, "were you in the company of Mr. Ellis Dyke?"

"Yes, ma'am."

"Were you, in fact, at Doogan's Saloon with Mr. Dyke?"

"Yes."

"And did you at that time observe Mr. Dyke and the defendant, Abner Malloy, engaged in—"

"Objection," Kit said. "Mrs. Price is leading the witness."

"Sustained," said Judge Trent. "Rephrase the question, Mrs. Price."

Looking like she'd almost slipped one by, Clara Dalton Price asked, "Tell us who else was present in the saloon at this time."

"Well, there was me and Billy and Doogan—"

"*Billy* would be Billy Rye?"

"God rest his soul. Mousy had no call to kill him!"

Kit shot to her feet in objection. "That is pure speculation, your honor, not based on any facts in evidence and prejudicial to the jury."

Clara Dalton Price folded her arms, a cat's smile on her face. "That is a rather scatter-gun objection, Your Honor."

"Nevertheless," said the judge, "the answer was improper. Mr. Hartrampf, you will confine your answers to the question that is asked. Do you understand?"

With a broad smile that showed his toothy gaps, Hartrampf replied, "Yes, I do."

Something about that smile and the cool visage of Mrs. Price speared Kit's mind. "Your Honor, may we approach the bench?"

Out of earshot of the jury, Kit said, "Your Honor, I believe this witness was coached by the prosecutor to give that statement about my client killing Billy Rye. The defense requests a mistrial."

Clara Dalton Price threw her hands in the air. "That is an outrageous accusation. I demand to know if Miss Shannon has any proof."

"The proof is sitting in the witness chair," Kit said. "If you would like me to cross-examine Mr. Hartrampf, outside the presence of the jury, I think I can make him talk."

Now Kit was out on the proverbial limb. But she had come to trust the instincts she'd developed as a trial lawyer. There were times when you just *knew* something was not right, and you bore into that hole like a gopher with hunger pangs.

"I sternly object to that," Clara Dalton Price said. "It will be a distraction and will disrupt my witness."

"Seems to me your witness already disrupted things," said the judge. "I don't want this to go any further. I will deny the motion for a mistrial and will admonish the jury to disregard that last answer. Mrs. Price, you had better keep a tight rein on Mr. Hartrampf. Is that understood?"

The prosecutor gave the judge a curt nod.

When the lawyers returned to their tables, Judge Trent looked at the jury. "Gentlemen, the last answer of this witness was an unfounded, improper expression without any basis before this court. You are instructed to disregard it. You may not take it into consideration in any deliberation of the facts. Do you all understand that?"

The impassive men in the jury box nodded their assent.

Sam Hartrampf sat in an attitude of disbelief, as if he couldn't fathom being the cause of such a commotion. Well, Kit thought, the real commotion is going to come soon enough.

Clara Dalton Price kept a stoic expression as she returned to her witness. "Mr. Hartrampf, you were telling us who was present with you at Doogan's on the morning of March 30. Mr. Doogan, Billy Rye, Ellis Dyke, and yourself. Anyone else?"

"Some others I didn't know were watching, too."

"Describe what they were watching."

"It was like this, see. Ellis saw Mousy in there, and he and Mousy got into it a little. Started with Mousy, I think, grousing about Ellis. There's some bad blood twixt 'em. Ellis made a joke about it, and we all laughed. Ellis, he's a good man that way."

"Objection," Kit said. "Irrelevant and immaterial."

"Sustained. Mr. Hartrampf, just answer the question."

Mrs. Price said, "What happened next?"

"Well, next Ellis tells Doogan to pour a couple of beers and send one of 'em to Mousy. Then Mousy says something like `You think you can hold your liquor like a man?' And Ellis says, `Why don't we find out?' And so there was a drinking contest on."

"How would you describe this contest?"

"Simple. Doogan poured, and Ellis and Mousy drank. Fast. And everybody started cheering and hollering."

"How many beers did each man consume?"

"I don't remember exactly. Maybe five or six."

"How long did this go on?"

"No more than five minutes or so. They were knocking 'em back pretty fast."

"What happened next?"

"Mousy, he gets to his feet and he's staggering all over the place. The rest of us are laughing and whooping it up because we thought Mousy was gonna hit the floor. But he didn't. He started screaming for Ellis to shut up. Then he started for Doogan."

"Why Mr. Doogan?"

"Because he was telling Mousy to take it easy, see. With Mousy making threats, Doogan was saying he didn't want any trouble. That's when I saw the gun."

"What gun?"

"Doogan had a gun, a revolver. He was sort of holding it in his hand, showing it to Mousy."

"Did Mr. Doogan threaten to shoot Mousy?"

"Nah. He just showed it. So Mousy would get the message."

"And then?"

"Mousy goes up to Doogan. Doogan is being careful, see, watching Mousy's eyes. He should have watched his hands."

"Why is that?"

"Because Mousy grabbed the gun right out of Doogan's hand. Quick as a cat. I never seen a drunken man move so fast."

"So the defendant had the gun now?"

"That's right. He points it at Ellis and he says, `I'm gonna kill you.' And Ellis, he says, `You won't shoot, you rummy.' Mousy says, `Is that a fact?' And Ellis says, `You never did have any guts.' That's when Mousy fired."

"How many shots did he fire?"

"Two. Then Doogan gets him from behind and takes the gun away. And that was that."

Clara Dalton Price said, "No more questions."

"You may cross-examine now," the judge told Kit.

Kit approached the witness, who gave her a gap-toothed smile. "What time did you arrive at Doogan's?"

"Oh, about ten, I'd say."

"That would be ten, in the morning?"

"Yes."

"You described some of the men who were there with you. Did you also see a man in a uniform?"

"Uniform?"

"Do you know what a uniform is, Mr. Hartrampf?"

Sam Hartrampf's cheeks flushed. "'Course I do. Seems to me there might have been a uniform in there."

"What sort of uniform was it?"

"It sure wasn't Salvation Army!" Hartrampf, pleased with himself, laughed.

Kit folded her arms and looked at the jury. Two of them were laughing as well. Kit's expression put a damper on that. They snapped back to attention.

"I'll ask you again, Mr. Hartrampf. What sort of uniform was it? A police officer? An army uniform? What?"

"I really didn't pay much attention to that. I was looking at Mousy and Ellis most of the time."

"Yes, I'd like to explore that further. Will you please step off the witness chair and show the jury where you were standing? Pretend the bar top runs along in front of the judge's bench here and that I am standing where Mr. Malloy stood when he held, as you say, Mr. Doogan's gun."

Tentatively at first, then with the bluster of a ham actor, Hartrampf stepped to the far side of the bench and turned toward Kit, who stood near the rail of the jury box.

"That's about how it was," Hartrampf said.

"Where was Ellis Dyke standing in relation to you, sir?"

Hartrampf indicated to his right. "He was next to me, here."

"Were you at the end of the bar and looking directly at Mr. Malloy?"

"Yes, ma'am."

"So if you bent down to pick up a coin from the floor, the bar top would have hidden you completely from Mr. Malloy's gaze?"

Hartrampf shrugged. "You could say that, I guess."

"I want to know what *you* would say, Mr. Hartrampf. You were there, weren't you?"

"Yes I was. And that's right, I was at the other end of the bar, looking straight ahead, so I could see everything."

"Could you see Mr. Doogan pouring the drinks?"

"Sure I could. I watched him."

"Isn't it true, sir, that Doogan poured horseshoes for Mr. Malloy?"

The witness looked stunned by the question.

"Objection," Mrs. Price said. "I do not understand the question. Horseshoes?"

The judge smiled. "A horseshoe, Mrs. Price, is a shot of whiskey poured into a glass of beer. Is that how you understand it, Mr. Hartrampf?"

"Yes, sir," Hartrampf said.

"Is the question clear to you now?" Judge Trent asked.

"I suppose," Mrs. Price said, looking none too pleased.

"You may answer," Kit said.

"No," Hartrampf said. "Doogan was just pouring the beer."

"Was he, now? For both men?"

"Sure. That was the contest, see."

"Are you sure the contest wasn't rigged from the start?"

Hartrampf shook his head, but his eyes were becoming a little less secure in his head.

"Isn't it true, sir, that Doogan was pouring something else for Ellis Dyke, something that only looked like beer, at the same time he was pouring whiskey into Mr. Malloy's beer?"

"No. I would have seen it."

"You saw a lot that day, didn't you?"

"I saw what happened. That's all."

"You saw Mr. Malloy take a gun from Mr. Doogan?"

"Like I said."

"You claim he just took it from Doogan?"

"Snatched it."

"Pretty hard for a drunken man to do, wouldn't you say?"

"I saw it."

"Did you ever think Doogan might have *wanted* Mr. Malloy to have the gun?"

"Huh?"

Kit kept the questions coming fast to keep Hartrampf from concocting answers. "You say my client pointed the gun at Dyke?"

"That's right."

"Who was standing right next to you?"

"Yeah."

"And the two of them exchanged words?"

"Some."

"You claim Mr. Malloy said, `I'm gonna kill you.' And that Dyke said, `You won't shoot, you rummy.' Is that right?"

"Yeah."

"Then Mr. Malloy said, according to you, `Is that a fact?' After which Mr. Dyke replied, `You never did have any guts.' Right so far?"

"Right as rain."

"Pretty brave of Mr. Dyke, wasn't it?"

"I guess so."

"He didn't seem to be in much fear, did he?"

Hartrampf slowly shook his head.

"Out loud for the reporter," said the judge.

"No," the witness said.

"In fact," Kit said, "it almost seemed like Ellis Dyke was daring Mr. Malloy to fire at him, didn't it?"

"I didn't see it that way."

"But you did see Mr. Malloy standing there with the gun, correct?"

"I just told you."

"Then tell the jury how it was that you did not drop down behind the bar?"

Hartrampf swallowed. "I didn't. That's all."

"Let us get this clear for the jury. An angry, drunken man who has threatened to kill the man standing next to you grabs a gun, points it toward you, and you just stand there, watching and listening? Is that what you expect this jury to believe?"

"That's what happened. I was there."

"Yet you did not duck, did you? Nor did Ellis Dyke."

"I told you just the way it was."

"We will let the jury decide that, Mr. Hartrampf. No more questions."

Chapter Twenty-Three

The next witness for the prosecution was Bill Doogan. He did not look comfortable. Perhaps having to sit outside the courtroom while Sam Hartrampf testified made him nervous. That was Kit's guess, anyway. He was wondering if their stories would match.

For the most part, they did. Doogan followed Hartrampf's line about pouring drinks—"Just beer," he told Mrs. Price—and watching the contest unfold.

"At some point," Mrs. Price asked, "did the defendant make a threat against Ellis Dyke?"

"He said he was going to kill him. And he had a mean look on his face."

"Objection," Kit said. "What look was on my client's face is a matter of opinion. It should not be taken by the jury as fact."

"Overruled," the judge said.

"Did the defendant's look and actions cause you any alarm?"

"They sure did. I thought there might be trouble."

"What did you do?"

"I got my revolver out from under the bar—the one I use to make noise when I need to stop trouble—and let Mousy see it."

"So it was never your intention to shoot the defendant, was it?"

"No, ma'am. Just to scare him."

"What happened then?"

"Well, Mousy's eyes got real big. He looked at the gun in my hand. He came toward me, looking at it all the while like he couldn't believe it was there."

"And you held it out for him to see?"

"I wanted him to know I meant business."

"Where were you pointing the weapon, Mr. Doogan?"

"Sort of at his feet."

"You were prepared to shoot?"

"If I had to."

"But you did not have the opportunity, did you?"

"No."

"Why not?"

"Because Mousy grabbed it from me. It happened so quick. I didn't expect it."

"What happened next?"

"Well, Mousy shouted `I'm gonna kill you' at Ellis Dyke. Some more words were exchanged and then he fired. Two times."

"What did you do?"

"I came out faster than a bat out of ... faster than you can say *Hey diddle diddle*. I grabbed Mousy and took the gun away from him."

"No further questions."

Kit was on her feet in an instant. "You waited until Mr. Malloy fired the gun, twice, before you took it away from him? Is that your testimony?"

Doogan nodded. "Yes, it is."

"Waited until someone could have been killed?"

"That wasn't what I was thinking."

"You weren't thinking much at all, were you?"

"It all happened so fast."

"Did it really? Mr. Hartrampf testified that at least four statements were made between Ellis Dyke and Mr. Malloy before he fired the gun."

"Well, there was—"

"You did not say anything, did you?"

"I might have said something."

Kit almost pounced at the witness. "This is the first time you or any other witness has made the assertion that you might have said something, isn't that true?"

"I don't—"

"Isn't that true, Mr. Doogan?"

"I haven't thought about it for a while."

"But your memory has suddenly improved?"

"No, I—"

"You did not say anything, isn't that a fact? You stood there as Ellis Dyke practically begged Mr. Malloy to shoot at him, didn't you?"

"That's not how I remember it."

"It's a miracle you remember anything at all."

The prosecutor's objection was sustained, but Kit moved on without pausing. She went to the counsel table and took out a pistol from her briefcase. "Your Honor, I would like the witness to examine the weapon I hold in my hand, a revolver, and ask if it is similar to the one he held on the date in question."

"Any objection?" Judge Trent asked.

"Only if it is loaded," said Mrs. Price.

"Is it loaded, Miss Shannon?"

"I assure you it is not, Your Honor."

"Then proceed."

"I will now hand this revolver to the witness," Kit said for the record, then placed the weapon in Doogan's hands.

The witness gave it a cursory look. "That looks about the same," he said.

"It is a six-shooter, is it not?"

"Yes."

"As is your own gun?"

"Yes."

"Now, when you are getting ready to fire a gun like that, how do you hold it?"

Doogan shrugged, in a way that said this was such an easy question anyone would know the answer. He smirked at the jurors as he held the revolver up in his right hand, finger on the trigger, careful to point the barrel at the floor.

"Just a little higher, please," Kit said.

Doogan complied.

"No," Kit said, "more like this." She grabbed the barrel of the revolver. And pulled. A loud *click* issued from the gun, which dangled loosely on Doogan's finger by way of the trigger guard. His mouth dropped open.

"If there had been a bullet in the chamber," Kit said, "it would have fired at me, isn't that true?"

Before Doogan could answer, Mrs. Price was on her feet, objecting. "Your Honor, this is a blatant attempt to sway the jury!"

Kit said quickly, "Your Honor, I submit that this demonstration proves my client could not have grabbed the revolver as the witness has testified—without it going off."

"It proves no such thing!" the prosecutor cried.

"Order," said the judge. He rubbed his chin. "I am going to overrule the objection, yet I will allow the witness to explain how this demonstration may have differed from what actually happened."

Giving the witness a chance to change his story, Kit thought. But the judge had ruled, and she had to see where it might lead.

A relieved Doogan cleared his throat. "It wasn't exactly like the way Miss Shannon thinks. I didn't have my finger on the trigger. I was just trying to scare him, that's all."

The judge nodded. "Go ahead, Miss Shannon."

"Convenient of you to remember that detail now," Kit said to Doogan. She knew he was lying and was pretty sure the jury did, too.

"I got a good memory of it, because I was there."

"Do you also have a good memory of doctoring Mr. Malloy's beer with whiskey?"

"I did no such thing."

"You deny it?"

"I do."

"So if I had a statement from a witness to the contrary, you would deny that as well?"

Clara Dalton Price interrupted, "If Miss Shannon has a statement to that effect, she should produce it."

"I am asking the witness a question, Your Honor. It is hypothetical."

The judge thought a moment. "Do you have a basis for the question, Miss Shannon?"

"I do, Your Honor."

"Then the witness will answer. Will the reporter please read back the question?"

The court reporter, a middle-aged man with eyeglasses, looked at his shorthand pad and read, "`So if I had a statement from a witness to the contrary, you would deny that as well?'"

Doogan shifted in his chair. Kit stared at him, waiting.

"Yeah," the witness said finally. "I was serving the drinks." But the way he said it was uncertain, exactly what Kit intended. Jurors judged the credibility of witnesses in part by how they looked when responding.

Clara Dalton Price said, "May we approach the bench?"

In front of the judge, the prosecutor said, "Now make Miss Shannon produce the statement, Your Honor. I don't believe she has one."

"Am I being accused of lying?" Kit asked.

"You are," said Mrs. Price.

"That is a very serious charge, Mrs. Price," Judge Trent said. "Nevertheless, Miss Shannon did tell the court she had a foundation for the question." He looked at Kit. "Do you have something to produce?"

"Your Honor," Kit said, "you asked if I had a basis for my question to the witness. I do. It is not a recorded statement. It is a statement that was made orally to me."

"By whom?"

"Billy Rye."

Kit could almost feel the steam shooting out of Mrs.

Price's ears. "That is uncorroborated, unsubstantiated, and out-of-bounds!"

"If Your Honor would like," Kit said, "I will gladly take the stand and swear to this statement, under oath, and let the jury decide if I am credible or not. I will gladly let Mrs. Price cross-examine me on the point. The jury, I am sure, would be quite interested."

Like wind dying from sails, Clara Dalton Price seemed to shrink back. The judge was looking to her for an answer. Finally she said, "I will withdraw my complaint. At this time."

The law offices of Sutter, Wingate & Finn took up half the building on the corner of Bush and Sansome. As Ted considered it from the outside, he thought it looked more like a house out of a gothic novel than a law office. Its windows were like eyes peering out over the city, passing judgment and looking out for the interests of its leading client, Western Rail.

Somewhere in this building was a lawyer who knew secrets. Ted did not know who, nor did he know the exact nature of the secrets; he only sensed an inner voice telling him that he could help Kit if he could crack through the wall of silence and client privilege that was no doubt strong within the place.

He was, however, invigorated by his purpose. He saw Kit's face in his mind's eye and smiled as he entered through the front door.

The receptionist for Sutter, Wingate & Finn was an older woman with firm Teutonic features and masculine-looking arms. While her accent was American, she might as well have said *Achtung!* rather than her actual words: "What is your business?"

"Good morning, madam. I am Theodore Fox, the aviator."

"I beg your pardon?"

"I am an associate of Miss Kathleen Shannon of Los Angeles."

"Do you have an appointment?" She glanced down at a

large appointment book that lay open on her spare desk. Two men of obvious means were waiting, sitting with legs crossed, smoking cigars in the reception area nearby.

"I am here to speak to one of the lawyers for Western Rail," Ted said. "It concerns the death of a boy, Samuel Franklin, by a trolley run by Los Angeles Electric. Surely you can—"

"You must make an appointment, sir."

"All you have to do is direct me to the—"

"Sir, as I already stated, an appointment is necessary."

"Well ..." Ted drew out the word. "I suppose I could sit right here and wait to catch somebody on their way out. Maybe I could hum a few tunes. Do you know `Mary Took the Calves to the Dairy Show'?"

"Sir, I—"

"It goes like this—"

"Please." The woman scowled at him. "If you will wait a moment, I shall see if Mr. Beaumont has any time on his schedule."

The receptionist disappeared through a door of frosted glass behind her desk. Ted took the opportunity to gaze at the portraits on one of the walls, a half dozen austere men, no doubt the partners of the firm. They all frowned back at him as if resenting his intrusion.

Soon the woman returned, faced Ted, and announced, "Mr. Beaumont cannot see you, sir."

"Cannot or will not?"

"Good day, sir."

"Is there another time?"

"No other time. Good day."

"Then perhaps you might answer a question for me."

She glowered at him.

Ted motioned toward the portraits. "Which one of these fine gentlemen is Mr. Beaumont?"

"Mr. Beaumont is an associate."

"Ah. Hasn't made it to the wall yet."

"Sir, I—"

"Suppose I wait for him?"

"You should know I was told to call the police if you do not leave," she said.

"In that case," Ted said with a tap of his cane, "I shall go. But tell Mr. Beaumont—"

"Good day!"

Ted nodded, turned, and headed toward the door, singing, "'Oh, Mary took the calves to the dairy showww....'"

Chapter Twenty-Four

When the trial resumed the next day, Clara Dalton Price surprised Kit—and everyone else in court—by resting the case for the prosecution. Without calling Ellis Dyke as a witness.

That told Kit there was something about Dyke that could hurt the prosecution's case. But what? She wouldn't have the chance to find out through cross-examination. Now she would have to decide whether to call Ellis Dyke as a hostile witness during her own case-in-chief.

Resting now was a good move. Kit could see the strategic hand of John Davenport behind the decision. First, it would give the jury the impression that the assistant D.A. was confident in her case. No more witnesses needed. All was proved.

Second, it caught Kit slightly off guard. She had her own decision to make, such as whether to put Mousy Malloy on the stand.

Jurors tended to be suspicious of defendants who did not testify. If innocent, they should have the guts to get up and swear to it, or so the thinking went. Even though the

Constitution guaranteed the right of a defendant to stay off the witness chair, in reality the men of the jury often held this against the accused.

In this case it was problematic because Mousy admitted his recall of the facts was fuzzy at best. He did not have a clear recollection of much that happened after he came through the door of Doogan's Saloon that morning.

Kit still had her opening statement reserved and so decided to approach the issue head on.

"Gentlemen of the jury, it is now the turn of the defense to present its case. You are all aware that it is not the burden of the defendant to prove his innocence. The law says that he *is* innocent, at this very moment, in fact, unless and until you twelve good and true men deliberate and reach a unanimous verdict to the contrary. Which you may not do unless the evidence convinces you beyond a reasonable doubt and to a moral certainty that Mr. Malloy is guilty of the crime charged.

"That crime, attempted murder, has two elements. There must be an act which may have caused an actual murder, and there must be an intention to murder. Both of these must be proved beyond a reasonable doubt.

"A defendant does not have to testify. If the evidence is such that a case has not been made against him, he may submit the matter to you without testimony. That is a right protected by the Constitution of the United States.

"With all of that in mind, gentlemen, I urge you to listen to the evidence presented, as you have sworn to do, with an open mind. And now the defense calls its first witness."

Kit turned toward the gallery. "Mr. Jack London."

A buzz of excitement swept through the courtroom. Necks craned as observers searched for the famous author. London looked more shocked than anyone else, as Kit well understood. She had not given him any indication he would be a witness for the defense.

Clara Dalton Price was also in a state of agitation, in part, no doubt, because London would hold great sway with the men of the jury. He was a man's man, a famous writer, and his words would be considered important.

With some trepidation, Jack London stepped through the gate and whispered to Kit, "You tricked me. You got me down here to call me as a witness!"

"Just tell the truth," Kit said.

After London was sworn as a witness, Kit asked him, "You are the author of *The Call of the Wild* and *The Sea Wolf,* are you not?"

"I am," London said, still looking unsure about his presence here.

"You served as a war correspondent in Japan during the Russo-Japanese war, is that true?"

"Yes it is. Back in '04."

"Is it fair to say that your writing has won wide acclaim?"

London smiled. "I leave that to the public."

"You base your writing on the close observance of detail, correct?"

"No one can hope to be a writer of any worth unless he can get details on the page that bring a story to life."

"You are a student of human nature, as well?"

"I try to be."

"In that regard, Mr. London, have you spent a good deal of your life in saloons?"

There was a collective gasp from some in the gallery, but Kit knew exactly what she was doing and was only a little less sure of Jack London's reaction. She was a student of human nature, too, and she felt London was not the type to let social graces interfere with literary honesty. Besides, if he were to hedge in his answer, Kit could always produce the piece he wrote for the *Examiner* that extolled the virtues of drinking. It was not necessary to do so.

"Yes, I have frequented many a watering hole in my time," London said. "But no more than many a man."

"Indeed, you have even written about how social drinking is a pleasure which society should be prepared to accept, have you not?"

"I am gratified, Miss Shannon, that you know of my work."

"In your estimation, there are two types of drinkers, is that right?"

"That is right, yes."

"How would you describe them?"

"There's the man who can hold his liquor, and there's the man who cannot."

"The dipsomaniac is the latter type?"

"Certainly."

"What is the effect on the mind of the man under the influence of alcohol?"

"There is the white logic, first of all."

"Please explain that to the jury."

"It is a sort of false seeing, like being overtaken by the pessimism of, say, German philosophy. Values are turned upside down. He sees God as bad, truth as a cheat, life as a joke. Even wife and children may be exposed to him as frauds and shams under the white logic."

"Anything else?"

"For the man in the grip of John Barleycorn, there is a correlation between inhibition and morality. Wrong conduct that is impossible to do when sober is quite easily done when one is not sober."

"Thank you."

Kit returned to her table as Clara Dalton Price stood to cross-examine.

"Mr. London, you do not know the defendant, Abner Malloy, do you?"

"No, ma'am."

"You've never seen him drink?"

"No."

"Have never observed him under the influence of anything."

"That's right."

"You are a drinking companion of Mr. Earl Rogers, is that true?"

"Objection," Kit said. "Irrelevant and immaterial."

"I wish to show the bias of the witness toward Miss Shannon," Mrs. Price said. "Her colleague is Earl Rogers. I want to know the connection."

"I will allow you to ask only a few questions on this matter," Judge Trent said.

Mrs. Price returned to the witness. "Did you hear the question?"

Jack London began to look peeved. "Of course I did. You were standing right there when you asked it."

"Your answer, please."

"Earl Rogers and I have chased a few together, and why not?"

"Did you ever, as you put it, chase a few in the presence of Miss Shannon?"

London looked at Kit, who returned the gaze impassively. If she objected now, it would seem she had something to hide. And she did not.

"I think there was one time," London said, "when Miss Shannon was present."

"Was this a social occasion?"

"I'm a socialist, so it's always that kind of occasion."

Laughter in the courtroom brought the gavel down from Judge Trent.

"Answer the question," Clara Dalton Price said.

"Dinner it was," said London.

"So you were acquainted with Miss Shannon, on a social basis, before you came into court today?"

"What's that got to do with the price of beans in Borneo?"

Again a ripple of laughter broke into the proceedings. Mrs. Price, however, was not amused. Kit could tell London's flippancy was beginning to wear thin with some of the jurors.

"Are you afraid to answer the question, Mr. London?"

"Afraid? Are you crazy?"

"Are you fond of Miss Shannon?"

"Who wouldn't be? You, perhaps."

Clara Dalton Price let the comment pass, even as more laughter ensued. She was allowing Jack London to hang himself with his own words. Now Kit wondered if calling him to the stand was a good idea after all.

"In your study of drunkards," Mrs. Price said, "is it your experience that this type of man knows he cannot take strong drink?"

"When sober, they do. When drunk, they don't think about much at all."

"Would you hold a man responsible for getting himself drunk if he went out and committed a crime under the influence?"

"I probably would. It's like a man who loads a gun knowing it is liable to go off somewhere."

With a polite smile Clara Dalton Price said, "No further questions."

"Is there redirect for this witness?" Judge Trent asked Kit.

"Yes," Kit said. "Mr. London, you know me, but did that in any way color the truth of what you have told us here today?"

"No, of course not. I'm under oath."

"Now, Mrs. Price asked you about a man getting himself drunk and committing a crime. What if a man knows his capacity for drink, but then someone slips him a stronger brew without his knowing it? Would you then hold that man responsible for his actions?"

"It seems to me the one spiking the drink would be the responsible one."

"Thank you. No further questions."

Chapter Twenty-Five

"You don't have to take the stand," Kit whispered to Mousy Malloy.

"Do you think I should, Miss Shannon?"

The decision had to be made. Now, during the short recess. Kit wondered if she had sown enough reasonable doubt in the minds of the jurors. She thought not. But as a witness, Mousy was a wild card. He could tangle himself up in his own testimony.

"Do you feel up to it?" Kit asked.

"I'm a little scared. I don't know what they think of me, those people in the jury."

"Mousy, do you remember what I told you about trusting God? We have been talking about that, you and I, for a long time, haven't we?"

"Yes, ma'am."

"Are you ready to trust?"

Mousy shook his head. "I'm a sinful man."

"You don't have to stay that way. The time is now. Are you willing to trust in God for once in your life?"

"I guess I can try."

"That's enough for now. God is listening in on our little conversation here. He wants to know if you'll keep on going."

"Will you help me?"

"Of course."

Mousy Malloy slapped the counsel table. "Then put me up there on the stand. I'll give God a chance."

When court resumed, Kit announced that her client would testify. This seemed to both amaze and please Mrs. Price. The chance to grill a defendant was something every prosecutor looked forward to. Kit would have to be on guard to protect Mousy any way she could.

A jittery Mousy Malloy took the oath. There was something pitiful about it, and Kit hoped the jurors would see him as a man first and a defendant second. That was her task.

"Mr. Malloy, what is your line of work?" Kit asked.

"Rail jobber. Work the lines." Mousy's voice warbled a bit as he answered.

"You are an independent jobber?"

"Right. Whoever needs the help. I can replace rail and tie, hammer spike, dig and fill. You name it, I do it."

"How long have you worked the lines?"

"Ever since '01 or thereabouts. Everywhere from Kentucky to San Diego."

"Before the day of the alleged shooting in this case, were you acquainted with Mr. Ellis Dyke?"

Mousy nodded, his expression turning dark. "We did some jobs together."

"He was working the lines in and around Los Angeles?"

"His daddy made him."

Some people in the courtroom laughed. Kit saw Ellis Dyke, sitting in the front row, give Mousy a deadly stare.

"How do you know Ellis Dyke's father made him work on the rail lines?"

"Because Ellis told me. One day he said—"

"Objection," Mrs. Price said. "Hearsay."

"No, Your Honor," Kit said. "There is an exception to the hearsay rule when the statement helps to explain the state of mind of the witness."

The judge nodded. "That is correct. I overrule the objection."

"What did Ellis Dyke say to you, Mr. Malloy?"

"He said he was only working because his father was making him do it. He said he was going to take over the whole line someday, and then said people like me would be shining his shoes."

"Was it your impression that Mr. Dyke was not, shall we say, fond of associating with you?"

"I thought he'd rather be sipping tea than getting his hands dirty."

"Did Mr. Dyke and you ever get into an altercation?"

"Ya mean a fight?"

"That's what I mean."

"Yeah, we got into it once. I wouldn't bow down to him, so he got mad."

"What do you mean you wouldn't bow down to him?"

"He thinks his money makes him worth listening to. He was sitting around telling a bunch of us what he was going to do with the railroad someday, and I got up and started walking away. He piped something at me about that, so I stopped and asked him if he wanted to back up his mouth with me. Because other guys were watching, he couldn't back down. We had a fight."

"What was the outcome of that fight?"

"I beat him like a drum."

"Liar!" Ellis Dyke, his face red, was on his feet in the gallery. "He could never best me!"

"Mr. Dyke!" Judge Trent pounded his gavel on the bench. "You will remain seated and quiet!"

"I want to tell my side!" he shouted.

"Quiet, sir, or I will have you removed from this courtroom."

His mouth open, Ellis Dyke froze as he seemed to realize he had made a spectacle in court. He sat down in a huff and folded his arms.

Kit waited a moment, letting the jurors get a full dose of Dyke's outburst. She turned again to her witness and said, "Tell the jury, as best you can remember, what happened when Ellis Dyke walked into Doogan's Saloon on the morning of March 30."

Mousy swallowed, looked toward the jury. Then to Kit he said, "I was having a drink, just a little beer and a couple of eggs before going on my way. Ellis and his friends walked in, at least I figured them for his friends. They were laughing and joking, you know. I didn't pay them any mind, until Ellis tried to get something started."

"What did he do?"

"Called over to me. Said things like `Look at the rummy over there. He thinks he can drink like a man.' That sort of stuff."

"Did it bother you?"

"It interrupted my breakfast, that's for certain."

"What happened next?"

"Ellis wouldn't stop with the comments. I may have said something back to him. Next thing I know, he's telling me to prove I can drink with the men. One thing I know—I can drink Ellis Dyke under the table. I've seen him drink before. So I took the bet."

"The bet was to match drink for drink until someone couldn't continue?"

"That's it."

"Who paid for the drinks?"

"I guess it was Ellis. I don't remember."

"So Doogan began pouring, and you and Mr. Dyke began to drink?"

"As soon as we drained a beer, Doogan served us another."

"Did the beer taste odd to you in any way?"

"Objection," Clara Dalton Price said. "That would be pure speculation on the part of the witness."

"He can testify about his impression," Kit said.

"I agree," Judge Trent said. "The objection is overruled."

Mousy Malloy thought a moment. "Now that I think about it, there was a difference. Stronger taste, maybe. I think Doogan was putting a shot of whiskey in my beer."

"How many beers did you consume and in what period of time?"

"I'm sorry, Miss Shannon. I don't have a good recollection of that. At least five, and then things started to get fuzzy on me."

"Do you remember standing up and moving toward the bar?"

"No, I don't."

"Do you remember Mr. Doogan standing at the bar with a gun in his hand?"

"No, ma'am."

"Telling Mr. Dyke you were going to kill him?"

"No."

Kit paused to allow the jury a good long look at Mousy Malloy. He seemed sincere, honest. A liar would try to color the facts, and Mousy was definitely not doing that.

"Would you ever shoot another man in cold blood?" Kit asked.

"Never."

"No further questions."

Clara Dalton Price jumped to her feet and walked toward the jury box. "The truth about that morning at Doogan's bar, sir, is that you got drunk, isn't that right?"

Mousy scowled. "I already said—"

"Yes or no?"

"You know I did."

"No one held a gun to your head and ordered you to drink beer, right?"

"No, but I—"

"You could have stopped at any time, correct?"

"This was something—"

"Please, you can answer my questions with a simple yes or no."

Kit stood. "Objection, Your Honor. The witness should be allowed to answer in the way he sees fit."

"The prosecutor may ask questions that call for a yes or no response," the judge said. "Overruled."

"You could have stopped at any time, isn't that right, sir?"

"I suppose."

"Does that mean *yes*?"

"Yes."

Clara Dalton Price was standing like a gunslinger in front of the witness stand. "You are a drunkard, aren't you, Mr. Malloy?"

Mousy Malloy ran his hand over his mouth nervously. "I drink some."

"You were, in fact, hospitalized recently for delirium tremens, or DT's. Isn't that so?"

"I ..."

"Yes or no?"

His head hanging, Mousy said, "Yes."

"DT's is what a dipsomaniac suffers when he can't have a drink, such as when he is locked up in jail?"

"So they tell me."

"You knew, did you not, on March 30 that you were a dipsomaniac when you walked into Doogan's?"

"I can handle my liquor."

"You handle it by pouring it down your gullet, don't you?"

Mousy's face was beginning to blanch. Kit had never seen Clara Dalton Price on the attack like this. "I object to the prosecutor's tone, Your Honor."

"Overruled," the judge said.

Clara Dalton Price did not back down one bit. "You are a plain drunk, isn't that right, sir?"

"I drink," was all Mousy managed to say.

"And what if you drink too much?"

Mousy shrugged. "I get drunk. Lots of men do."

"Lots of men do terrible things when drunk, as Miss Shannon's star witness, Jack London, has testified—isn't that true?"

"I guess."

"Have you ever done anything when drunk that, later, you regretted doing?"

Mousy looked down. He might have been searching for a hole to crawl into.

"Answer the question," Mrs. Price demanded.

"Sure I have."

"Because you were not in control of your faculties?"

"Yeah."

"You are not drunk now, are you?"

"'Course not."

"So in this sober, reflective state you are able to tell this jury that you drink, and when you drink too much, you are capable of doing things you might otherwise regret?"

"I admit it."

Mrs. Price looked directly at the jury. "You knew, then, on the morning of March 30, that if you drank too much you could very well end up doing some destructive act, isn't that true, Mr. Malloy?"

"I didn't think I would ..."

"And you claim now to recall that the beer tasted like it may have been spiked, wasn't that your testimony?"

"I think it might have been."

"An even greater reason for you to stop. But you didn't, did you?"

Mousy did not answer, nor did he have to. Clara Dalton Price let him sit there in silence. Then, after a long moment, she said, "No more questions."

The shoeshine man looked as if he'd been on the job since the Comstock Lode silver strike. He was gaunt, with a face of white whiskers, blackened somewhat by the polish he slapped on fancy shoes.

Ted's weren't so fancy, but they were black and needed a shine. For a nickel the price was right.

So was the bootblack's location, which was directly across Bush Street from the offices of Sutter, Wingate & Finn. It was almost noon, and the business crowd started to emerge for their lunch plans.

Ted sat on the chair and the shoeshiner started his work.

"Don't think I've done you before, stranger," he said,

opening a can of black polish and wiping some of it out with a cloth.

"I'm from out of town," Ted said. "Los Angeles."

"Ah, that's a wild place. Too many gunslingers down there."

"Not anymore." Ted laughed. "They actually have the law there now."

"You don't say?" The man began to smear the polish on Ted's shoes.

"You must know some lawyers up this way."

"You lookin' for one? You in trouble of some kind?"

"No, just looking for a name. I don't suppose you'd know of a Mr. Beaumont, from the law firm across the street."

The man peered up at Ted. "You know Charlie? He comes here almost every day."

"You don't say."

"Sure I do. What would you be wanting with Charlie Beaumont? He's a company man. Does work for Western Rail and the telegraph lines, like that."

"You seem to know all about him."

"Man's got to know his customers if he expects to make a living." He hesitated, looked at Ted's left leg, and knocked on it with his knuckles. "Cedar?"

"Pine."

The man nodded.

"You think Mr. Beaumont might come this way soon?"

"Might."

"I'd like to meet him."

"Why?"

"To discuss the law."

"You a lawyer?"

"No, but I'm going to marry one."

The man's eyes nearly popped out of his head. "A woman lawyer?"

"That's right."

"Next thing you know a woman'll be shining shoes."

"Think Charlie will come by today?"

The man eyed Ted suspiciously. "You aim to do him any harm? You have a gun on you?'"

"I assure you, my intentions are honorable. This is the only weapon I carry." Ted produced a small Bible from his coat pocket.

"Preacher?"

"Only when the opportunity presents itself."

"You aiming to preach to Charlie?"

"I just might."

"Won't work. Charlie's not a God-fearing man."

"Maybe he's open to reason."

The man stood up. "You're all done. If you want to talk to Charlie, you might try Monday morning, about nine o'clock."

"Thank you." Ted gave him a quarter. "Keep the change."

"A preacher giving away money? Now, that is news."

Chapter Twenty-Six

On Saturday morning, as Kit was about to read the *Times* with her morning coffee, the telephone rang in the Fairbank mansion. When she picked up, the crackling voice of the operator told her she had a connection from San Francisco.

"Ted!"

"Is that you, Kit?"

"Yes. I can barely hear you."

"IS THIS BETTER?"

"Much better. Darling, it is so good to hear your voice!"

"I keep reading about you in the papers."

"The locals?"

"You're news even up here."

Not a pleasant thought. "What are they saying about the trial?"

"That it is not easy."

"No, not easy."

"Perfect! The kind of case Kit Shannon likes to win."

"When are you coming back?"

"That's what I'm calling about. I've got a lead on Western Rail. I'm going to try to talk to one of the lawyers."

"Who is it?"

"Fellow named Beaumont."

"Be careful, Ted."

"What do I have to be careful about?"

"You can't trust lawyers."

He laughed. "Miss me?"

"Terribly."

"What was that?"

"TERRIBLY."

"I still can't hear you."

"Ted... ?"

A static sound, like distant firecrackers, came over the wire. Then the line went dead.

"No!" Kit hit the plunger, trying—willing—the line to come back. It didn't.

Well, at least she'd gotten to hear his voice. That was something.

She returned to the library and took up the *Times*. So now she was making it into the San Francisco papers! Publicity was becoming a potent force in the world. The ability to reach so many people. She began to wonder what that might mean for the future of trying cases.

Her eyes fell to the story in the *Times* by Tom Phelps. As Kit read it, she could almost feel Tom's desire to give her some benefit of the doubt. But he had to write what he saw and heard, and it was the same thing she'd experienced in court.

> The Malloy attempted-murder case continued to unfold in the prosecution's favor yesterday as the defense lawyer, Kathleen Shannon, gambled by putting her client on the stand.
>
> Abner "Mousy" Malloy testified on his own behalf in the courtroom of Judge Alton Trent. It seemed the only thing Miss Shannon could do, considering the state of the evidence. Clara Dalton Price, the deputy district attorney who is prosecuting, has built a simple and straightforward case against Malloy.
>
> After Miss Shannon guided her client through a somewhat shaky direct testimony, Mrs. Price began her

cross-examination. It was an attack as swift as it was deadly. The witness squirmed on the stand under the relentless questioning of the prosecutor.

Court observers have been riveted by this, the second meeting of the county's leading female advocates in court. The last time was in the Harcourt murder case, when Miss Shannon convinced the court to allow testimony at the scene of the crime. Her restaging of the event, with the help of the magician Harry Houdini, was a sensational twist that unraveled Mrs. Price's case.

No such unraveling appears to be in the offing here, unless Miss Shannon has her own magical bag of tricks from which to draw.

Kit put down the paper as Corazón entered the library for their morning conference. "We are, as they say, behind the eight ball," she said.

"Eight?" Corazón asked.

"An old expression. How is our young charge this morning?"

"Bobby is ready to begin school."

"That is grand. Monday morning, then?"

"Yes. The Halifax School will take him."

"Our next task is to find him a good home. Are we continuing to make inquiries?"

"I have begun," said Corazón.

"Let us turn to the two cases before us. First, Mr. Malloy. If you were a juror, how would you see it?"

Corazón frowned and looked sheepish.

"The truth now," Kit said. "That's what I need."

"It is not looking so good."

"Did the cross-examination go as poorly as the newspapers suggest?"

"Mrs. Price, she is very good at what she does."

Kit nodded. "And she wants this case badly. The answer, then, is that Mrs. Price tore a very large hole in our defense yesterday."

Sadly, Corazón nodded.

"Do you know what Abraham Lincoln's advice to lawyers was?"

"I do not."

"He said, `When the facts are against you, argue the law. When the law is against you, argue the facts. When both are against you, pound the table and shout for justice!' I am beginning to think pounding the table is what we must do." Kit stood and began to pace, which was the way she best thought out loud. "The facts are against us, at least in the minds of the jurors. The law is not for us, either. We must show that Mousy's intoxication was involuntary, or we cannot argue that point. What have we got left?"

Corazón thought a moment, then put an index finger up in the air. "A fact," she said. "We need a fact that is very good, yes?"

"Yes! But what are we missing?"

"Someone to say that Doogan—he was not playing fair. Only it was Ellis Dyke's friends around. They will not say."

"Who else?" Kit said, deep in thought. "The man in the uniform—the cop, or whoever he is—was he part of Dyke's crowd? I don't think so. If only we could find that man!"

"There is the matter of the gun."

Kit stopped and looked at Corazón. "Tell me what you're thinking."

"I am thinking of the part where the man Hartrampf said he did not, how do you say, duck behind the bar. He was not afraid of the gun."

"Yes, that bothers me, too. What was on his mind? Was he drunk?"

Corazón furrowed her brow. "I do not think so. The men with Ellis Dyke did not have the time to get, how you say, stewed?"

"You're picking up the lingo pretty well, I think."

Corazón beamed.

"You're probably right," Kit added. "Hartrampf most likely was not drunk enough not to notice a gun being pointed at him. I wonder if we can find out who sold the gun to Doogan. Perhaps there's something about it we should know. Check the gun shops in town. And take Raul with you. Some of the characters in those places can be rough."

"I will do it."

Ted saw the bootblack giving a shine to a young man in a sharp brown suit. At once he knew it was the lawyer Beaumont, because this was the type of man who kept appointments, and now was the time the shoeshine man had told him he would be here.

With a confident tapping of his cane, Ted crossed Bush Street.

The lawyer sat reading a copy of the morning *Chronicle*. He was perhaps thirty, with the serious scowl of a man twenty years his senior. He seemed to be practicing the solemn face that would one day be a portrait hanging on the wall of Sutter, Wingate & Finn.

He did not bother to look up upon Ted's approach. The bootblack, however, noticed Ted's shoes. "Here's the fella I was telling you about," he said.

The lawyer glanced up from his paper. "I have no interest," he said.

"You must be Mr. Beaumont," Ted said.

"I am. Digger here says you want to discuss something legal with me. If you make an appointment, and can pay for a consultation, I shall see you in my office."

"Did Mr. Digger here tell you I am a somewhat clumsy preacher?"

"He said you carried a Bible with you. I don't mean to be rude, but—"

"No offense taken." Ted took the Bible out of his coat pocket.

"Excuse me, I—"

"Let me tell you what the Bible thinks of the law and lawyers."

"See here—"

"Jesus did say woe to ye lawyers, but I think He was thinking only of a certain kind."

"Certain kind?"

"As it says in Proverbs, `A false balance is abomination to the Lord: but a just weight is his delight."'

Beaumont twisted in his seat. "May I please read the paper and—"

"You are a lawyer for Western Rail, is that not so?"

"What has this to do with Western Rail?"

"Western is the parent of Los Angeles Electric."

The lawyer's lower lip twitched as he said, "I don't know what you're about, sir, but I will no longer listen to this."

"Hold on there, Mr. Beaumont. I want you to hear another Proverb."

"But—"

"`The integrity of the upright shall guide them: but the perverseness of transgressors shall destroy them."'

"What on earth are you talking about?"

Ted looked the lawyer in the eyes. "I am talking about something deceitful in the handling of the case in Los Angeles, the death of a little boy at the hands of Los Angeles Electric." His voice rose in the manner of the hellfire preachers he'd heard in revivals. "I am talking about the wrath of God being delivered to those who are part of the deception!"

Beaumont's eyes grew round with anger. He looked down at the bootblack. "Digger, I'm through!"

"There's more to do," Digger said.

"Not today." Beaumont dug a coin out of his pocket and dropped it into Digger's hands.

"Come clean before it is too late!" Ted said, caught up in the moment. Enjoying it, in fact.

Beaumont walked briskly away, heading across Bush Street toward his law office.

Ted smiled. "Say, I didn't know I had that in me."

"You're some hellfire and brimstone preacher, all right," Digger agreed. "But would you mind doing me a favor?"

"Certainly, friend."

"Find a different corner. You're bad for business."

Chapter Twenty-Seven

On Monday morning, the press and what seemed to be half of Los Angeles gathered for the final showdown between Kit Shannon and Clara Dalton Price.

Both morning papers, the *Times* and *Examiner,* ran stories about the dire condition of Abner "Mousy" Malloy. Closing arguments were expected, they said.

Kit had other plans. They were no doubt going to rile the judge, but there was nothing in the code about riling being a criminal offense. She was ready.

As was Clara Dalton Price. She was dressed this morning in a beige skirt and a white shirtwaist with floral trim. Kit had never seen her looking so ladylike. Usually Mrs. Price dressed for business and eschewed all but the most utilitarian ruffles or pleats. Today, however, she might have been on her way to an afternoon tea at the women's club. She wore a wide-brimmed hat, which matched her dress, topped with a fluffy white feather.

For her part, Kit had chosen a biscuit-colored suit of English tweed, the skirt ankle high. This morning it was Kit who was all business.

Judge Trent took the bench and called the case, asking Kit if she was ready with her closing argument.

Kit stood. "I have one more witness to call," she announced.

Looking a bit surprised, the judge said, "Fine. Proceed."

"The defense would like to recall Bill Doogan."

Kit saw the look of dismay run across Doogan's face. He was sour enough, no doubt, at being here and not at his business establishment. Yet he also knew what a subpoena was.

"You are still under oath, Mr. Doogan," Judge Trent cautioned. "Do you understand that?"

Doogan grumbled his assent and then sat heavily in the witness chair.

Kit whispered to Corazón, "Get ready," then approached the witness. "You do know that it is a crime to give false testimony in a court of law, do you not, Mr. Doogan?"

"Of course." Even Doogan's eyebrows seemed belligerent.

"It is called perjury."

"I know that."

"Good. Now we can continue with the questions, knowing you will tell us the truth, the whole truth, and nothing but the truth—or face jail."

The tavern owner shrugged. "I tell the truth."

"Then answer this, Mr. Doogan. Do you know a man named Laird Rawlings?"

Doogan's eyes gave the merest flicker of apprehension. "Sure, I know him."

"What is his line of business, sir?"

"He's a gunsmith."

"In fact, he is the one from whom you bought the very revolver at issue in this case, correct?"

"Well, yes."

Kit turned and nodded at Corazón, who got up from the counsel table, then walked through the gate and out of the courtroom. The chamber was silent, watching the scene with a collective anticipation. Kit let the drama build. She did not ask another question until the courtroom doors opened again.

Corazón walked in with Raul Montoya. She brought him to the rail and stood there, both facing Doogan.

"Isn't it true," Kit said, "that the day before the alleged shooting, you were at Mr. Rawlings' gun shop?"

Doogan's eyes darted from Kit to Raul and back again. "I do some business with him. I can't recall when, though."

"Isn't it also true that, on the day of the alleged shooting, you—"

"Objection!" Clara Dalton Price blurted. "Your Honor, Miss Shannon is misrepresenting the facts by using the term *alleged shooting.* It has already been established that there was a shooting. Only the intent of the shooter is in question."

"No, Your Honor," Kit argued. "There was no shooting."

While Judge Trent opened his mouth to speak, Kit whirled around to the counsel table and pulled from her briefcase the same gun she had shown Doogan in court. She pointed it at the ceiling and fired.

Screams in the courtroom. A feeling like an electric jolt crackled through the air. Judge Trent's expression was one of shock.

And Doogan looked as though he was going to have a heart attack. That was what Kit needed.

"There was no shooting," said Kit, "because your gun was filled with blank cartridges. Mr. Raul Montoya, an associate in my office, spoke to Laird Rawlings yesterday afternoon. If need be, we can summon Mr. Rawlings to testify. He will say that he sold you blank cartridges on March 29, the day before the incident. That's why no one ever found another bullet hole in your saloon. That's why Sam Hartrampf and Ellis Dyke didn't duck behind the bar. There was no possibility of anyone being shot."

Doogan's breathing grew rapid. From the corner of her eye, Kit saw Judge Trent holding his gavel aloft but not bringing it down.

"The truth, Mr. Doogan," Kit all but shouted. "You are under oath."

"It was Dyke's idea!" The witness pointed at Ellis Dyke, seated in the front row. "He put me up to it."

"You lying—" Ellis Dyke said, the last part cut off as he leaped over the rail and charged Doogan.

It was all happening too fast for the bailiff, who appeared frozen on the other side of the courtroom. The only person between Doogan and Dyke was Kit.

She acted without a second thought. As Dyke made a lunge toward the witness-box, Kit turned her body into him. The force knocked her backward into the rail of the witness-box. For a moment she was face-to-face with Ellis Dyke.

He gritted his teeth at her.

Then he was being pulled off of her by the bailiff.

"Arrest that man!" Judge Trent ordered. He looked at Kit and said, "I am very close to having the same done to you, Miss Shannon! I want to see you and Mrs. Price in my chambers at once."

After the two lawyers were alone with the judge, it was difficult for Kit to tell who was more upset, Judge Trent or Mrs. Price.

To Kit, Trent said, "What was that stunt you pulled out there?" The judge stomped around his desk, arms waving. "You could have gotten yourself shot! If my bailiff was half awake, you should have been."

"She should be held in contempt," Clara Dalton Price said.

"That sounds like a very good idea. My courtroom has been turned into a madhouse."

"Your Honor," Kit said quietly, "I had a lying witness on the stand and needed to do something drastic to get him to admit it. Without that shot I don't think he would have."

"Why didn't you prepare me?"

"Frankly, Your Honor, I think Mrs. Price would have thrown a ... would have strongly objected."

"You are right about that," the prosecutor said.

"And I did not want her getting to the witness in some way."

"I resent that!" Clara Dalton Price's eyes were watering with fury.

"Now, now," the judge said. "We must keep our heads about this. We still have a trial to conduct."

"I move for a mistrial!" Mrs. Price said.

"Well, I move the charges be dismissed," Kit fired back. "The *actus reus,* the bad act required for an attempted-murder charge, has been eliminated by the prosecutor's own witness. I want to go back out and finish my cross-examination, now that Doogan has admitted to a scheme involving Ellis Dyke and using blanks in his gun. I don't want to wait for another trial, giving Mrs. Price a chance to coach the witness."

A livid Mrs. Price slapped her sides. "Your Honor, do I have to put up with—"

"Hold on." The judge raised his hand. "Perhaps you'd better talk to John about this."

Yes, Kit thought, *go running back to Davenport for your dancing orders.* Problem was, the D.A. could not take back what Doogan had just admitted.

Clara Dalton Price adjusted her hat. "That is just what I'll do."

"I'll give you half an hour," Judge Trent said. "Then we'll reconvene."

Judge Trent took to the bench almost thirty minutes later to the second. He had Bill Doogan resume the witness chair. Ellis Dyke had been removed from the courtroom. To Kit's way of thinking, his outburst could not have been a better form of evidence for the jury. But the jury had not yet been summoned back into court.

Kit put a hand on Mousy's arm, reassuring him. She had no idea what was going to happen next. Clara Dalton Price had, by now, conferred with Davenport. Kit could read nothing in her expression.

"Very well," the judge said, "we are in the middle of cross-examination. Before we call the jury, does the prosecution have anything they wish to say?"

"Yes." Clara Dalton Price stood up. "We would like to make a motion."

For a mistrial, Kit thought. *Well, let them. I will object and—*

"The People move that the charge of attempted murder against Abner Malloy be dismissed."

The inhalations of surprise came mostly from the reporters. Kit herself issued a muted yelp of shock.

"What's that mean?" Mousy asked. "Am I free?"

Before Kit could answer, Clara Dalton Price added, "And we would serve an information against Abner Malloy for the murder of William Rye."

"Murder?" Mousy grabbed Kit's hand, a gesture that cried out for her to do something. "I didn't kill anybody!"

"Order!" Judge Trent banged the gavel until quiet was restored.

Kit looked at Mrs. Price. "What is the basis of this new charge?"

"You will find out in due course," the prosecutor said. "Right now I ask that Mr. Malloy be removed to his jail cell."

Mousy's eyes went wide with fear. "But, Miss Shannon, I didn't kill anybody! You can't let them do this to me!"

The bailiff was already approaching Mousy with shackles for escort back to the jail.

"I'll find out what's going on," she said, taking his hand. "And I will see you later. I promise."

"You'll come see me?"

"I promise."

The bailiff slapped cuffs on the wrists of Mousy Malloy.

Chapter Twenty-Eight

Kit stormed into Davenport's office and found him looking smug, his thumbs casually inserted into his vest pockets. Clara Dalton Price was there, too, and also had a countenance of satisfaction. Both seemed to have been waiting for her arrival.

"You made good time," Davenport said.

"Do you want to tell me what is going on here?" Kit would not be bothered with social graces now; there was something afoot that was foul, not deserving of her courtesy.

"Going on?" said Davenport with a feigned innocence.

"Yes, what are you trying to do, Mr. Davenport? If you had evidence of murder, you would have charged my client before now. Why did you wait until Mrs. Price here lost the case?"

Kit could feel the heat rippling off Clara Dalton Price. "What makes you think we've lost?" the prosecutor asked.

"New evidence has surfaced," Davenport explained. "I simply wanted to wait for the right time to inform you of it, that's all. Now you know."

"What new evidence?" said Kit.

"You are asking me to reveal it to you? Before a trial? How sporting is that?"

"This isn't sport." Kit took a deep breath in an effort to calm herself. Davenport liked to do this whenever he could—put the needle to her. Only this time she could not allow him such a victory. *Hold that temper,* she told herself.

Davenport took up a pipe from his desk and began filling it with tobacco. "Why should we share anything with you, Miss Shannon? What have you ever done for this office?"

"I've always tried my cases openly and aboveboard."

Clara Price pounced. "You call that little stunt with the gun aboveboard?"

Kit faced her. "I did nothing unethical, and I exposed a liar on the witness stand. I would think your office would be pleased about that."

"Well, your tricks have become tiresome," Davenport said.

"You call them tricks; I call them the defense lawyer's arsenal. You hold all the cards as prosecutor. You don't have to reveal your evidence—you can wait to spring surprise witnesses and you can withhold evidence that might help the defense. All we have is our wits in order to find out when you've put on false witnesses and—"

"That's enough, Miss Shannon! We all know the system."

"The system is stacked against the innocent man accused of a crime. And I will do everything the law allows to give such a man an honest and fair defense. You are supposed to seek justice, not convict the innocent."

"Suppose that man is not innocent?" Davenport said. "What if you yourself were convinced of his guilt? What would you do then?"

Kit paused. It was a critical question for her, and she'd always had some difficulty answering it. If she were Earl Rogers, the answer would be simple: try and win the case anyway. But Kit did not see the law in that fashion. For her, the search for truth had always been the primary goal of her practicing law.

"If the evidence was overwhelming," Kit said slowly, thinking out loud, "I would discuss it with my client and first see what he said about it. I would listen for an explanation. If I thought it made sense and could be corroborated, I would move forward with the trial."

"Even if the evidence suggested he might be convicted?"

"All defense lawyers take that chance."

"And what if you knew that a guilty plea would result in a lesser sentence for your client than if you had a full-blown trial that resulted in a verdict of guilty? You know the judge will listen to the recommendation this office makes with regard to sentencing."

That was true. And if a prosecutor wished to punish a defense lawyer for going to trial, that prosecutor could later urge the judge to hand down the harshest sentence allowable.

"It would then be my duty to inform him, of course," Kit said. "But the decision would be the client's on whether or not to go to trial."

Davenport gave a knowing glance to Mrs. Price before returning to Kit. "Then I will make you a little deal. I will show you the evidence we have against your client. If it looks persuasive to you, you discuss it with Mr. Malloy. If you have your client plead guilty, I will arrange with the judge to be lenient, say to the tune of a mere twenty years in prison."

"A *mere* twenty years?"

"It is better than the noose."

Kit took a breath as she thought this over. "And if I am not convinced of his guilt?"

"You will be. Do we have a deal?"

More like a trap, Kit thought. But what harm could there be in listening? The chance to hear evidence from a prosecutor was one to jump at. Then again, what if she did become convinced Mousy was guilty? Well, that was a risk she would have to take. Better to know the truth, the whole truth, and nothing but.

"All right," Kit said. "What have you got?"

Davenport nodded at Clara Dalton Price, who reached to the floor for a leather satchel. She handed it to the district attorney. Davenport pulled out a paper and gave it to Kit.

It was a note, written in a rather chaotic hand. It read:

I'm giving you until noon Tuesday to make good. Not moving till then. You don't come up with all the money, there's gonna be some trouble. R.

"What's this mean?" Kit asked.

"The *R*," Davenport said, "is Rye. That's a note from Billy Rye."

"How do you know that?"

Davenport took out another paper, this one a longer letter in the same odd handwriting. Kit looked at the signature. *Wm. Rye.*

"We got this letter from Rye's effects," Davenport said. "It looks like it was to a lady but was never sent. It doesn't have anything to do with the case. If you look at the writing, however, you can see it's the same as the threatening note. Both were written by Billy Rye."

"Who was the threatening note written to?"

"Your client."

"How do you know that? There is no designation on the note."

"We found it in a box of Mr. Malloy's things."

Kit felt a chill grab her throat. "Where?"

"Oh, didn't your client tell you?"

"Tell me what?"

"The place where Billy Rye met his untimely death? It's a little house—a shack, really—and is owned by one Abner Malloy."

Kit was speechless.

"That's right, Miss Shannon," Clara Dalton Price said. "Billy Rye was in Malloy's house, and it was Malloy who planted the hatchet in his head."

"Why didn't you tell me?"

Kit worked hard to keep the anger as well as the hurt out of her voice. The man she'd committed herself toward exonerating had not been honest with her.

At the moment Mousy Malloy looked less like a mouse and more like a sheep. A sheep in a jail cell, looking at his feet.

"Look at me, Mousy," Kit demanded.

The reluctant prisoner raised his head.

"The D.A. has strong evidence against you. It is circumstantial evidence, but men have been sent to the gallows on less. There's both motive and opportunity, and it all lines up as nicely as a vaudeville chorus line. Billy was one of the witnesses against you in the Dyke matter, and now the D.A. has Billy Rye dead on property you own. Now, how did that item escape mention?"

Mousy rubbed his dry lips. "I didn't kill him, Miss Shannon. You got to believe me."

"I don't know what to believe, Mousy. Suppose we begin with you telling me the whole truth? Or else I can't help you."

"You have to help me. Nobody else will."

"Why didn't you tell me about the shack in Glendale?"

"I was afraid."

"Of what?"

"It's all I got in the whole wide world. I thought I'd lose it."

"Lose it how?"

"Maybe you'd take it from me. I got no money to pay a lawyer, and you took my case 'cause you thought I was innocent."

"Are you innocent?"

"I don't know anymore!"

Kit tried to find a vein of mercy for him. "You have to trust me, Mousy. I never said I wanted a fee from you."

"I been trusting people all my life, and what's it got me?"

"The past is done with. You can begin right now to start anew."

"Will you still help me?"

"Do you want the truth from me?"

"'Course I do."

"Then I will tell you this. I am going to listen to what you have to say, and if I think you are lying to me again, I'm going to suggest you get another lawyer. But if I believe you, I will do everything in my power to help you. If I believe you are guilty, I will tell you that the district attorney has offered leniency in exchange for a plea of guilty."

"But I didn't kill Billy!"

"Convince me. Start with the shack."

Mousy rubbed his hands on his pants and sighed. "This is the truth. I got the place from my old man. It was his, and he left it to me when he died. That and sixty acres."

"Sixty acres? You own all that land?"

Mousy nodded. "I thought maybe someday I could make something out of it, but I never did. 'Cause of the drink, and 'cause I never found me a woman to settle down with. Never had any reason, I guess. Can you understand that?"

"Yes, Mousy. I can."

"Drink takes away most of my money. I gamble, too. You know, a man should never gamble. But he sure shouldn't gamble when he's drunk. Drinking makes you think you can draw to an inside straight. Which is what I did one night in a game with Billy Rye. I gave him my marker. He took it, and I lost."

"How much?"

"More'n I could ever earn. A thousand."

Kit shook her head.

"Billy told me maybe we could work something out, but that in the end if I didn't pay up he'd make sure something bad happened to me. He started asking me about my land."

"How did he know about it?"

Mousy frowned. "That's a good question. I don't know. I must've said something when I was drunk once. I just don't know. Anyway, he came out to see it and said he'd use the shack for a while. I had no way to argue with him about it. I was trying to buy some time, and letting him stay there did the trick. For a while."

"And then the incident at Doogan's happened?"

"Yes, ma'am."

"It's all a little too neat," said Kit. "Ellis Dyke and Doogan set you up for a false attempted-murder charge. I don't think it was just because Dyke didn't like you or that he wanted to make you out a fool, either."

"Think it had something to do with Billy? And my land?"

"Something, yes. I don't know what, though. Tell me this; where were you at approximately eight o'clock on the night of April 15, when Billy was murdered?"

Mousy swallowed, looked upward, then back down at Kit. "Honest, Miss Shannon, I don't know."

"Think! Do you remember how you got out of the hospital?"

"I went through the window."

"After you unstrapped yourself?"

Mousy's eyes narrowed. "I don't remember doing that. I just got up out of bed, looked around, didn't see anybody, and then lit out of there."

"Then what?"

"I ... I got me a bottle of whiskey."

"Where?"

"A place down by the Plaza."

"How? You didn't have any money, did you?"

Mousy scratched his chin. "Seems to me ... no. I met a fellow. He offered to buy me a drink."

"Who was this man?"

"I never saw him before. Or since."

"So out of the goodness of his heart he bought you whiskey?"

"I can put on a pretty good sob story, I guess."

Kit sighed heavily. "Where did you drink it?"

"I started down there, and I remember hopping a trolley later."

"Where to?"

"I don't know. It all gets muddy after that."

"Then how do you know you didn't go to your place and kill Billy Rye? You didn't remember shooting at Ellis Dyke."

"It's not something I would ever do—that's how I know."

"That's just it, Mousy. Under the cloud of drink you are

apt to do things you never would do when sober. And when this debt you owed Billy comes out in court, the jury is not going to believe that you conveniently forgot where you were at the time of the murder."

"But it's the truth!"

Kit gazed into Mousy's rheumy eyes. He did not look away from her. "I believe you, Mousy. I believe you are telling me the truth."

For a moment there was silence, and then Mousy's eyes began to tear. "Thank you, Miss Shannon."

"Now the hard part begins," she said. "We are going to have to go over everything you can remember, and I mean everything. No detail is too small. Because when this is all over, we're going to have to find out who really killed Billy Rye. That's our only defense."

"Miss Shannon? I'm afraid of them DT's. Can't you get me to a hospital?"

Kit shook her head. "They won't allow it. You'll need to weather that storm."

"I can't do it!" Mousy's eyes were filled with fright.

"We can make it," Kit assured him.

"We?"

"I'll stay and pray with you, Mousy. As long as it takes."

Chapter Twenty-Nine

It was well past dark when Kit returned to her office on First Street. She had hoped to find Earl Rogers still in. She wanted his advice on Mousy's indictment. Her mind was tired from the long interview with her client in jail. Now would come the sorting out process.

But he was not working tonight. She knew he was probably out on the town. She would try to catch him tomorrow.

She unlocked the door to her office, turned on the electric light, and sat in her wooden swivel chair. She was about to reach for a copy of the penal code when something disturbed her spirit.

Kit immediately turned to the framed photograph of Ted Fox that sat on her desk. She wondered if God was telling her to pray for Ted. She did not like his being away. Twice before when he had left Los Angeles she had almost lost him.

The first time he had been on a spiritual journey, shortly after losing his leg in the monoplane crash. He had to find God on his own; Kit could not make it happen by herself. And he had, one Sunday at church, after hearing the guest preacher, G. Campbell Morgan.

The second time was when Ted had pursued the German operatives in San Diego as they tried to get plans for the monoplane design from him. For a short time the federal government thought Ted was a traitor. Kit managed to convince a judge otherwise.

Kit closed her eyes. *Heavenly Father, keep Ted safe tonight. Give him strength to complete his tasks in San Francisco, then bring him safely back to me. Grant us a marriage that will honor you. Thank you for your provision in all things.*

She opened her eyes and placed her hand on the worn leather of her father's Bible. It was her most beloved possession in the world, and it always brought her comfort. It almost made it seem like Papa was still alive, still guiding her with his wisdom and warmth.

She would need that wisdom in the coming weeks as she tangled not only with Davenport over Mousy Malloy but with Western Rail over Winnie Franklin.

You have called me to the law, Lord. Help me to see justice done. Help me know what to do!

She opened the Bible and began to read the Gospel of John. She had not read more than a few verses when a soft knock on the door startled her. Who could be calling at this hour? Maybe it was Earl, seeing the light in her office. He often stopped in to check on her.

She opened the door.

A man, perhaps thirty, stood there. He was nicely dressed, hat in hand. "Miss Shannon?"

"Yes?"

"Pardon the lateness of the call. I may have some information for you. Do you represent a Mrs. Franklin?"

"Yes, I do." She opened the door farther. "Would you like to come in?"

"Just for a moment. I would rather show you what I have. It concerns the trolley line."

"Show me what?"

He smiled nervously. "I am so sorry. I've forgotten my

manners. My name is Robert Nolan." He bowed slightly. "I used to work for the line. As a motorman. When I heard about what happened, the little boy and all, well, I had to come see you."

"What is it that you have, Mr. Nolan?"

"I know this is rather mysterious, but I've been reading about the matter in the newspapers and thought you needed to see what I have."

"My curiosity is aroused, I will say that. Where is this item?"

"It is around the back of the building. I did not want anyone to see me coming here." He looked out at the darkened hall. Kit noticed his hands were shaking. "I think the company will stoop to anything, Miss Shannon. They are very powerful."

"I am aware of that. Why are you doing this?"

Nolan pulled at his collar. "I could not sit back and let them get away with this, not after what I found. It's a type of mechanism ... I can't explain it, really. But if you saw it ... it came directly from one of their trolleys."

Kit read fear in the man's face when he said this, yet she hesitated.

"If you would prefer," said Nolan, "I can use a telephone to contact you tomorrow. I will try to explain. But the company simply cannot find out I have contacted you."

"Take me to it."

Nolan sighed with relief. "Thank you, Miss Shannon. I don't think I would have been able to sleep."

Kit followed the man down the stairs, around to the back of the deserted building. In the blackness of the alley she saw a horse-drawn carriage waiting.

"Now you can see what I mean," Nolan said, opening the carriage door.

Kit took a step toward it. "We don't have a lantern," she said.

"Here, let me." Nolan reached into the carriage, and Kit saw the small illumination of a match. Presently the greater light of a lantern inside the carriage created an aura strong enough for them to see.

"There," Nolan said, pointing into the carriage.

Kit peered in. On the middle of the seat was a single bottle. The label was clear in the light: Kentucky Home Whiskey.

Whiskey? Kit thought. *What can this possibly mean?*

Something covered her face. Her head was yanked back. Pain exploded in her neck. She reached out, catching nothing but air. She kicked back with her right foot, hitting something—a leg?—and heard a wail from the man who held her.

The smell ... like a hospital, she thought. Like a linen sheet in a hospital. The man's hands were strong, and she couldn't breathe. Her head started feeling light; her eyes rolled upward.

God help me....

Corazón pointed to the words of Scripture, and Bobby read them slowly. "`The Lord is my Shepherd; I shall not want.'"

He looked up at Corazón, her face reflecting the soft glow of the oil lamp. They were alone in the study and waiting for Kit to come home.

It had become their routine to read the Bible together. Corazón used the time to brush up on her English, and at the same time, Bobby was learning to read. The Beasley home had done little in that regard.

"What's it mean, `not want'?" asked Bobby.

"It is to not be without." Corazón puzzled a moment over her syntax. "It is to have all that you need. From God."

"Honest?"

Corazón smiled. "Honest." But Bobby's eyes reflected doubt. She brushed a bit of his hair with her hand. "What is wrong?"

"I want ..." His voice fell, like a rock over a cliff.

"What is it you want?" In the short time Bobby had been living with them, Corazón had come to feel a great affection for this boy. He had a quick mind about him, and with help he might someday overcome the circumstances that had overtaken him.

"I can't have it, anyway," Bobby said.

"What?"

Bobby's shoulders went up and down with a deep breath. "A mother."

The word came out of his mouth like a lament, cutting Corazón to the heart. She could not speak.

"I know God can't do that," the boy said.

"God can do anything," Corazón said without pause.

"Even that?" Now Bobby's voice squeaked with vague hope.

Which only hastened Corazón's heartbeat. She felt she'd opened a door to a huge room and the boy was following her into it, trusting. "God, He is ... he can do anything," she said.

"At Beasley, the older kids say it can't be done. Once you're there, you're too old. Nobody wants you. I tried not to believe it."

"Believe only in God," Corazón said softly.

"Do you think Miss Shannon might?"

"Might ... ?"

"Be my mother."

Corazón's heart warmed as she hugged him close to her. "I do not know. She likes you very much. That I do know."

"And I like her. And you, Corazón."

The grandfather clock in the hall, one of Aunt Freddy's prized possessions, began to toll ten o'clock.

"My, is it that late?" Corazón stood and went to check it herself. Indeed, that was the hour. Bobby scurried up to her.

"Where is Miss Kit?" he said.

"I will call to the office." Corazón cranked the wall phone, picked up the earpiece, and asked the telephone operator for Diamond 3979.

Two long minutes passed, timed by the ticking of the clock. Then Corazón heard the operator's voice. "There is no answer at that location."

"Please, try it once more," Corazón said.

Another two minutes. Same response.

Corazón hung up the phone and looked at Bobby. "This is not like Kit. I must go to the office. You will stay here."

"Is something wrong?"

"I am sure there is a reason." But the reason could be trouble.

Kit's head felt like a sandbag, her eyelids like bricks. She tried to open her eyes, fought to do it, then wanted to go back to sleep. Sweet sleep.

No. Have to wake up.

Where was she?

Outside. She felt the cool air on her arms and cheeks. Night. Barely any light. Her lids closed again.

She willed them open.

On her tongue she tasted something stale, bitter. An acrid odor hitting her nostrils helped her fight for wakefulness.

And in that awakening she knew she wasn't dead but thought she should have been.

What had happened?

Hard ground. She was lying on cold, hard ground. What place was this? A wall next to her. The smell of dirt. A distant clanging, like a trolley car.

She was somewhere in the city, and it was night, and she was alone.

On her back, now seeing stars in the small patch of sky. She heard herself moan as she tried to turn over, every part of her held down as if by strong hands.

The man. At her office. He had done this.

What was his name?

Nolan.

Yes, he had done something to her. But what?

Kit's chin angled down on her chest as she fought to raise herself on one arm. She smelled her shirtwaist, and on it was the strong odor of liquor. What was this? Her blouse was wet with whiskey.

How could that be?

God, help me.

She heard voices laughing, and music. The sounds of men having a good time. The sound of a saloon. Why was she on the ground outside a bar? At this time of night?

Up, up! she commanded herself. She shook her head to clear the cobwebs from her mind. The man Nolan, he had knocked her out. Yes. With something sweetly medicinal. Chloroform?

But why?

The scuffling of feet sounded near her. Kit managed to push herself up on her hands and peer upward. The shadowy forms of men gathered around her like dark ghosts. She heard them talking but couldn't make out the words.

"Help ..." she managed to say, the word seeping out slowly like tar from a barrel. Then she heard a man's voice, as thick as her own.

"She didn' wan' dance wi' me. And after I treated her nice."

Kit sensed the men pushing in closer to her. What did they mean to do?

"Let's get her up," another voice said.

"I treated her real nice," the first voice said again.

And then another, more familiar voice. "Hey, that's Kit Shannon!"

Who was that? Where had she heard that voice before?

"One side, one side." Another voice, coming up close for the first time.

She felt something on her. Hands.

Her head was pounding, and the images around her started to swirl.

These men, they were going to do her harm.

Why? Why?

"I treated her nice...."

Who was that?

The strong hands gripped her arms, and soon she was on her feet. She saw a man's face near her own. It was unfamiliar and frightening.

A rush of adrenaline hit her. She was in danger. With that surge of energy she put out her leg, and with a quick motion she had her attacker on his back.

The other men burst into laughter.

"Hey, that's a good one! Did you see her?"

Kit was unable to distinguish the voices. All became a jumble along with her thoughts, which had only one purpose—survival. She turned to run, her legs feeling like sacks of grain but her determination overcoming her infirmities.

She went two steps before falling on her hands and face. Someone had grabbed a handful of her dress.

Kit smelled the dirty ground again. She cried out.

The office was as dark as a tomb.

Corazón flicked on the light and saw only an empty chamber. A law book lay open on Kit's desk, the only sign of recent use.

Corazón locked up the office again and hurried down the hall to Earl Rogers' office. It, too, was empty. At least, no one answered the door.

Now what should she do?

Do not panic, she told herself. There is a reason. Where had Kit said she was going?

Corazón walked down the dark steps. A figure jumped at her presence. She screamed.

"Miss Chavez!" the figure said. "It's me!"

"Mr. Lowden?"

"Yes. You almost scared me to death!" Harlan Lowden was a furrier on the first floor.

"I am so sorry," said Corazón. "I was not seeing anybody."

"You and Miss Shannon are sure acting funny lately."

"Funny?"

"Sneaking around. You're going to get yourselves shot or something. You know I carry a gun on me, don't you? Have to, with the furs and all."

"What do you mean we are sneaking?"

"Like earlier, I saw Miss Shannon slip out of here with some fella."

"Fella?"

"I heard steps outside so looked out my door. Funny thing was, they were headed out the back. I figured she was off with her beau, only ..."

"Yes?"

"It wasn't that flyin' fella, her fiancé. He had no limp. Thought it was curious, but it's none of my business."

Kit had not mentioned a meeting with any man. Who could it have been? "What time was this?" Corazón asked.

"I don't know, a couple of hours ago. And now here you are, sneaking around in the dark. What do you suppose—"

"Thank you!" Corazón bolted out the front doors.

Chapter Thirty

"Let me out!"

Kit's voice echoed off the cold stone walls of the women's jail.

"Quiet!" The woman in the next cell, whom Kit had heard snoring but a few moments before, was an ample, hard-looking sort.

"I'm sorry," Kit said. "There's been a mistake."

"You telling me? Life was my mistake."

"I need to see the jailer." Kit's head throbbed. As far as she could tell, it was morning, but she had no idea what time it was—or how she had ended up here.

"Put in a good word for me, would ya?" the woman said.

Kit was about to call out again, then hesitated. "What are you being charged with?" she asked the woman.

"This is where they let me dry out. Only they don't let me know when I can go."

"You mean they've held you here before?"

The woman nodded.

"Without formal charges?"

"That's how they do business," she said with a shrug.

"Not if I can help it." Kit picked up the wooden stool next to the cot and held one of the legs like a club. She reared back and brought it down on the bars of her cell. It splintered into chunks, leaving Kit with a solid piece of wood in her hands.

With it she began banging on the bars of the cell.

"Say, who are you, anyway?" the woman asked.

"Kathleen Shannon."

The woman peered at Kit with a narrowed gaze. "The lawyer?"

"That's right."

The door at the end of the corridor opened and a matron entered, her expression foul.

"What's all the noise about?" the matron yelled. She held her large ring of keys in beefy hands.

"I demand to be taken to a judge," Kit said.

"Judge? Who do you think you are, the president?"

"Why am I not being released?"

"That's up to the chief."

"Chief?"

"Of police. He's the one said you should be held."

"On what charge?"

"Drunk and disorderly."

Kit gripped the stool leg tighter. "That is an outrage!"

"Lawyers got a right to drink, too," the neighbor woman said.

"Quiet, you!" the matron warned. Then to Kit she said, "I'll tell the chief you've come around."

"You unlock this cell," Kit said. "I want to see him."

"Oh, you will, honey." The matron jangled her keys but made no move to open Kit's cell.

Corazón felt dead from lack of sleep. No sign of Kit. Something was terribly wrong.

And the police proved to be of little help. A tired desk sergeant regarded her with suspicion and did not seem interested in doing anything immediately.

"Your friend will probably show up today, and then you'll feel mighty embarrassed," the sergeant said. The stationhouse was just coming to life, with a few policemen wandering the halls.

"No," Corazón said, "she is not like that. She would never stay gone without telling me of it."

"You never know. I had a husband in here just a couple of days ago, saying his wife was missing. Turns out she was with his neighbor, just a couple of doors down. Of course, they had a lot to talk about when she—"

"Please, what will you do?"

The sergeant sighed. "It's like I said. I got to give this report to the captain, and he decides what to do after that."

"But she may be hurt!"

"What else can I tell you? Now, I got other business to attend—"

"Corazón?"

Turning around, she saw it was Ed Hanratty, the officer Kit had defended on murder charges. He wasn't called "Big Ed" for nothing. His girth was every bit as imposing as his broad shoulders. In his police uniform he looked like a thick blue wall.

"What's the trouble here?" Hanratty asked.

The desk sergeant spoke first. "This one thinks her friend has gone missing, but I'm trying to tell—"

"Miss Shannon?" Hanratty said.

"Sí!"

"What are you doin' about it, Jim?"

The sergeant scowled. "It's going to Cap, same as everything else."

"You don't understand," Ed Hanratty said. "This is Miss Shannon we're talking about."

"I don't care who—"

"Tell Cap I'm reportin' in later." Hanratty took Corazón's arm. "Come on, we'll go find her."

Chief of Police Horace Allen was in John Davenport's office, along with the D.A., both standing there as if waiting for Kit to try and blow them over. Well, she was going to do her best.

"Thank you for the audience!" she said.

Allen was the first to bark. "I'd advise you to calm yourself."

"I don't think I shall. Before I drag both of you before a magistrate, I want to hear—"

"Drag *us* before a magistrate?" Davenport huffed. "I am afraid you do not understand the situation."

"Oh, I understand perfectly. And I am going to make sure that the entire city, nay, the state, understands, as well."

Horace Allen stuck out his chest. "Miss Shannon!"

"I am not finished!" Kit pushed back a lock of hair, not caring for the moment that she resembled a London charwoman. She faced Allen. "You have a woman locked up in a cell right now without cause, and that's a matter for the state's attorney. You may wish to consider your resignation right now."

The look of shock on Allen's face was exactly what Kit wanted. Before he could recover, she shifted her attention to Davenport. "Whatever trumped-up charge you try to level at me, I'll make sure it is recorded in the official reports. It should make a fascinating chapter in my memoirs."

"Memoirs... ?" Davenport said.

Memoirs? Kit thought. Not a bad idea.

"This is nonsense," Allen said. "Let's get to it."

Kit glared at the chief. "So this has been discussed and planned? What are you two cooking up?"

Both of the men seemed to expel the same breath. Allen, his ruddy face starting to glow, threw his hands up in the air. "I am the chief of police of the city of Los Angeles! I will not have a defense attorney accusing me of—"

"Malfeasance?" Kit said. "Fraud? Perjury, perhaps?"

"Enough!" Davenport cried. "Don't you want to do yourself some good here?"

"I don't see any good coming out of this office," said Kit.

"Regardless of that, you'd better listen, Miss Shannon, because something very bad is hanging over your head."

Davenport's threatening tone made Kit stop for a moment. "Fine," she said. "I'll give you two minutes."

"The temerity!" Allen said. "I have a good mind to—"

"It's all right, Horace," said Davenport with a raised hand. "Two minutes is all we need. There is still a chance, Miss Shannon, that this episode will not reach the newspapers."

"What episode?"

Davenport gave a half smile and said, "In view of your very public, shall we say, positions on matters of moral conduct, it would come as quite a shock to the city of Los Angeles that you were found drunk and in the gutter, outside a saloon. That might do more than a little damage to your credibility."

And then, like a lighthouse beam through a night fog, the direction became clear to Kit. "I see. A nice little setup. You had a man knock me out with some anesthetic, pour liquor into me, and deposit me outside a saloon."

"Drunk and disorderly," Horace Allen said. "You attacked a policeman."

"Police—"

"You remember, don't you? Witnesses saw you throw him to the ground. Good thing he caught you by the dress."

"That's a fact," said Davenport. "We have the cop and three other men who will testify about your condition. Not to mention the gentleman who was your escort for the evening, a Mr. Nolan, I believe? It seems you were more than happy to make his acquaintance."

A cold fury nearly sent Kit reeling. "No one will believe you! No one who knows me will believe—"

"You want to take that chance? You want your name spread about by the gossips of your social class?"

"I don't frequent that crowd."

"What about your own crowd? What about all the people who look up to you as some moral beacon in the darkness of this city?"

Kit felt short of breath. In her anger and mounting

incredulity over what was happening, she felt unable to put coherent thoughts together. Only one thought came to her, which was that these men had something to offer. She waited, looking at the two of them like a cornered animal. "What are you proposing?" she asked.

Allen now took the lead. Apparently he had recovered his equilibrium and pride. "Now you're talking sense. I gave you this chance once before, and you threw it back in my face. So now you're ready to listen, eh? It is like this. We can keep all this to ourselves. In return, you will drop your actions against the principals of Western Rail."

"That again," Kit muttered. "Tell me, what does Western Rail have to do with you?"

"It is the entire city we are talking about," Allen said. "I tried to explain it to you the last time. There is a stiff competition going on at the present time for urban transit, and the city fathers believe Western Rail is the best company for the job. We'd like to help them out."

"I am getting in the way, is that it?"

"Plain and simple."

"That's blackmail," Kit said.

Allen stiffened. John Davenport pointed at Kit. "You are in no position to make accusations."

"Then let me understand my ... position. You want me to drop a lawsuit. In return, you'll not press any charges for this charade you set up, for my kidnapping and drugging. Is that the deal?"

Davenport nodded brusquely.

"You two must sleep well at night," Kit said.

"This has gone far enough," Davenport said. "You know what we're discussing here. What is your answer?"

"You are asking me to abandon a woman who lost a child, and also the attempt to make things safer for others who might suffer."

"But your reputation will remain intact," Davenport said quietly. "And you will be able to help others in the future. You don't want your career to end when it is just beginning, do you?"

What jumped into Kit's mind next was the feel of Carry Nation's hatchet. She thought taking it to this office, chopping at the corruption, would be a tonic. But then, for a second, she contemplated what Davenport and Allen had said. To have people believe she was a hypocrite? She thought of the line from Shakespeare about losing a purse being nothing, but losing a reputation being everything.

She then thought of another line, one from a much greater book. *"Blessed are ye, when men shall revile you, and persecute you, and shall say all manner of evil against you falsely, for my sake."*

"My answer is no," Kit said. "Will there be anything else?"

For a moment the silence in the room hung as heavy as an Irish haze. Then Davenport said, "So be it."

Corazón was comforted by the presence of Big Ed Hanratty. She knew he would move heaven and earth to find Kit. Also, he knew the city much better than she.

However, now they were frustrated at where to turn next. Hanratty had questioned two of his informants—denizens of the streets who shared information with the cops when there was a benefit to them, usually in the form of money for drinks.

No help.

"What was Miss Shannon doing the last time you saw her?" Hanratty said. They were on the corner of Temple and Main, near the Plaza.

"It was about Malloy and the death of Billy Rye," Corazón replied.

"Yeah. Where might she have gone on that?"

Corazón thought a moment. "To Glendale?"

"Why?"

"That is where she met with the man Rye."

"Could be. Any other place?"

"Maybe the place it started? Maybe Doogan's?"

"Doogan, eh? I know him well. I also know he'd lie about his mother if it got him a good deal on hooch. Let's give him a try."

Doogan's was around the corner and half a block away. When they entered, Corazón saw a smattering of men drinking, with Doogan at the bar serving up a beer. He looked up and spotted them, and his face turned a shade lighter.

"Hello, Doogan," Hanratty said, leading Corazón inside.

"What's she doing here?" Doogan stared at Corazón as if she were a mangy dog.

"This is a public place, ain't it?" Hanratty took out his billy and began to twirl it by its leather strap.

"What do you want, Hanratty?"

"That's Officer Hanratty to you."

"This isn't your beat."

"The whole city's my beat when it comes to lookin' out for my friends. We're here to ask you if Miss Shannon has been by. You wouldn't happen to know, would you?"

Corazón watched as Doogan's expression became one of devilish glee. "You mean you haven't heard?"

"Heard what?"

"Shannon was here, but it wasn't today. It was last night. And she was with a man."

"Who?" Corazón blurted.

Doogan shrugged. "I've never seen him before. But I wasn't really looking at him. I was looking at her. She was drunk."

Corazón wasn't sure she'd heard the word correctly, yet the grin on Doogan's face confirmed it. "No," she said. "Never."

"If there's one thing I know, it's when somebody is drunk or not. They were only in here for a few minutes—didn't order anything, then went outside. I hear tell she was picked up by the police." The bartender looked at Hanratty with a challenging gaze.

That's when Hanratty with his big fists grabbed Doogan by the shirt. "You're a liar!" he said.

With wide eyes Doogan said, "Go see for yourself! Go back to the station and ask!"

Hanratty pulled Doogan closer. Corazón touched the policeman's arm. "No, do not," she said. "Let us go see."

Chapter Thirty-One

It was 10:30 a.m., and Kit was almost home when she remembered the hearing on Winnie's case was scheduled for eleven o'clock.

Not even time to freshen up! She had a suit of clothes in her office for emergencies, in the event something spilled on her or a dress ripped. So she stopped by her office and quickly changed clothes.

Corazón was not there. Kit knew she was probably sick with worry. She called the house and told Angelita that she was all right.

She rushed into the courtroom at 11:15.

"I am sorry, Your Honor," Kit explained. "I had a little trouble last night."

The judge studied her, a scowl on his face. "Nothing serious, I hope."

Kit felt as though she'd been washed up on some beach. "Nothing that will affect this matter, I assure you."

"Very well. But in the future, please try to arrive to my courtroom promptly."

"Yes, Your Honor."

The judge cleared his throat. His name was Owen Renner, and he had a reputation for fairness. "We are here for the motion by the defendant, Los Angeles Electric and Western Rail, for summary judgment. Mr. Mill, are you ready to proceed?"

"Thank you, Your Honor." Western Rail's lawyer stood and smiled broadly at Kit. "Miss Shannon has alleged a tort based upon negligence. However, she has not proffered any factual basis other than the accident itself. The plaintiff has failed to state a cause of action. And, I would remind the court, the coroner found no blame on the part of Western Rail or Los Angeles Electric."

For the next ten minutes Mill discussed a string of cases from other states that supported his position. Because of the previous night, Kit had not been able to brush up on the law like she would have otherwise. She took copious notes as Mill spoke.

After Mill had finished, the judge looked over at Kit and said, "Miss Shannon, your reply."

Still a bit woozy, Kit got to her feet, holding firm on to the counsel table. "Your Honor, the fact of negligence is at issue here, and it is a matter for a jury. Nor are the findings of the coroner relevant to this proceeding."

She glanced down at her notes. The letters seemed to swim around the page. As best she could, Kit pieced together her thoughts, trying hard to get them to make sense to the judge, and then, when done, took her seat again, spent.

Judge Renner waited for what seemed an hour before speaking. "While this is a close case, I am convinced there is nothing here for a jury to decide, the law being as it is squarely on the side of the defendant. Therefore, I am going to grant the motion for summary judgment."

Kit was not sure she'd heard the words correctly. The next ones came with a thundering finality.

"This case is dismissed," the judge said.

"So it's over?" Winnie Franklin's eyes filled with tears. She had come to Kit's office at the appointed time, unaware of all that had happened to Kit.

"There is always an appeal of the judge's ruling," Kit said gently.

"I wanted this to help others." Winnie shook her head. "Now I fear there will be more accidents like the one that took Sammy."

The door opened and Bobby entered, carrying the cup of soda water Kit had sent him out for. He handed it to Winnie Franklin, who took it without a word.

An uncomfortable silence settled on the office for a few moments. Finally Bobby spouted, "I hate 'em!"

His words startled Kit and brought Winnie Franklin to wide-eyed attention.

"I hate 'em all—for what they done to Mrs. Franklin."

Rather than looking more despondent, as Kit thought would happen, Winnie Franklin actually put on a wan smile. "Thank you, dear boy." Then she added, "The Bible says we must not hate. Isn't that right, Miss Shannon?"

Kit only nodded in reply.

"Can't I hate 'em just a little?" Bobby pleaded. "Can't we fight 'em?"

"I would not be able to stand that, I fear," Winnie said.

"But you have to!" Bobby's vehemence matched what Kit felt inside, only she didn't express it in deference to Winnie's condition. Yes, there was the avenue of appeal, though that could take months, even a year or more. Would Winnie be able to stay the course that long?

"Can't we do something about those guys?" Bobby was practically begging Kit with his eyes. "They're no better than Mr. Beasley! Nobody cares about nobody."

"I'm thankful that you care," Winnie said to Bobby. "Truly." She appeared to delve deep into her thoughts. She looked at Kit. "Is there any other way that is open to us?"

"If there is," said Kit, "I will find it. That I promise."
"Now we're talkin'," Bobby said.

17 April, 1906

My Darling Kit,
They tell me the bay here is wide and deep, with currents that are too much for any man to resist. Funny, I say, how that describes my love for Kathleen Shannon—wide and deep and irresistible. Both are forces of nature, although I prefer the one in Los Angeles.

This city is not unlike others, I suppose, yet it has a spirit about it that is troublesome. While passing the Knickerbocker Hotel on Van Ness Avenue, I noticed a party of ladies and gentlemen who were elegantly dressed. They were very much excited and chattering about their personal effects or some such. A ragged man sat nearby, his hand extended in the mode of begging. The small party stopped, laughed and said, "You'll do." They then proceeded to try to make him sing. It appeared to be some sort of game or sport.

It burned me to see this. So I intervened. I told them this was no way to treat a fellow human being, and so on. They castigated me and then walked away. The ladies, I am sorry to say, had the more expressive language in the group.

Afterward, when I offered to buy the poor fellow a meal, he scolded me for my interference! He said that he had expected to make a substantial sum from the party and that my meddling had cost him a day's pay! He was so indignant he did not wish to accept my invitation for food.

I cannot help but think things are upside down in this burg.

But I digress. I write to tell you that you shall be fascinated with my progress on the Western Rail controversy. I believe I may be closing in on something. I spoke with Addison Dyke himself and found it strange that, while he professed ignorance of Western Rail's interest in the boys' home property it owns, he knew all about you. I trust I will have more to share with you upon my return, which, God willing, will be soon.

You see, I have decided that my next trip will be with you and you alone—to the Hawaiian Islands, for our honeymoon. We must be about finalizing the wedding plans, and then we must be about our married life.

No more interferences! No more business but that which will join us as husband and wife! If anything should try to get in the way, I would, as the saying goes, move heaven and earth to get to you.

For now, the United States mail will have to suffice to send you this small expression of all my love for you. Wide and deep it is. They could never build a bridge across it. God has made it a wonder in this world.

Your loving,

Ted

Chapter Thirty-Two

Ted fell out of bed, his head hitting the floor with a numbing thud.

Was he dreaming? Was this some vivid nightmare?

No. It was dark, and the house was shaking.

A low rumble, like the passing of a train, hit his ears. He knew then what it was.

Earthquake.

The shaking became so violent that it threw down a large bookcase in his chamber. Ted heard the shattering glass and knew it had only missed him by a hair. An armoire fell beside him. More sounds of glass breaking. And the cracking of walls.

Ted was helpless on the ferociously quavering ground. He thought of the time he had crashed in his plane. There was a moment when the air had battered the fabric and frame, shaking both plane and pilot like a child's kite caught in a storm.

That was the feeling he had now, on his back, as the earthquake continued to rumble.

How long it lasted he was not sure. Less than a minute perhaps. When suddenly it was over, the silence felt as ominous as a cave at midnight.

He heard Harlow Hayes shouting from another part of the house.

"Mr. Fox! Are you alive?"

The question seemed oddly funny to Ted, sprawled out as he was. If the answer had been no, how then could it have been given? "Yes!" he answered.

"Thank the Lord! I'm coming for you."

A moment later, candle in hand, Hayes forced open the door. He had to push against the broken bookcase but managed to fight his way in.

Ted struggled off the floor. Other than the blankets from his bed, nothing had fallen on top of him.

"What about Mrs. Hayes?" Ted said.

"She's fine. God was watching over us." His face changed in the candlelight. "The boys!"

"Yes. I'll go with you if you'll help me find my leg."

Ten minutes later they were out the front door. Dawn's light was just surfacing, and in front of them Ted saw that the air had become filled with white dust.

Across the street, where St. Luke's Church had been, Ted now beheld a ruin. The roof and the points of the gables, along with the ornamental stonework, had all caved in. Debris covered the adjacent sidewalk and lay piled up against the sides of the church building to the depth of eight to ten feet.

Next to the church stood a mansion, its chimney now gone, the stone balustrade and carved stonework wrecked.

"This is unbelievable!" Reverend Hayes said.

Indeed it was. Black smoke rose up and cast a thick haze over the skyline, the unmistakable sign of large fires burning.

Ted, with all the speed he could muster, kept up with the reverend. There would be no trolleys today. Maybe not for a long time.

Devastation surrounded them. The sidewalks in many places were heaved up, chimneys from houses strewed about on the ground, with all manner of walls cracked and crumbling. Ted noticed that St. Mary's Cathedral and Grace Church gave no outward sign of their being damaged. He wondered how it was that certain buildings had escaped the disaster.

As they zigzagged onward down California Street and over Nob Hill, Ted caught sight of the business district below. There were as many as a dozen fires raging in the lower part of the city. Smoke ascended in great columns, obscuring the sun, which from here looked like a large copper disk.

Crowds of people were standing around on the streets. Some of them appeared to be dazed, others wildly agitated.

And then Hayes stopped in his tracks and pointed toward a cloud of black smoke. "That's near the boys' home!" he shouted.

Earl Rogers' voice sounded troubled over the phone. "You'd better get down here," he said.

"What is it, Earl?" The phone call had rousted Kit from bed. It was seven in the morning.

"You need to come see me immediately. There was an earthquake early this morning."

"Earthquake? I didn't feel—"

"In San Francisco."

Ted.

"A big one," Rogers added. "And something else."

"What?"

"Just get here."

Kit flew through her morning preparations, sticking her hair up hurriedly and stuffing it under a hat. She told Corazón to meet her later and then hopped in the Ford. She was inside Earl Rogers' office ten minutes after leaving the house.

"Sit down, Kit." Earl was all seriousness, not a sign of his usual jovial self.

Kit stayed standing. "Can we get any word to San Francisco?"

"No. All lines are down."

"But Ted is up there."

"Please, Kit, sit down."

She gave in and plopped into a leather client chair. "What can we do?"

"Nothing right now. I'm sure your fiancé will come through it."

"We don't know that."

"No."

"Any idea of damage?"

Rogers frowned as he sat behind his desk. "A lot of it, first reports indicate. Much of the city is on fire."

"What about phone calls?"

"No phones working at the moment."

"How about telegraph?" Kit was nearly mad with the uncertainty of it.

"I don't know. We'll get more information later. Right now you have other things to worry about, like a murder case and Western Rail."

Earl was right. She couldn't just drop everything and leave her clients in the lurch. She'd have to put aside her concerns for now. That much she could do, she thought, at least for a little while. She was not prepared for Rogers' next bit of news.

"And you need to know about this." Rogers tossed her the morning edition of the *Examiner.* The paper had not had time to report on the earthquake, so the front page was dominated by the report of 2,000 dead in an uprising in Moscow and a scandal involving the family of Adolphus Busch, the millionaire beer baron from St. Louis. "Down at the bottom," he said.

Kit flipped the paper to look below the fold. Her heart went numb.

KATHLEEN SHANNON SUCCUMBS TO DRINK
Local Attorney Falls to Demon Rum, Says Companion

She looked up from the headlines, tears stinging her eyes. "They did it," she whispered. "They went and did it."

"I don't believe a word of it, Kit. I want you to know that."

She flung the paper across the office. "They tried to blackmail me!"

"Who?"

"Allen and Davenport. They said if I didn't withdraw from the Western Rail case, they'd do this! But the judge threw the case out yesterday. They went ahead with it anyway."

Rogers' eyes gleamed with fresh malice. "I can see Davenport's fingerprints on this. But he wouldn't let this story out unless he had all of his ducks in a row. With Allen in on it, he's practically got everything covered."

"What am I going to do?" Kit said.

Rogers lifted a copy of the *Times* from his desk. "It's not in the *Times,*" he said. "My guess is Tom Phelps may have been approached with it. Why don't we go find out?"

"We?"

"You think I'm going to let the powers that be defame my protégée? Come along, Kit, we'll fight 'em together."

"Before we go anywhere," Kit said, "we're going to send a wire."

The boys' home had avoided the fires but had sustained much damage. Ted thanked God that all of the boys had managed to make it out of the building without injury.

With the children now safely out on the lawn, Ted could relax for the moment. The fires continued to burn down below. The city was in complete chaos. A horse pulling a trundle ran past the boys' home, scared out of its wits. As it passed by, the trundle tipped over, spilling its contents—newspapers.

The news was dated already, Ted thought. The papers would have been printed late last night, well before the earthquake. It was the *San Francisco Chronicle,* the Hearst paper. Ted shook his head. Hearst, with all his sensationalism, couldn't have foreseen this. Although if anyone was going to manufacture this sort of story, Hearst would be the one. He glanced down at the front page, which carried a story out of Russia. Some uprising that was put down by the Czar's army. He turned the paper over. At the bottom right, the type jumped off the page.

L.A. ATTORNEY, VOICE FOR TEMPERANCE, FOUND DRUNK
Kathleen Shannon Went on Binge, Male Companion Says

His heart in his throat, Ted read the article with a growing sense of disbelief.

> The noted Los Angeles lawyer, Kathleen Shannon, was discovered drunk outside a saloon late last night, apparently after hours of carousing with a male companion.
>
> Police arrested Miss Shannon for public drunkenness. Her companion, an unidentified man, was questioned and released. According to police, the man is a traveling salesman who had called on the attorney earlier in the evening.
>
> *Miss Shannon is well-known to Los Angeles as a devout Christian and, more recently, a voice for the temperance movement. She is currently representing a man, Abner Malloy, on the charge of murder.*

"I've got to get out of here," Ted said. He looked up and noticed no one was around to hear him.

The city was in turmoil. And so were his thoughts. He found he was wandering now, walking toward downtown. Toward the fires.

Chapter Thirty-Three

The telegraph office had turned into a madhouse. Men and women, young children, and every other type of citizen were stuffed inside the Western Union building and spilling out into the street.

Kit tried to squeeze inside but couldn't make it past the outer row of people. She saw, just inside the doorway, a man in a visor gesticulating wildly with his hands. He was saying something, but Kit could not hear him over the din of the crowd.

Desperate, she grabbed the shoulder of the man in front of her and asked if he had heard of any way to get in touch with people in San Francisco.

He shook his head. "Lines are all out is what I'm hearing."

"Surely there's a way to get a message somewhere up there."

"Carrier pigeon maybe," the man said.

"Has there been any report of casualties?"

"You mean the names?"

"Anything posted in the window?"

"No, ma'am. My sister's up there, and I know she would have called me if she could. Do you have someone up there?"

"Yes. My fiancé."

"God help them both," the man said.

Kit turned back to Earl Rogers and said, "This is going to tear me apart."

Rogers patted her on the shoulder. "I promise you I will check back here every hour on the hour. Right now, though, I want to talk to Tom Phelps."

They found Phelps in the midst of a clamor; the city room of the *Los Angeles Times* resembled a beehive after being poked with a stick.

"Tom!" Kit attempted to flag down the reporter, who was rushing from one desk to another, screaming at people, trying to get information. "Tom!"

He stopped and turned when he finally heard his name. "Kit, I can't talk to you now!" The reporter saw Earl Rogers standing next to her. "Unless you have reports for me from San Francisco, that is."

"Ted is up there," Kit said.

"I'm sorry."

"Are you getting any news?"

"One of our people just called in from Stockton. He says an insane asylum fell to the ground and now the streets are rampant with crazy people who are breaking windows and screaming their heads off."

"Is there any way to contact anyone in the city?"

"I'm afraid not."

Kit held her anxiety in check. "Then can you tell me about the story in your rival paper?"

Tom looked at her with a knowing gaze. "Are you talking about the claptrap that portrays you as a drunken hypocrite?"

"Thank you for softening the blow, Tom."

"I think it stinks."

"That makes two of us," Earl Rogers interjected. "What I want to know is if you were approached with this story."

"I was going to tell you, Kit," Tom Phelps said. "But then the earth shook up north, and I haven't had the chance."

"What do you know?" Rogers asked.

"Only that I got an anonymous note with the names of several witnesses who said they saw Kit stone-cold drunk. I didn't believe it for a second."

"Do you have any idea who might have written that note?"

"None."

"Do you still have the note?"

Before Tom could answer, a voice shot out from the other side of the city room. "The trains aren't running! There's no way to get out except by catching a ferry to Oakland!"

Kit pictured Ted in her mind, trying desperately to escape. If he wasn't dead.

"Can't talk now!" shouted Phelps. "Later." He turned back to his business.

"One good thing about the earthquake," Earl Rogers said.

"What is that?"

"People won't be caring too much about your story."

"I'd rather know where Ted is," Kit said.

Ted hurried past an almost solid wall of flame on the north side of the street. The heat was near to unbearable. He paused, wondering why there were no fire fighters in sight. Most of them were probably down in the financial district, Ted thought. Save first the money.

Then Ted recognized the shoeshine man, the one known as Digger. He stood off to one side, gawking at the flames that shot up like silks blown by the wind. The poor man's eyes had a wild look in them.

"Where is your gear?" Ted said upon approaching him.

The man did not so much as twitch.

Ted grabbed his shoulders and spun him around. The crazed stare of the bootblack was indication to Ted that this man was not going to be of any help, to himself or to others. "Come along," Ted said. He took the man's arm and started leading him away from the fire.

"No!" Digger jerked his arm away and ran like a scared rabbit.

Ted had no way to catch him. He watched as Digger disappeared around a corner. Ted uttered a silent prayer for the man, and then he thought of something.

Turning around, Ted saw the damaged building that was the home of Sutter, Wingate & Finn. Men were scampering in and out of the building. Then Ted spotted Beaumont. He was not the immaculately dressed lawyer he had seen on Monday. Now he was a man who looked like his whole world, and not merely his city, was on fire.

His coat was gone, and his white shirt was smudged with soot. His face was a picture of fear. In his hands was a box. He began running down the street, toward some unknown destination.

Ted followed him.

Beaumont continued around a corner and seemed to be heading for a cart that was waiting for him. Suddenly he stopped, put the box down, and fell to his knees.

Ted reached him. "Can I help you?"

Beaumont reacted as if a ghost had screamed in his ear. He fell backward onto his haunches and stared up at Ted, eyes wide.

"What are you doing here?" he said.

"May I help you?" Ted repeated.

"No! Get away from me!"

Ted didn't budge. "Please, give me your hand."

Beaumont ignored the offer. His look became one of sadness. "Why is this happening?" he asked.

Ted reached down and grabbed Beaumont's arm, helping the man to his feet. Beaumont let him, clearly shaken.

Once up, however, Beaumont snatched his arm away from Ted and screamed, "Leave me alone!"

The lawyer picked up the box he'd been carrying and staggered toward the cart. Ted watched as Beaumont thrust the box into the cart and turned back. Seeing Ted still there, he took to the street rather than the sidewalk so as to avoid him.

Ted noticed that, here under the orange-and-brown glow

of a narrow side street, he was alone. His eyes turned to the cart. It held perhaps a half dozen boxes. Boxes from the law firm, he figured. Boxes containing what?

Ted did not hesitate. He practically charged the cart. Beaumont, or someone else from the building, would be back soon. If they should catch him rifling through the boxes, what then?

He knew a good defense lawyer.

He opened a box.

Chapter Thirty-Four

The next morning Los Angeles seemed to have found its equilibrium again. Which meant that the preliminary hearing in the case of Mousy Malloy was going to take place, no matter Kit's anxieties about Ted's predicament. Corazón joined Kit and Mousy at the counsel table, ready to take notes.

Clara Dalton Price called the coroner to the stand, and it seemed to Kit that Dr. Smith took great pleasure describing the cause of death. His comparison of the victim's brain to a sliced grapefruit was a bit much, she thought. Kit wasted no time in getting to the heart of her cross-examination.

"Dr. Smith, you have no way of knowing the identity of the killer, do you?" Kit asked.

"No."

"There is nothing in the condition of the body of the deceased that would offer any clue about the killer's identity, is there?"

"Well, it was a man."

"You don't know that for certain, do you?"

"I do," the doctor stated. "The force of the blow had to be dealt by a very strong person."

"Is it the contention of the coroner's office that women are unable to deliver blows of sufficient magnitude as to cause death?"

"That is not what I am saying."

"Are you not making a great leap in logic when you say only a man could have killed the victim in this matter?"

"I don't deal in logic."

"That much is certain," said Kit.

Laughter erupted in the courtroom. Clara Dalton Price objected, yet this seemed a formality and nothing more. It was quite clear the prosecutor remained confident in her case.

"The murder weapon was a hatchet, isn't that correct?" Kit asked.

"Yes."

"And you have no way of knowing who wielded that weapon, do you?"

"I don't deal with evidence, either."

"My question in this case is—" Kit spun around to look at Clara Dalton Price—"who does?"

Before Mrs. Price could object, Kit addressed the court by saying, "I withdraw the question," and sat down.

Next in line for the prosecution was a police officer, the one who found the hatchet that had been used to kill Billy Rye. Mrs. Price produced the weapon and asked the officer if in fact it was the one he'd found. After he answered in the affirmative, Mrs. Price moved that the hatchet be admitted into evidence.

"I object on chain-of-custody grounds," Kit said. "The prosecution has not shown who had possession of this weapon from the time it was found until it reached court today."

Mrs. Price scowled. "We will have to call more witnesses to establish that, Your Honor. This is only a preliminary hearing."

"Nevertheless," Judge Trent said, "the rules of evidence still apply."

With a sharp look at Kit, Mrs. Price replied, "Very well. We have only one more witness to call—Eli Autry."

A name unfamiliar to Kit. And she did not recognize the man who came forward. He wore the clothes of a neatly dressed wrangler—denim jeans, boots, and a string tie that was in fashion in the 1880s. His face had a weathered look, as one who spent a good deal of time in the sun.

"Mr. Autry," the prosecutor began, "what is your line of work?"

"I'm a cowhand."

"Work for hire?"

"Yep."

"And where were you on the evening of April 15, at approximately nine in the evening?"

"I was at the corner of Aliso and Main."

"Down near the Plaza?"

"That's right."

Kit watched the man's eyes as he spoke. A little too glib, she thought.

"What were you doing at that time?"

"Heading home."

"Where is home?"

"Out in Glendale. I was waiting for the Glendale trolley."

"While you were waiting, did you happen to see anything odd?"

The witness nodded. "I sure did. I saw him." He pointed at Mousy Malloy.

"Where did you see the defendant?"

"Across the street, staggering toward me."

"Did you say *staggering*?"

"Yep. The man had a snoot full—that is for certain."

"Objection," Kit said. "Mere opinion."

"Sustained. Continue, Mrs. Price."

Clara Dalton Price did not hesitate. "Did you see anything in the defendant's hand?"

Kit leaned forward, watching Autry's eyes.

"I sure did. A hatchet."

"How did you know it was a hatchet?"

"Because I saw it. And then I saw him put it under his coat and get on the trolley, same time as I did."

"Did you see anything else after that?"

"I glanced at him a couple of times, but when we got to Glendale he jumped off and stumbled into the night."

"Thank you. Your witness."

There was something overly smooth about this testimony and also the way Mrs. Price handled it. Kit had several ideas swirling in her mind as she went to question Autry.

"Sir, you said you were at the corner of Aliso and Main at nine o'clock, is that right?"

"Yep."

"What were you doing downtown at that hour?"

The question seemed to take him slightly by surprise. "Nothing in particular."

"You just happened to be there?"

"I'd had a meal."

"You live in Glendale but came downtown for a meal?"

"Sure."

"Where did you eat, sir?"

Autry scratched the back of his neck. "I can't rightly remember."

"Think harder."

He looked at Kit like a man insulted. "I told you ... I don't exactly remember."

"Yet your memory is clear enough to recall what Mr. Malloy was doing and holding in his hand?"

"Well, yes."

"Isn't it true that there are several saloons along Aliso that cowhands like to frequent?"

Autry shrugged. "I don't know that, ma'am."

"I see. And if we were to show your photograph around there, none of the barkeeps would recognize you, is that right?"

Again Autry reached for the back of his neck. "Hey now, I'm just in here to tell what I saw."

"Your Honor, please direct the witness to answer my question."

Judge Trent said, "Mr. Autry, please, just answer Miss Shannon's question."

"I don't know," the witness said. "I may have been in a few places down there."

"Do you drink, sir?" Kit asked.

"Why, who doesn't?"

"Sober people," Kit said, to the delight of the gallery. "You'd had a `snoot full' yourself, hadn't you, sir?"

"No, ma'am. I was as sober as a judge." Autry glanced over at the bench and added, "In a manner of speaking."

There was no way to disprove the witness's testimony, Kit knew. Not at this time, anyway. But perhaps later there would be a crack to open wider. "Tell us," she asked, "how did the D.A. find you?"

"I beg pardon?"

"Find you as a witness, how?"

"I went to them, told them what I seen."

"What prompted your concern?"

"Just what I read in the papers."

"Very convenient for the D.A., wasn't it?"

"Objection!" said Mrs. Price.

"Sustained."

"Sir, you claim to have seen my client with a hatchet. At night. From across the street. After you may or may not have had a few drinks—"

"I said I didn't drink that night!"

"Still, isn't it possible that what you saw could just as well have been something else, say, a bottle?"

"No, ma'am. It was a hatchet."

"Nothing further," Kit said, then added, "at this time."

When she sat down she whispered to Corazón, "Follow Autry after he leaves the courthouse."

Corazón nodded.

Mrs. Price rested the People's case. Kit argued to the judge that there was not enough evidence to bind Mousy over for trial on murder charges.

The judge disagreed. Trial was set for two weeks later.

It was dynamite.

The documents inside the leather satchel Ted had looped around him had the potential to blow the city of Los Angeles, and maybe the whole state, wide open.

If he could get them to Kit in time.

The Oakland train depot was overflowing with people who looked like refugees from Russia. Having finally managed to get over to the other side of the bay, he now faced the challenge of finding a place on the next train heading south.

Meanwhile, he'd tried to get in to send a wire to Kit, but the office was overwhelmed. If he caught a train, he'd probably get to Los Angeles sooner than a wire.

If.

Lord, find me a spot!

Ted almost fell a couple of times, his false leg little help in dealing with the jostling throng. At least he'd made it this far, to the platform, though getting aboard would be another matter entirely.

And was it just his imagination—troubled as it was by the explosive material he had procured off Beaumont—or was someone on this platform following him?

How could that be? He'd been left alone on the ferry over, had even struck up a conversation with a friendly, dutiful policeman.

Now, however, as he made his way closer to the train, the thought occurred to Ted that the policeman might have deterred a phantom tracker.

Ted stopped for a moment, looking quickly behind him. Only a sea of faces, all locked within their own desperate circumstances, met his gaze.

You're daft, man. Get on the train.

"No more room!" a conductor shouted from the steps.

But there has to be! Ted struggled forward, his cane barely keeping him upright. He had to get to Kit.

Chapter Thirty-Five

The telephone jangled Kit out of her prayers. It was Corazón.

"The man Autry went to the office of the trolley line," Corazón said. "He went there after the courtroom."

"What would he be doing there?" Kit wondered aloud.

"He does not work for the trolley."

"Or maybe he does. Corazón, meet me back here at four. I have a business call to make."

Before leaving her office, Kit prayed once more for Ted's safety. Her spirit was troubled for him, and she wanted God's hands firmly around him. *Bring him back home soon.*

She prayed all the way to the office of Los Angeles Electric, both for Ted and for her mission here. It was sure to be a brash bluff, but she was counting on the surprise factor. Before Stanton Eames could formulate a story, she wanted to observe his face.

The place was as cold and unwelcoming as it had been the last time Kit had come here. The austere woman behind the desk recognized Kit immediately and stood up to block her entrance.

Which is why Kit merely nodded and then burst through the door behind the desk without an invitation.

The last thing she saw was the chin of the receptionist dropping in shock. "You can't!" the woman said.

But Kit already had.

She remembered the way to Eames' office at the end of the corridor. She did not bother to knock on his door before entering.

"Woman, what is the meaning of this?" Stanton Eames bellowed. As he stood up from his desk his knee hit an open drawer and rattled the entire surface.

Before Kit could answer, the receptionist stumbled into the room. "I'm sorry, sir, I couldn't stop her."

Eames gave her a curt nod. "It's all right. Close my door and call the police down here."

With a look of satisfaction, the receptionist huffed from the room, slamming the door behind her.

"Your intrusion is not appreciated, and I shall press charges," Eames said, rubbing his knee. "If you leave now, without further trouble, I may decide to let it go. But if you—"

"I would like to know what business you had with Mr. Autry," Kit said.

Eames stopped rubbing his knee and froze, staring at her.

"My assistant followed him from the courthouse, and he came here. Paying a witness to give false testimony is a felony, sir."

"Are you accusing me of bribery?" Eames pulled himself up to his full height and stuck his chest out like a boxer.

"But if I get a statement from you, *I* may decide to let it go."

Eames' jaw twitched. "Do you honestly think the authorities are going to listen to you?"

"Perhaps they will listen to Mr. Autry."

"Do not try to bluff me, Miss Shannon. I play poker for high stakes."

"There are many ways to get at the truth," Kit said.

"Such as the fact that Kit Shannon is a drunkard?"

"You know that is not true."

"What I know and what the public believes are two different things."

"Sir, you can believe me when I say you won't be keeping your position of influence for very long, for it is based on lies and corruption."

"Lies when used judiciously are some of the most valuable currency we have."

Kit could scarcely believe the outright crookedness of the man. "You are not going to get your hands on Mousy Malloy's land," she said emphatically.

Stanton Eames raised an eyebrow and said, "And who is going to stop me?"

"The truth will stop you."

"Your version of the truth has been thrown out of court."

"The world is a courtroom, Mr. Eames, and all men stand before the Judge."

"I'm not interested in debating theology with you, Miss Shannon. Your reputation in this community is not what it once was. Any hope you have of recovering it will involve leaving the men of business alone so that they may do their work."

"Well, if my reputation is at such a low ebb, then I have nothing to lose by going forward and doing anything I can to bring you down."

Eames blinked twice before Kit turned her back on him and walked out of his office.

"What are you calling this?" Earl Rogers said.

"A press gathering," Kit said. "Or a conference. Something like that."

"You are planning to call all the reporters in town and ask them to gather on the steps of city hall?"

"Precisely."

She had just briefed Rogers in his office on the face-off she'd had with Eames.

Rogers shook his head. "I have been known to court the press while working a trial, but I've never conducted a trial outside the courtroom before."

"Why shouldn't we?"

"There are laws against slander, although those are suspended when a trial is in session."

"The truth is a defense. And with all of the reporters there to act as part of the public jury, there will be plenty of witnesses to what we do and say."

With a grin Rogers said, "I never dreamed you would outdo me in audaciousness. If you get away with this, they're going to have to start sculpting a statue of you to place in the center of town."

"I doubt that," Kit said. "All I want is justice for Winnie Franklin."

"Then you need something more, Kit. It can't just be your word out there."

"I've got a little evidence."

"But have you got a witness?"

Kit sighed and shook her head.

Rogers stood and moved to one of the windows of his office. "Let's find one," he said.

"A witness? How?" Kit asked.

He turned to face her. "Like the old days, eh? When you and I used to hash out cases together. Let's start from the top. Go over everything up to this point. I've found that if you dig hard enough, you can always find a nugget. So let's start digging."

Chapter Thirty-Six

"Everybody ready?" Earl Rogers called out to the reporters.

The men of the press, all of them smiling, nodded. They were happy to be here, even if it was early on a Saturday morning. This was news. This was Earl Rogers and Kit Shannon.

They were gathered, as planned, on the steps in front of city hall. A few other interested onlookers joined them. But mostly it was reporters, the majority of whom Kit knew by sight. Some were strangers, yet at least they were here. Kit didn't care if they came from the city room or the society page. All she wanted was as many of the press as possible to show up. Earl's reliable assistant, Bill Jory, had made the calls.

"Then I give you Kathleen Shannon, attorney-at-law." Earl waved his hand toward her, and Kit took her place on the top step.

"Gentlemen, I thank you for coming," she said.

"This better be good!" a reporter shouted.

"It will be," Kit promised. "We are here to conduct a trial. We are not in a court of law, because the court here has decided this matter is not sufficient for the system. So we are going to create our own system, right here on the street. You will be the jury; you will decide whether this is an issue that will go away or remain. Therefore, you are the last line of defense for what is right and just in this matter."

"You gonna swear us in?" a voice said.

"Why should I do that?" said Kit. "You gentlemen always tell the truth, don't you?"

They roared with good-natured laughter. There were no further protests.

"I give you now my opening statement," Kit began. "On the morning of April 2, a woman named Winnie Franklin, a widow, was walking with her young son, Sammy, down Broadway. She intended to buy him a suit of clothes that day. Along the way they stopped to watch an organ-grinder and his monkey. A neighbor of Winnie Franklin's happened to be there and swooned due to the heat.

"In the next few moments Sammy ran out into the street, after a coin that a boy had thrown. When Winnie went to look for him, she heard a scream coming from the street. Sammy was standing on the trolley tracks in the middle of Broadway.

"It was, by then, too late. Winnie saw the trolley hit her son and kill him."

There was not a sound rising from the steps of city hall. It seemed for a brief moment that all activity in the city had come to a halt. Then, from behind, Kit heard the voice of an agitated man, who shouted, "What is the meaning of all this?"

Kit recognized him as one of the aides to the mayor. "A public meeting," Kit answered, "as provided under City Ordinance 110. So long as there is no interference with the orderly operation of city activity, a public gathering shall be allowed to operate. We have the city police on hand to keep order."

"We were told nothing of this," the aide huffed, his pince-nez glasses nearly falling from his face.

"Notice is not required," Kit said. "But if Mayor Tillinghast would like to come out here for the festivities, we would be more than happy to have him. In fact, his name just might come up."

"What? In what fashion?"

"Perhaps as a material witness to wrongdoing."

The aide looked over the crowd of reporters, who all smiled at him and took notes. This seemed to disturb the assistant enough that he swiftly turned and retreated back into the city hall building.

"I am now ready to call my first witness," Kit said.

The call came to Stanton Eames as he was lighting his third cigar of the morning. "What is it, Tillinghast?" he barked into the phone.

"That attorney, Shannon. She is staging some sort of spectacle outside my doors!"

"What the devil are you talking about?"

"I can see her from my window! She's got a bunch of reporters and even Earl Rogers out there with her."

"What is she doing?"

"I don't know. Some sort of mock trial. Hunsucker's in here and looks as though he's going to have a heart attack."

"Calm down," Eames said, even as cigar ash fell onto his shirt. He quickly swept it away. "What can she possibly do?"

"I don't know!" Tillinghast's voice was rising into a squeal. "But she said she might bring up my name!"

"She's bluffing. Besides, her reputation is mud. We took care of that."

"All those reporters out there don't seem to think so."

"Don't worry yourself. I'll phone Allen and have him put a stop to it. Just don't put your foot in your mouth, where it always seems to reside. You've got half a year until the election."

"Hurry up, will you?"

"This is my assistant, Corazón Chavez," Kit said to the

reporters. "She did some digging into the Los Angeles Electric Trolley Line and found out about their work routine." She turned to Corazón. "Tell us what the normal hours for a motorman are during the day."

"They work for two hours in the morning, beginning at eight o'clock," Corazón said. "They are then given a break for one hour. After that, they are back to work for three hours. Another break, then two more hours' work."

"If you gentlemen want to verify that," Kit said, "you may do so at your leisure."

Kit put her hand out, and Corazón handed her a sheaf of papers. "I have here the official transcript of the coroner's inquest in the death of Sammy Franklin."

The reporters listened; Kit could feel it. Like when a jury was hanging on her every word.

Slowly she flipped the pages until she came to the one she wanted. "According to the transcript, the accident took place at 11:22 a.m. on the second day of April. The motorman was one Norman Bittaker. He was putting in his third hour, after taking his morning break. And where did he take his break? Where was Mr. Bittaker immediately before taking charge of his car?"

"Where?" a reporter wanted to know.

"I call my next witness, Mr. Sam Hartrampf."

A sheepish Hartrampf stepped nervously forward. Kit gave his arm a reassuring pat before facing the reporters again.

"Mr. Hartrampf was a witness in the Malloy trial, a part of the scheme that resulted in a trumped-up attempted-murder charge against Malloy. Mr. Malloy will not file a civil complaint against Mr. Hartrampf, however, because he has come forward today to tell you what else he saw in Bill Doogan's saloon."

The reporters seemed to lean forward as one.

"Go ahead," Kit said.

The gap-toothed drugstore clerk cleared his throat once. "It's true what Miss Shannon says, about me being in on what happened at Doogan's. There were others there, too. And—"

He was interrupted by the loud clang of bells raking through the air. The reporters' heads turned toward the street.

Kit thought at first it was the fire brigade but then knew exactly who it was.

"Listen," Kit shouted to the reporters, gaining back their attention.

"It's the chief, Kit," Tom Phelps said. "Why do I have a feeling he's coming for you?"

"I have the same feeling," said Kit. "Tell them, Mr. Hartrampf."

As if having difficulty finding his words, Hartrampf sputtered, "Like I said, I—"

Just then the paddy wagon of the Los Angeles Police Department, pulled by two angry horses, jerked to a stop in front of the city hall steps.

"Go on!" Kit urged her witness.

"Stop!" The booming voice of Chief Horace Allen ricocheted up the steps. "This is an illegal gathering!" He stormed forward, a very large cop right behind him.

A reporter shouted, "Hey, Chief, we're busy here. There is a trial going on."

Chief Allen ignored him. "Kathleen Shannon, you are under arrest."

Kit's chin dropped. "Arrest? There is nothing illegal about gathering on the steps of city hall in the middle of the day."

"I'll let the D.A. figure that out," Allen said. "I have a duty to keep order in this city. Now, are you coming along peacefully?" He nodded at the big cop, who immediately took Kit's arm.

"Tell them, Mr. Hartrampf," Kit pleaded.

Sam Hartrampf looked as scared as a cornered cat.

"You," Allen said to the nervous witness, "don't say another word, unless you want to go to jail yourself!"

Kit struggled in the cop's iron grip. "You can't stop him from speaking."

"Let's go," Allen ordered.

A press photographer managed to discharge a flash as Kit was being pulled toward the wagon.

She looked at the reporters. "Be sure to spell the chief's name correctly," she yelled. "That's two *L*'s in Allen!"

"Don't worry, Kit," Earl Rogers called after her. "We'll have you out in no time. And we'll get a statement from—"

Rogers interrupted his own words with a look of astonishment. Kit saw why. Sam Hartrampf had taken off and was running as fast as he could down the street.

The last face Kit saw before stepping into the back of the paddy wagon was that of Jack London. He was eagerly scratching down notes.

Chapter Thirty-Seven

It was ironic, Ted noted, that the train belonged to Western Rail. It seemed one of the slowest and most inefficient modes of transportation on the face of the earth. It was packed to bursting with all manner of desperate people.

And it was heading down the coast toward Los Angeles at a pace a man walking briskly could have matched.

No matter. That he had snatched a seat was miracle enough. Soon he would be back at the depot in Los Angeles, able to deliver into Kit's hands the ammunition one panicked lawyer had provided to him.

Ted held the leather satchel to his chest, in part to save room. He was sitting on a bench between a man, whose girth about equaled his height, and two young boys—somewhere between eight and ten—who chattered continually of baseball.

The smell of tobacco smoke, mingled with the smell of sweat from the horde of passengers all around him, was almost too much for Ted to bear. At least the large man next to him, who sat by the window, had lowered the glass so the outside air, though tinged with coal dust, might come shooting into the railcar.

Ted closed his eyes and thought of Kit. He prayed he would reach her soon. He dared not get off the train when it stopped, for fear he would lose his spot.

One of the boys shouted that Ty Cobb was the best hitter in baseball, to which the other answered back in no uncertain terms that it was Nap Lajoie and anyone who thought different was a rube.

With a smile Ted leaned over and said, "Honus Wagner led the National League three of the last six years in batting average. That's no small potatoes."

Both of the boys looked at him with mouths half open, but before either of them could speak, they were distracted by a tough-looking man who had approached them after pushing his way through the unruly crowd. Ted glanced up and saw a face full of serious business staring down at him.

"Can I help you?" Ted asked.

The man nodded. "I believe you have something that does not belong to you."

The back of Ted's neck began to tingle. He kept his face calm. "I'm afraid I don't know who you are or to what you're referring."

The man took two quarters from his pocket and handed one to each of the boys. "You two run along for a little while," he said. "I have some business I need to discuss with this man."

The boys were eager enough to take their gifts and leave lickety-split.

The stranger sat on the bench next to Ted, turned, and said, "I believe you do know me, or at least you know my employer. A prominent law office in San Francisco."

"There are a number of law offices in San Francisco," Ted said, keeping his eye on the tough man's hands. The man wore a large overcoat and kept his hands in his pockets.

"I think you know which one I mean," the man said. "I'm here for the documents you have in your possession. Give them to me now and there won't be any trouble."

Ted let his gaze linger on the man for a moment. "Let us suppose I knew what you are talking about. You are hardly in any position to do anything untoward on a crowded train."

"I have other alternatives. You forget that you are riding as a guest of Western Rail."

"I must say, then, as your guest, your hospitality leaves much to be desired."

The man blinked a couple of times. "Give me the satchel or I will be forced to take it." His hand moved in his right coat pocket.

"Are you going to shoot me?" Ted said. "What will *that* do to guest relations?"

Speaking so as not to be heard by anyone else, the man said, "Now, Mr. Fox."

"If you want the documents that much, I suppose you won't mind a little inconvenience." And then, with a swift motion of his arm, Ted tossed the leather satchel out the open window of the train.

With a look of shock and outrage, the man in the overcoat jumped to his feet and began scrambling toward the back of the train.

Ted knew, however, he would be back.

"This is getting to be a habit with you, Miss Shannon." Chief Allen stared at her through the cell bars.

Kit felt that if her eyes could throw flame, she could burn her way out of the cell.

"You should rest now," the chief suggested. "After that I will decide what to do with you."

"We will decide right now!" Earl Rogers said, storming into the corridor, followed by Jack London.

"How did you get in here?" Allen bellowed.

"Unlike you," Rogers said, "your jailer knows the law. I'm here to see a prisoner, as her lawyer."

Allen smiled. "Very well. You may have a conference with the prisoner, and then you will be free to go. But Miss Shannon's status will still be left up to my discretion."

"We will let a judge decide that," Rogers said, "I can promise you."

Allen left the cell chamber with a curt nod.

"I will have a writ of *habeas corpus* before Allen sneezes," Earl assured Kit.

"I'm not worried," she said. "Allen is just buying time."

"Buying time for what?"

"I suspect for the Los Angeles Electric Trolley Line. He has no other interest in shutting me up."

Jack London was busy writing something on a pad of paper. He looked at Kit. "This is going to make a great story once the dust settles."

"The only problem is," Kit said, "I don't know where all the dust is coming from."

"We may know where some of it's from," Earl said.

"What do you mean?"

"Jack here caught up with your boy Hartrampf. He's ready to testify that the motorman was drinking in Doogan's."

London smiled. "It was fun, like the old days in Oakland, when I used this—" he held up a fist—"instead of this." His pencil. "But what was it tipped you off that Bittaker might have been there?"

"Mousy thought he saw a cop in Doogan's, or at least a man in a uniform, and it was the right area."

Jack London wrote some more. *"The Legend of Kit Shannon* should make a good title."

"Just get me out of here," Kit said.

The train jolted. Ted fell forward into the lap of an older woman and just barely avoided being impaled by knitting needles.

Someone had pulled the brake. No doubt the man in the overcoat.

The train had come to a stop in the middle of farmland. Ted knew what he had to do. With a gracious apology to the lady across from him, Ted stood and made his way toward the door of the railcar, opened it, and walked out onto the platform. He leaned around the corner of the car and saw three men, one of whom was the man in the overcoat, running down the tracks. They would find the leather satchel soon enough.

Ted stepped to the other side of the train and lowered himself to the ground. Nearby a scrawny black cow regarded him with a bored expression. Ted moved as best he could along the uneven ground and before long he reached a small shed not far from the tracks.

Now what? he thought. He had no doubt the man in the coat was going to return for him. It would be inevitable once he looked in the leather satchel and saw it contained only air.

Ted patted the documents he had folded once and stuck in the waistband of his pants.

He pushed open the door of the shed. A smell so foul it almost knocked him over issued from inside.

Despite the smell, what he saw inside made him think of Jesus. And escape.

When Kit heard the voice coming from the other side of the lockup doors, she knew immediately who it was.

"I will see her, young man!" Carry Nation was screaming. "Out of my way!"

A moment later Mrs. Nation bolted in, her black dress flowing behind her like an ocean wave. She hardly acknowledged Rogers and London.

"There is something most foul and sinful afoot," Carry Nation said. "You got me out of here once, Miss Shannon, and I intend to do the same for you."

Kit saw Earl Rogers smiling. "I would bet a good twenty dollars that you do it," he said.

"Sir, gambling is also a sin!" Carry Nation whirled on the famous lawyer. "I will not be made the object of sport. I will not be bullied again, nor will I be run out of town by thugs and bullies!"

Earl Rogers bowed to her graciously.

"Thugs?" Kit inquired. "What do you mean?"

"My girls are being hounded by the rabble of this city," Mrs. Nation said. "In some cases roughed up a bit. Property stolen, too! And the police do nothing about it! Is there no law here?"

"How long has this been going on?" Kit said, visibly upset by what she'd just heard.

"Since my girls and I were locked away, remember? It seems the word has gone out into the streets and byways that the voices of reform are not welcome here. Well, I intend to stay! And you, Miss Shannon, will be my lawyer, won't you?"

Kit's mind started spinning. "Earl, get me out of here at once!" she said.

"It's Saturday, Kit," Rogers said. "Allen can keep you here till Monday."

Kit stomped her foot on the floor of her cell.

"If there is some place I can smash for you," Carry Nation said, "just tell me!"

Chapter Thirty-Eight

So this was how Jesus entered Jerusalem, Ted mused. *Well, if it was good enough for the Savior, it is good enough for me.*

The donkey's back was bony, even with the blanket. At least, though, it was moving with some speed, and Ted wasn't falling off.

While the train still waited to resume its trip, Ted had his sights set on a grove of trees perhaps a quarter of a mile away. If he could get there before anyone noticed, he might just have a chance. Of course, riding a donkey across an open field was not the most inconspicuous way to make himself scarce, but he had no other choice.

The grove of short and stocky trees was straight ahead. It would provide him cover, for how long he did not know. He prayed as he jounced, *Lord, get me out of this. And off this animal.*

Behind him the train whistle scorched the air.

He was safe, the train about to set off again. Or was it?

Ted looked back again and saw that the train was not moving. Then three figures appeared in the open space between train and donkey, heading his way.

"Come on," Ted urged the undernourished animal. To its credit, the donkey tried to obey. Within a few minutes Ted was in the grove of trees, though he had no idea which way to go.

Branches reached out and scratched him as the donkey pressed on. Maybe this donkey knew where it was going, he thought. So he decided to hold on and see where the animal would take him.

The donkey's destination turned out to be the other side of the trees, where there was a farmhouse. It was a modest affair, serviceable but not much else. Made of clapboard, it sat atop a knoll and had a well in the front yard. This reminded Ted of how thirsty he was. Grateful, he lowered himself off the donkey, just a couple of feet from the well.

He wondered if the men were far behind him. He estimated it would take them at least ten minutes to reach this point, even if they knew the direction.

Ted was peering over the side of the well, searching for a bucket, when he heard a loud *click* behind him.

Spinning around, he saw a hefty woman in blue overalls, standing on her porch and pointing a shotgun at his stomach.

"What're you doing with my Matilda?" she said. The woman had what appeared to be a chaw of tobacco in her cheek.

"Matilda?"

"You don't like that name?"

Ted patted the donkey on the head. "Oh, Matilda. A nice name, yes."

The woman wiggled the gun at Ted. "Now answer my question. You stole my animal, and I—"

"No, I only borrowed your animal."

"Stole!"

"Well, may I tell you why?"

"That's what I'm asking you for."

"My name is Ted Fox. And you would be?"

"Mighty upset."

"Yes, I can see that." Ted looked behind him, then back at the woman. "I must be brief. Some men are after me."

"What did you steal from them?"

As fast as he could, Ted told the woman the entire tale, up to Beaumont's flight.

When he had finished, the woman lowered the shotgun slightly. For a long moment she studied Ted. "Mister, I think you're tellin' me the truth," she said. "Nobody coulda made up a story like that. My name's Kate and this is my place. Now the question is—"

She raised the shotgun once more.

Ted raised his hands in the air.

Kate said, "Hold it right there!"

Ted turned and saw three men, including the one who had cornered him on the train.

"You can put that gun down, ma'am," the man in the overcoat said, almost out of breath. "He's the one we're looking for."

Kate stepped down off her porch, shotgun still at the ready. "You just keep your hands where I can see 'em."

The three men looked at each other.

"Now!" she said. "This buckshot can do a lot of damage to the leg bones."

The three men slowly put their hands up.

Ted still had his in the air when Kate turned to him and said, "Take Matilda back to the train. Leave her by the tracks. She'll make her way home. I'll keep these gentlemen company until I hear the whistle."

"You can't do that!" said the man in the overcoat.

Kate spat tobacco juice on the ground. "Watch me."

Chapter Thirty-Nine

On Sunday Kit held a church service for the other two girls in jail. The service consisted of a song, "Rock of Ages," and a sermonette.

Kit chose Genesis 39 as her text. The account of Joseph's fall from Potiphar's house to prison. It held the interest of the young women—both prostitutes—who listened quietly and without skepticism. They especially perked up when Kit, preaching from memory, described how Potiphar's wife had tried to seduce Joseph.

"Hussy," one of the girls remarked.

And when Kit got to the part about Joseph being thrown into prison, the girls were positively rapt.

"The Scripture says that the Lord was with Joseph and showed him mercy and favor. He will do the same for you if you seek Him as your God."

The two prostitutes looked at each other. The one who appeared younger—Rose, she called herself—said to Kit, "I don't see how the Lord has helped us much. You, especially. How come they can haul off and throw a lawyer in jail?"

The second woman, Alma by name, pointed at Rose. "Don't you be disrespectful," she said.

"I wasn't tryin' to be," Rose objected.

"But you were. Miss Shannon is telling us how to get right with God, which, if you're wanting my opinion, we need to do."

"I don't believe in God anymore," said Rose matter-of-factly.

Alma snorted. "How can you say that? God hears everything you say."

"That's what I'm afraid of," Rose said. "I still don't see how He's been any help to—"

The door to the cell corridor creaked open. Kit looked up, expecting the jailer. Why would he be coming? It was too early for soup, or what they called soup here.

But it was not the jailer who entered.

"Ted!" Kit reached through the bars of the cell. Her fiancé, looking like he hadn't slept or changed clothes in days, rushed to her and took hold of her hands.

"Earl told me you were here," Ted said.

He held her hands tenderly. Kit felt a warmth race through her entire body. For a moment the bars of the cell disappeared.

That's when the jailer hit the steel with his baton. "No touching there."

"Leave 'em alone!" Alma protested.

The jailer pointed his stick at her. "Quiet, you."

"Go away," Rose said to the jailer.

"Kit, I've got something for you," Ted said. "Earl says you'll be out tomorrow. In the meantime, you can read this."

He held out a folded sheaf of papers. Kit reached for it but never touched it.

The jailer snatched them. "What have we got here?"

As he opened the papers, Ted grabbed them back. Rose cried out with delight.

"Give those back to me," the jailer cried.

Ted threw them into Kit's cell. "Legal correspondence," Ted said. "That's protected, isn't it, Kit?"

No. In truth, the jailer had the right to demand that all

property be inspected before it was passed to a prisoner. But he was not, in Kit's estimation, the smartest of men.

"You have heard of *de minimis non curat lex,* have you not?" Kit said to the jailer.

"The what?"

"You best look it up before you go taking away privileged information."

The jailer looked as if he were lost. He said to Ted, "You. Out."

"Until tomorrow," Ted said.

Kit blew him a kiss.

"Let that be a lesson to you!" Alma shouted at the jailer just before he slammed the door behind him.

Kit picked up the documents off the cell floor.

"Hey," Rose said, "what was that fancy thing you said to the jailer?"

"De minimis non curat lex," Kit said. "It means the law does not deal with trifles."

"It sure spooked him! I gotta remember that one."

While her two jail mates laughed, Kit started to read the papers in her hands. She saw immediately that what they contained was no trifle.

Chapter Forty

John Davenport, the district attorney of the county of Los Angeles, tried to look defiant. But Kit felt her own rising sense of defiance, which seemed to overwhelm her constant opponent.

"You had better sit down," Kit said. It was Monday, late in the morning.

"If it's about your case, we decided not to file charges," Davenport said.

"But you taught me a lesson by letting me sit in jail for a couple of days?"

"You are free now, Miss Shannon."

"This is not about my case, sir. Again, I advise you to sit down."

Davenport regarded her for a moment and, without a word, lowered himself into his chair.

From her briefcase Kit took out one of the pages Ted had given her the day before. "I have here a copy of a memorandum, memorialized via carbon paper. It was issued from the office of Sutter, Wingate & Finn, in San Francisco. You have heard of them, of course."

Davenport swallowed. "Go on."

"The memorandum references the criminal prosecution of my client, Abner Malloy. It urges that the case be prosecuted to the full extent of the law, without dismissal or settlement. It also directs that a sum of ten thousand dollars be placed in a certain account, number 1273, in the Merchants Bank and Trust. I am prepared to subpoena the records of that account as part of a civil action against Sutter, Wingate & Finn."

The D.A. took a labored breath. "Why would you want to do that?"

Kit looked him in the eye and said, "To prove that Addison Dyke funneled money into the private account of the district attorney in order to ensure the felony conviction of Abner Malloy."

"You cannot hope," Davenport said in a subdued tone, "to make a case against me."

"Cases of bribery have been supported on less than this. Even if it does not end up in a courtroom, I am sure the state bar would have something to say. You will never practice law in this state, or perhaps any other, again."

"And you will never get to use that against me. The internal memoranda of a law office are privileged information."

"Not if they contain evidence of criminal acts. There is an appellate-court decision on this point. Shall I look it up for you?"

For the first time since Kit had known him, John Davenport looked as if he had no further cards to play. His face, normally a granite-like visage etched with scorn for all who stood in his way, now had a soft, pale countenance to it.

"Kit," he said, "surely you can't be prepared to make this known. There must be some way we can work together on this."

Now she held all the cards. "There may be something," Kit said.

Davenport's eyes begged her.

"First," she said, "you will drop all charges against Abner Malloy."

The D.A. nodded.

"Second, you will bring to justice the real killer of Billy Rye."

He looked at her, seemingly confused, but more out of some inner dilemma, Kit thought. Finally he said, "What makes you think I know who did it?"

"Call it a hunch," Kit said. "I do not believe, however, that you had anything to do with it or had any previous knowledge. That would make you an accessory before the fact."

"I didn't know; I swear it."

"But you do now, and that makes you an accessory *after* the fact."

Davenport's cheeks began to twitch. "Do you know who did it?" he asked.

"I have a very good idea. I spoke with a few of Mrs. Nation's associates before coming here today. One of them told me that a man broke into her room at the Lancaster Hotel and stole some of her things. Including, it turns out, a hatchet."

"That man could have been your client," Davenport said.

Kit shook her head. "Not from this woman's description. She only caught a glimpse of him as he darted out the window, but what she was able to describe fits someone we both know."

Davenport ran a hand over his mouth as if he were parched. "You don't understand. I can't ... if I ..."

Kit held the memorandum higher. "What choice do you have?"

Several seconds of silence followed in which Davenport seemed poised on the edge of a cliff.

Then he said, "Do you swear to keep what I tell you in confidence?"

"You have my word," said Kit.

Davenport stood, unsteadily. "Come with me."

Davenport was tight-lipped during the drive. The D.A. drove a Peerless, and the auto must have been doing twenty miles per hour at one point. He stopped in front of a small wood-frame building on the northern edge of the city limits, almost as far as Glendale.

Kit followed him to the front door, which Davenport unlocked with a single key. They went inside.

The interior was spare, smelled musty, with cobwebs veiling the corners.

"Come on out, Ellis," Davenport called.

Kit heard a shuffling sound coming from behind a door on the other side of the room. The door opened, and Ellis Dyke, his hair unruly and eyes wide, walked in and faced them. His suit was disheveled, and his tie hung loose around his neck. He looked back and forth between Davenport and Kit.

"What's this all about?" Ellis Dyke said.

"It's over, Ellis," Davenport replied.

"What are you doing with her?" Dyke pointed a shaking finger at Kit.

"She knows."

"Knows what?"

"Enough to figure out the whole thing."

"How could she?"

"Ellis, she knows you stole the hatchet."

"No! That was Malloy! You are supposed to—"

"There's a witness who can describe you."

Dyke flashed his eyes at Kit. "You ought to be shot. You high-and-mighty—"

"Now, Ellis," Davenport said, "that's not going to do any good. I can't protect you anymore. I got you out of jail for that stunt you pulled in court, but I can't keep the lid on the rest. She knows about the whole scheme at Doogan's, the plans to—"

"My father will hear about this!" Dyke said.

"You can tell your father he'll get his money back. I'm going to come clean. And you're going to confess to killing Billy Rye. I will try to—"

"You can't ..." Ellis Dyke started to sputter, losing his words. "We trusted you! My father said you were a man he could count on."

"Things have changed."

"You mean you are going to side with her?" Dyke glared at Kit once more.

"No, I am siding with myself. I have to do what is in the best interest of the county. And this county needs a strong district attorney."

"You won't get away with this," Dyke said. "You are not powerful enough. You know there are others involved."

"The way I see it, you are out on a limb all by yourself and I'm holding the saw!"

An air of wild desperation took hold of Ellis Dyke. How far had he fallen from being the privileged son of a wealthy family? Deceit exposed does ugly things to a man's face.

Suddenly Ellis Dyke looked behind himself like one expecting to see a ghost. He turned back to Davenport and Kit and whispered, "I can give you more. I wasn't alone." He faced Kit. "You have to believe me. I will not take all of the blame. I didn't kill Rye. Please, take me out of here now."

"Take you?" Davenport said, even as Ellis Dyke grabbed him by the coat and, with a frantic look on his face, pulled the D.A. toward him.

"Take me out!" Dyke repeated.

The same door that Dyke had come through now swung open again, this time with great force as it slammed against the wall. Into the room stepped Clara Dalton Price, the gun in her hand pointed straight at Dyke. "You have said quite enough, Ellis," Mrs. Price said.

Dyke looked at Davenport. "She made me do it!" he confessed. "Made me steal the hatchet so she could set up Mousy and—"

The pistol in Mrs. Price's hand exploded. Ellis Dyke fell to the floor, a red blotch spreading across his chest.

For a moment Kit could not believe what had just happened. Not just the gun blast, but the fact that it was Clara Dalton Price who had pulled the trigger. Dyke's groans snapped Kit back to reality. She knelt beside the wounded man, took the handkerchief from Dyke's own coat pocket, and tried to stop the bleeding.

Ellis Dyke's mouth opened and closed as he struggled to

take in air. Kit placed her hand on his cheek. His eyes looked at her with yearning and fear.

"Lord, have mercy," she said.

Dyke's head rolled to the left. He stopped breathing.

Kit stood and faced Clara Dalton Price. "That was cold-blooded murder!"

"No," Mrs. Price said. "Mr. Davenport is a witness. He saw that Ellis Dyke went for a weapon as we were trying to bring him in. So I had to shoot him. The man who killed Billy Rye is now dead. The state is spared the expense of the trial. Isn't that right, John?"

Davenport said nothing.

Clara Dalton Price pointed the gun at Kit and said to Davenport, "It's our word against hers. Besides, she is a hypocrite and a drunk. No one will believe her against the D.A. and his deputy."

"There will be too many questions," Davenport said. "In fact, I have one—why did you do it?"

"You know why!" Clara Dalton Price spat. "I did it for you. And for me. For the office. We cannot have the likes of her"—Mrs. Price waved the gun at Kit—"making fools of us! We both needed a successful conviction of Malloy."

"Why didn't you tell me?"

"There was no need to tell you. I knew sooner or later someone would accuse Ellis here of the deed. I was trying to assure him that all would be well. He was really desperate at the end."

Davenport shook his head sadly. "You shouldn't have done it."

"Don't fold on me now!" Mrs. Price's voice held a large dose of fear all of a sudden.

"We have to come clean."

"Clean? Has she gotten to you?" Mrs. Price looked incredulous. "Then where does that leave me?"

"This has to end."

Clara Dalton Price slowly moved the gun to take aim at the D.A. "Do you think I'm going to take the blame for any of this?" she said.

"I won't be a party to murder," Davenport said.

"You already are. The only question now is whose side are you going to be on, ours or Kit Shannon's?"

And then Ellis Dyke's body jerked violently. Later Kit would come to realize that it was but a spasm. Yet a miracle of timing, too. Mrs. Price looked down at the body and she herself jerked, with what appeared to be fright. Perhaps by instinct she pointed the gun at Dyke.

Kit did not hesitate. Mr. Hancock had taught his ladies to move with quickness and exploit any momentary weakness in an attacker. Combining a leap forward with a cry to wake the dead, Kit sprang into action. She saw Mrs. Price's face turn white at the same time she raised the gun.

Then Kit heard the sharp report of the pistol as her right foot struck Clara Dalton Price's left knee. The prosecutor shrieked in pain.

And Kit felt a burning in her ribs as she fell backward to the floor.

Chapter Forty-One

Stanton Eames could not help thinking that events were spinning out of his control.

Looking out of his office window, waiting for a call from Allen, he knew he would have to strengthen his grip. Tillinghast, for one, was beginning to buck the machine, and such a thing could not go unpunished.

Furthermore, the earthquake in San Francisco had thrown the home office into a tizzy. Couldn't the Dyke family handle a little shaking of the earth? If not, perhaps it was time to make his own move—snatch up the Glendale properties for himself and start his own rail line. Why not? This was America, and America was a land of opportunity.

At least the Shannon woman was being taken care of. Her little stunt at city hall was a direct affront. Now that she was cooling her heels in jail, maybe she'd learn a lesson in power politics.

His office door flew open and his secretary rushed in, her eyes full of alarm. "Sir, I—"

"What is the meaning of this?" Eames said. Before she could answer him, a large uniformed policeman stepped into the office.

Eames' blood chilled. "What ... who are—"

"My name's Hanratty, Mr. Eames, and I'm here to take you in."

"In? What on earth are you talking about?"

"Arrest, sir. You are under arrest."

Speechless, Eames stared at the policeman, waiting for him to break into a grin. This had to be a practical joke. But the officer remained expressionless.

Eames said to his secretary, "Get Davenport on the line."

"Yes, sir," she said and darted away.

"We'll soon get to the bottom of this," Eames said.

"We're already there, sir. It was District Attorney Davenport who ordered your arrest."

"Did I almost die?" Kit asked.

"The doctor said you lost a good amount of blood," Ted said. He sat on the edge of her bed in Sisters Hospital, holding her hand. "It was mainly your head hitting the floor that did it. I told him you have a hard head, though. Irish rock."

She smiled, even as her head continued to ache. "How did I get out of there?"

"You apparently assaulted the deputy district attorney of Los Angeles."

Vague pictures formed in her mind. "She shot Ellis Dyke."

"Yes, and you, too. But it was only a flesh wound."

"Davenport was there," she said.

"He said that you brought Mrs. Price to her knees, and he got the gun and her."

Kit blinked a couple of times, trying to make sense of it all. "When did you talk to the D.A.?"

"He was here earlier, asking about you."

"John Davenport was asking about me?"

"He mentioned something about `cleaning house.' Mrs. Price is in jail, but somehow I think he was talking about the entire city."

Another voice came from the doorway. "That is exactly what he's talking about," Tom Phelps said.

"Who let the press in here?" Ted said.

"It's all right," said Kit. "Tom, what do you hear?"

"That Mayor Tillinghast is singing like a lark about Stanton Eames. Davenport's going after Eames. I'm working on the story. Can I ask you some questions?"

Kit felt her side. It was sore and bandaged. Even so, she felt she should oblige Tom for his having stopped by and wanting to uncover the truth. "Go ahead," she said.

"Do you know a fellow named Nolan?"

"Nolan!" Kit started to sit up, pain knifing through her side. She winced.

"Hold on there," Ted said. "You're not going anywhere."

"Nolan is the man who knocked me out, dropped me outside Doogan's Saloon."

"Tillinghast says Nolan's not his real name. He's a friend of Doogan's," Phelps said. "Doogan wanted you out of his hair and so concocted a scheme to make you look like a hypocrite. I think Tillinghast knew about it, maybe even went along with it, only now he's expressing his concern for your well-being. And he handed Nolan over to the cops."

"Tillinghast has his finger in the wind," Ted said.

"Kit, can you give me the whole story? Exclusive? Before the *Examiner* gets it?"

"What story?"

"I can't figure out how Eames and Dyke and Billy Rye all tie together."

Kit closed her eyes for a moment. Several puzzle pieces jumbled in her mind. "I'm not sure I have it all figured myself," she admitted. "I think it began because Mousy Malloy owns a prime piece of property in Glendale. Not much of a place to look at, just a shack and some undeveloped land. When his grandfather got it in a trade with the mestizos back in 1868, no one had any idea that Los Angeles would soon begin to boom and that people would seek to live outside of the city limits but still find work downtown."

Tom Phelps scribbled furiously. "Slow down, will you?"

But Kit was following after her thoughts as quickly as they came. "And how would people get downtown from places like Whittier and Glendale and Pasadena? By trolley. The horse is too cumbersome, the automobile too unreliable. This is what the railroad men—Addison Dyke, Stanton Eames, and Harrington—are up to. The idea is to get the land rights and then build rail systems to serve that land, which in turn would provide them a constant stream of profit. Not from the fares alone, but from the real-estate ventures."

"How did Malloy's murder trial figure into this?" Phelps asked.

"Mousy did not want to sell his land. I suppose he might have had his price, but at some point the elder Dyke, Addison, felt it was not worth paying. The Dykes, after all, are royalty. The Malloys of this world are supposed to obey and bow down. Mousy didn't do that, so Dyke decided to remove him.

"Murder would have been too obvious, so Ellis Dyke came up with what he thought was a great plan. He set it up so Mousy would be convicted of attempted murder. A convicted felon's land can be acquired by auction, and Western Rail had the money to take it. It would remove all suspicion from Western Rail and Los Angeles Electric and would put Ellis back in good standing with his father, who thought he was a bit of a wastrel."

Phelps kept writing. Kit did not slow her pace.

"The plan was nearly foolproof," she said, "that is, until it began to unravel at the trial. That brought in some uncertainty from the others involved in the scheme."

"What others?" Phelps said.

"I'm guessing Mayor Tillinghast and Chief of Police Allen, along with Stanton Eames. Eames hoped to reach a position where he would take over the lion's share of the rail business in the city. In return, his influence would keep Tillinghast and Allen in power. It would also keep the flow of money coming in from the saloons."

"For protection from legislation against them," Phelps added. "So long as people like Doogan were funneling money to Eames, and through Eames to the mayor's office and police department, they were going to be kept safe from the likes of Carry Nation."

"And Kit Shannon," Ted said.

Kit smiled, then continued, "With Mousy beating the attempted-murder charge—"

"Thanks to you," Phelps said.

"That's when Mrs. Price got involved. I suspect Mousy's escape from the hospital was set up. There was a cop outside his room, yet Mousy still got out the window. I should think Mrs. Price had something to do with pulling the cop off his watch. You'll need to check that. She probably had a man follow Mousy, who ended up talking to him and buying him the whiskey that got him drunk. Mrs. Price knew he wouldn't be able to account for his actions after that. The murder took place within that time frame."

Phelps was breathing rapidly now. "This story is going to make me famous!"

"Tom," Kit rebuked, "you have to check the facts."

"I trust that mind of yours, Kit, but I promise I'll make a few inquiries."

"Are you going to write about the trolley line?" Kit said. "What I was talking about at city hall before Allen hauled me in?"

"Oh, that," Phelps said with disappointment. "The *Examiner* beat us to it."

"The story's out?"

"Today. Tell me, how did you get Jack London on your side?"

Los Angeles Examiner
April 24, 1906

KATHLEEN SHANNON'S NOBLE CRUSADES
by Jack London

I've eyed many a place in my sojourn upon this globe.

I've been to the Klondike and out at sea. I've been a war correspondent in Japan and lived among the people of the abyss in the East End of London. As you can readily imagine, I have seen some tough customers along the way. Men of bravery. Strong men.

But never have I come across a customer as tough as the lawyer Kathleen Shannon. Single-handed she has stood up against Western Rail and Los Angeles Electric and has shown them to be callous and indifferent to the plight of the citizens of this city.

How did she do it? Let us begin with a look at the case of a little boy struck dead by a trolley....

Chapter Forty-Two

"It is nice to see you looking so well," Judge Brander Matthews said.

"Thank you, Your Honor," Kit said. She had been released from the hospital a week earlier, and her side was mending fine. So was her reputation. Tom Phelps's story on the conspiracy against her and Abner Malloy had hit the streets and caused a sensation. Even the New York papers had sent reporters to interview her, and Clyde Fitch, the noted playwright, had sent a telegram asking for permission to turn her life into a theatrical production. There were also offers for her and Carry Nation to go on a national lecture tour together.

But Kit had turned them all down. She did not desire celebrity. What she wanted to do was practice law, here in Los Angeles, for the benefit of clients who needed her help.

People such as Abner Malloy, who was now free—and had returned to the Lord. He had also come through the DT's and sworn off drink.

And people such as Bobby Whitlove.

Judge Matthews looked to the other side of the courtroom, where the lawyer for Chester R. Beasley and the

Beasley Home for Boys sat. "State your motion," the judge said to the lawyer.

"It is quite simple, Your Honor," said the lawyer, whose name was Thompson. "In the absence of a formal wardship, one which would legally grant temporary custody of the boy ..." Thompson then lost his train of thought for a second.

"Whitlove!" Chester Beasley, sitting next to the lawyer, said in a loud whisper.

"Whitlove, yes," Thompson said. "In the absence of such a wardship, the boy must legally be returned to the Beasley Home. It is our understanding that the boy Whitlove is currently in residence with Miss Shannon—on a strictly informal basis."

The judge turned to Kit. "Do you have a response?"

"Yes, Your Honor." Kit moved to the middle of the courtroom. "The laws of California grant preference to the family bond over orphanages. In *Logan v. Superior Court,* it was held that an application for adoption by a single parent is to be given presumptive acceptance against the claims of a public orphanage."

"Yes, Miss Shannon, I am aware of the law," said the judge. "However, in this case you have not sought adoption but wardship. Even that has not been given legal recognition."

Kit caught sight of Beasley leaning back in his chair with a satisfied grin.

"That is correct, Your Honor," Kit said, "although an application for adoption has been filed this morning."

Beasley lurched forward in his chair.

"By you, Miss Shannon?" the judge asked.

"No, Your Honor." Kit motioned to Corazón, who stood at the back of the courtroom. Corazón pushed open the door for Winnie Franklin to enter with Bobby Whitlove. The pair walked forward to the rail.

"This is Winifred Franklin," Kit said. "It is she who has filed for adoption."

"No, this can't—" Beasley began but was cut off by the judge.

"You have no standing to speak, Mr. Beasley," Judge

Matthews said. Turning to Winnie he asked, "Is it true, ma'am, that you have filed for adoption of this boy?"

"Yes, Your Honor," Winnie said, squeezing Bobby's hand.

"Is it your wish to live with this woman as your parent?" the judge asked Bobby.

Bobby nodded and smiled.

"That's it, then. I dismiss the action in this matter. Every boy needs a mother." The judge pounded his gavel on the bench.

Outside the courtroom, Beasley was waiting for Kit. He ignored Bobby and Winnie. "Now I trust you will keep out of my affairs," he said.

"I am only just beginning," Kit replied. "Sir, I would advise you to retain legal counsel. Your days of whipping boys are numbered."

"What? You can't—"

"Oh, but I can."

Beasley's eyes narrowed when he said, "You are a menace to the people of this city."

At which point Bobby Whitlove hauled off and kicked Chester R. Beasley square in the shin. The man screamed out in pain. Kit's initial shock gave way to a smile she could not suppress but quickly hid behind her hand.

"Bobby," Kit said, "you will apologize to Mr. Beasley this instant."

The boy shook his head. "I have the right to be wrong!"

Kit almost laughed out loud but again managed to keep herself in check. "Apologize, Bobby," she insisted.

"I'm sorry," Bobby said, then added, "Sorry I didn't kick your other leg, too."

"Well, what are you going to do about this pup?" Beasley all but screamed.

"Send him home with his mother," said Kit, "where you can't get at him."

Beasley touched his tender leg. "I won't forget this."

"I hope you think about it every waking minute," Kit said.

The man gave one last huff, turned, and limped down the steps of the courthouse.

Then Winnie threw her arms around Kit. "Thank you, Miss Shannon," she said. "You've done so much."

"And so have you."

Pulling back, Winnie looked confused.

"I got word from Tom Phelps this morning," Kit explained. "He found Sam Hartrampf and got the whole story. He went to Mayor Tillinghast with all the evidence from our case, to get him to comment on the story. Apparently the mayor knows what's good for him politically. Tillinghast and the city council are pushing a law through that would require all trolleys in the city to have safety guards."

Winnie Franklin's eyes began to mist and she embraced Kit once more.

"Hey," Bobby said, "we should celebrate."

Kit tousled his hair. "Now, isn't that a fine idea!"

"Come on," he said, grabbing each woman by the hand. "I know a place where they have hot dogs as good as the ones at Coney Island."

Chapter Forty-Three

"Dearly beloved," Reverend Macauley began, "we are gathered together here in the sight of God and in the face of this company to join together this man and this woman in holy matrimony, which is an honorable estate, instituted of God, signifying unto us the mystical union that is betwixt Christ and His Church."

Kit basked in the warmth of the sun's rays touching her through a stained-glass window. She could hardly believe she was finally here. Ted stood beside her, looking so handsome in his black tie and tails, and standing next to Ted, Gus Willingham, Ted's best man, looking quite uncomfortable in a suit devoid of any oil stains.

Kit wore the peau de crepe wedding dress Mrs. Norris had made just for her, while Corazón, her maid of honor, looked as lovely as any flower in Los Angeles in her gown of blue silk.

Kit felt beautiful and more than content. She felt complete.

" ... and therefore is not to be entered into unadvisedly or lightly, but reverently, discreetly, soberly, and in the fear of God ..."

Yes, Kit thought, *the goodness of God is what has brought us here.*

"Into this holy estate these two persons present come now to be joined," continued Macauley.

The church was filled with the fragrance of white magnolias, Kit's favorite flower. Corazón and Angelita had worked on most of the decorations, and the results were stunning. Broad, white silk ribbons adorned the aisles; ropes of greenbrier, with immense bunches of chrysanthemums, festooned the church walls.

And the sanctuary was brimming with those who meant the most to Kit. From Earl Rogers, her mentor and friend, to Jack London, who the day before had told her that he was going to begin writing a memoir entitled *John Barleycorn,* which would bring to light what the liquor culture could do to children.

Many of Aunt Freddy's old friends were present, as well, some weeping for joy, knowing it had been Freddy's wish to see her great-niece hitched, like a respectable woman. They did not seem to notice that also in attendance, at Kit's insistence, were two of her newest clients, Rose and Alma, who had made Kit's acquaintance while in the county lockup. At first they had refused to come, citing their "place" in the order of Los Angeles society, but Kit would have none of it. So here they were in the house of God. Miracles abounded.

Reverend Macauley turned slightly toward Ted. "Theodore Fox, wilt thou have this woman to be thy wedded wife, to live together after God's ordinance in the holy estate of matrimony? Wilt thou love her, comfort her, honor and keep her in sickness and in health, and, forsaking all others, keep thee only unto her so long as ye both shall live?"

Ted, his smile incandescent, answered, "I will."

The minister looked at Kit, his kind eyes glistening. "Kathleen Shannon, wilt thou have this man to be thy wedded husband, to live together after God's ordinance in the holy estate of matrimony? Wilt thou love him, comfort him, honor and keep him in sickness and in health, and, forsaking all others, keep thee only unto him so long as ye both shall live?"

"I will," she said. Never had she spoken more earnest words in all her life.

Macauley took Ted's right hand and guided it to Kit's. "Theodore, please face Kathleen and repeat these vows. I, Theodore, take thee, Kathleen, to be my wedded wife ..."

Ted repeated the vows as Kit gazed into his eyes. "... to have and to hold from this day forward, for better, for worse, for richer, for poorer, in sickness and in health, to love and to cherish till death us do part, according to God's holy ordinance; and thereto I pledge thee my troth."

Then it was Kit's turn. "I, Kathleen, take thee, Theodore, to be my wedded husband, to have and to hold from this day forward, for better, for worse, for richer, for poorer, in sickness and in health, to love and to cherish till death us do part, according to God's holy ordinance; and thereto I pledge thee my troth."

"The ring," Reverend Macauley said.

Gus removed the gold band from his vest pocket and handed it to the minister. Macauley gave it to Ted, who slipped it on Kit's finger.

"With this ring," he said softly, "I thee wed. In the name of the Father, and of the Son, and of the Holy Ghost. Amen."

Kit felt Ted's hand caress hers.

"Bless, O Lord, this ring," said the reverend, "that he who gives it and she who wears it may abide in thy grace and continue in thy favor through Jesus Christ our Lord. O God, look mercifully upon these thy servants, that they may love and honor each other and so live together in faithfulness and peace, in wisdom and true godliness, that their home may be a haven of blessing. Amen."

The minister joined the couple's hands, placed his own on them, and said, "Those whom God hath joined together let no man put asunder. Forasmuch as Theodore and Kathleen have consented together in holy wedlock and have witnessed the same before God and this company, thereto have given and pledged their troth, each to the other, and declared the same by giving and receiving a ring, I pronounce that they are man and wife, in the name of the Father, and of the Son, and of the Holy Ghost. Amen." With a broad smile Reverend Macauley added, "Ted, you may now kiss the bride."

Ted paused but a second, his blue eyes adoring his bride, then lifted Kit's veil. His lips met hers in a perfect communion of heart and soul. Husband and wife at long last.

Outside, the day was clear and California-golden. Rice flew around the couple like confetti as they exited the church building. Parked along the street, waiting for them, was a roadster. Gus had tied a bunch of old shoes to the auto's rear bumper.

Shouts and whoops went up from the guests lining the church's front steps. Kit and Ted waved to everyone, both smiling and laughing.

"Hurry up!" Gus said behind them. "You don't want to miss the boat, do you?" He was referring to the liner bound for Hawaii and their honeymoon.

They made their way toward the street, Ted holding on to Kit's arm as she helped him down the steps. At the bottom stood Winnie Franklin with Bobby. The boy tossed the last bit of rice at Kit.

She heard her name being shouted. A girl's voice. Desperate.

"Kit Shannon!"

She felt Ted's grip tighten on her arm. Kit turned to the girl, who ran up to her, breathless. She was nine or ten years old and had a tired, fearful look about her. Her modest yellow dress was dirty and worn.

"I'm Kit Shannon Fox."

"Thank goodness," said the girl. "You've got to help my mama!"

Kit took the girl's hands. "What is the matter with your mother?"

"She's been beaten and thrown in jail." Tears streaked the girl's face.

"Who beat her?"

"A policeman."

Kit stiffened.

"She said to fetch Kit Shannon," the girl said. "Said you'd understand."

"Can't you see she's just got married?" Gus spouted.

"Please, Gus," Kit said.

Then she heard Earl Rogers at her side. He said, "Kit, I can handle this for you."

"No!" the girl practically screamed. "My mama said she had to see Kit Shannon!"

Kit touched the girl's cheek. Now what? Never before had she refused a cry for legal help. This was her calling. But then again, never before had she been married. This was her duty now.

Kit felt an arm around her shoulders. It was Ted. He drew her to himself and whispered, "There will be other ships. But there is only one Kit Shannon Fox. Come along; I'll drive you to the jail."

Author's Note

The story of the electric trolley system in Los Angeles is, in this work, a fictionalized account based on actual fact. Part of the reason Los Angeles grew so quickly in those early years was its remarkable transit system.

The electric trolley was perfected in the 1880s, primarily because of the efforts of a man named Frank J. Sprague, who worked closely with Thomas Edison. Throughout the 1890s the electric system replaced, slowly but surely, the horse-drawn trolleys that were common in Southern California.

A company trying to exploit the new system went bust in 1898, and in stepped Henry Edwards Huntington, the nephew of railroad magnate Collis P. Huntington. Henry built up the system dramatically and profited by buying up real estate, then selling it at a huge profit once the area was linked to his trolley lines.

Henry's chief competitor was Edward H. Harriman, president of the Southern Pacific Railroad. His rail line was the Los Angeles Railway, and he was also one to use political sway to accomplish his aims. The character of Stanton Eames is not based upon Harriman, except in the sense that both were men of immense wealth, influence, and ambition.

Kit makes reference to sixty-seven fatalities, the result of rail accidents, at the coroner's inquest. This is an accurate number. The *Los Angeles Examiner* listed these findings in 1906. The power of the railways was so great that there was not a single attachment of blame made by a coroner's jury in any of these deaths.

Jack London, of course, was a real person. His views on socialism were based on his own life experience in poverty and his observance of the dire lot of the working class. His writings, along with those of people like Upton Sinclair, helped turn the tide of public opinion concerning the conditions of working people.

His cautionary tale about alcohol, *John Barleycorn,* was published in 1913. It is my artistic license that has Kit as the voice that inspires London to think about the evils associated with free-flowing alcohol. It was very much a social issue in 1906, when this novel takes place.

John Barleycorn was a sensation, and Jack London became a leading proponent of Prohibition (he was even urged to run for president by the Prohibition Party). London's book remains a powerful indictment of the culture of alcohol. It was written, London himself once said, primarily to keep children from being swept into the drinking life, as he had been. His testimony in court in this story is based almost exclusively on the views expressed in *John Barleycorn.*

For biographical information on London, I relied most heavily on Russ Kingman's *A Pictorial Life of Jack London.* London was, by all accounts, an active social drinker up to the time of *John Barleycorn.* And though he tried to quit, entries from the diaries of his wife, Charmian, indicate he never managed a complete break from the bottle. Late in his too-short life he was not a drunkard (what we today would call an alcoholic), but one gets the feeling he was absolutely sincere when he wrote: "I regret that John Barleycorn flourished everywhere in the system of society in which I was born, else I should not have made his acquaintance, and I was long trained in his acquaintance."

The reference to Fundamentalism is also historically based. In 1906, Christianity was in crisis, torn between those who extolled traditional faith and those who sought to accommodate Christianity with the modern world. Those in the first camp became champions of "the fundamentals" of the faith—doctrines such as the Incarnation, the Atonement, the bodily resurrection of Christ, and so forth.

The two leading institutions defending the fundamentals were the Moody Bible Institute in Chicago and the Bible Institute of Los Angeles, or BIOLA. The Institute of the Bible in this novel is fictional but draws its inspiration from Biola. A series of scholarly booklets entitled *The Fundamentals* was published between 1910 and 1915. The term *Fundamentalist* became a derogatory term among liberal theologians and later, from the 1920s and beyond, in the common language. However, it is important to note that the original movement was founded on the best scholarship of the time.

Carry Amelia Moore Nation—her first name sometimes spelled *Carrie*—is a historical figure who wielded a very real hatchet in saloons, mostly in and around Kansas. She did make guest appearances in lecture tours and did sell souvenir hatchets. She cut an imposing figure. It was reported that no less than John L. Sullivan, the former heavyweight boxing champion of the world, went running like a scared mouse when Carry Nation burst into his New York City bar one day.

It was marriage to an alcoholic, and a mighty religious conversion, that turned Carry Nation to the temperance movement. She was arrested some thirty times in "joint smashing" episodes; she really did utter the cry, "Smash, ladies! Smash!" For an entertaining and authoritative account of Mrs. Nation's life, see *Vessel of Wrath: The Life and Times of Carry Nation* by Robert Lewis Taylor.

I have a feeling that Carry Nation and Kit Shannon would have made a dynamite team on the lecture circuit—Mrs. Nation with her hatchet, Kit with her Bible. No town would have been left the same.

Made in the USA
Columbia, SC
20 August 2025

61472586R00202